THE VIOLET VEIL MYSTERIES

A CASE OF MISFORTUNE

SOPHIE CLEVERLY

THE VIOLET VEIL MYSTERIES

A CASE OF MISFORTUNE

HarperCollins *Children's Books*

First published in the United Kingdom by
HarperCollins *Children's Books* in 2022
HarperCollins *Children's Books* is a division of HarperCollins*Publishers* Ltd
1 London Bridge Street
London SE1 9GF

www.harpercollins.co.uk

HarperCollins*Publishers*
1st Floor, Watermarque Building, Ringsend Road
Dublin 4, Ireland

1

ISBN 978–0–00–830801–8

Sophie Cleverly and Hannah Peck assert the moral right to be identified as
the author and illustrator of the work respectively.

Typeset in 11/18pt Plantin by
Palimpsest Book Production Ltd, Falkirk, Stirlingshire
Printed and bound in the UK using 100% renewable electricity
at CPI Group (UK) Ltd

A CIP catalogue record for this title is available from the British Library.

MIX
Paper from
responsible sources
FSC™ C007454

This book is produced from independently certified FSC™ paper
to ensure responsible forest management.

For more information visit: www.harpercollins.co.uk/green

For Dominic Baker-Smith,
because he wanted his name in a book

CHAPTER ONE

My name is Violet Veil, and I am an undertaker's daughter.

More importantly, though, I'm also a detective.

'You're not,' said my younger brother, Thomas, at the breakfast table through a mouthful of toast and butter. The butter was dripping on to his school shorts. 'You don't work for the police.'

'I'm independent,' I told him. I was working on an advertisement as I spoke, poking my tongue out of the corner of my mouth as I carefully inked the letters.

'But you're a girl,' he insisted. 'Girls can't be detectives. You need to be a man with a funny name, like Sherlock Holmes or, or . . .'

'Jack Danger,' suggested my friend Oliver with his usual cheeky smile.

'Oh hush, you,' I said and blotted the ink carefully. 'Just because something has never been done before doesn't mean you can't start.'

I'd had the idea after the events of last October, when Oliver had come crashing into our lives. Or, more accurately, when he'd turned up in a coffin – only to wake up alive, much to his own surprise, as well as everyone else's.

He had asked me to solve his 'murder', which we soon surmised was linked to others that had recently taken place. We had the help of Bones, my greyhound, who had appeared mysteriously one day in the cemetery behind our home, and my equally mysterious sixth sense that allowed me to communicate with ghosts (although whether they felt like communicating back was another matter). And together we had done it. There were a few bumps along the way, of course – including my father being thrown into prison on suspicion of committing the Seven Gates Murders. Yet my catching the real culprit had led to his freedom. (At that moment he was already long since out in the stable yard, preparing for the day's work.)

But solving the mystery had given me a taste of something that I never could have imagined. Suddenly I was no longer doomed to a life of embroidery and attending social events with eligible bachelors. I had always dreamed of being allowed to become an undertaker like my father, which had filled my parents with varying degrees of horror. But that was Thomas's and perhaps Oliver's lot, not mine. Now I'd seen an opportunity to create my own destiny.

I leaned back and admired my handiwork on the small piece of white card.

VEIL INVESTIGATIONS
Detective Services
(Mysteries Solved Within)

ASK FOR MISS VIOLET VEIL

Oliver peered over at it. I'd been helping him with his reading. 'Veil . . . In-ves-tig . . . ations,' he read, and then grinned at me.

'Precisely.' I grinned back.

His smile slowly faded. 'Just you, then?'

'You're Father's apprentice. And, besides, you don't enjoy this whole mystery business.'

He wrinkled his nose and said nothing.

'Mother will be cross with you,' Thomas said as he jumped down from the table. Bones barked and ran over to scoop up any stray crumbs.

'She told me to investigate,' I shot back. It was true – although, to be precise, she had only been referring to exonerating Father. But there was no reason, I had decided, that I couldn't interpret that as permission.

'What're you going to do with it, Violet?' Oliver asked, pointing to the card.

'I'm going to put it in the front window of the shop,' I said. 'Come on.'

* * *

The business had been doing considerably better these past few months. Father had received some compensation from the newspapers who had falsely accused him. He'd also sold an exclusive interview to the *Weekly Bugle* about his wrongful conviction, and not only made a tidy sum but advertised his services at the same time. He'd been so busy that his debts were decreasing rapidly, and he had been able to hire some more staff. The first of these was Ernesto, who now manned the shop (as we called it, though it wasn't really a shop) whenever Father was out directing funerals.

'Morning, Miss Violet,' he said with a tip of his hat as we entered. 'We've had two arrangements made alre—'

He was interrupted by Bones, who barrelled in through the back door from the house, skidded on the wooden floor and leaped up to greet him. Ernesto was rather afraid of dogs but, unfortunately for him, Bones loved him. The dog had his paws on the young man's shoulders and was wagging his tail vigorously. Ernesto's expression was one of pure horror.

'Down, boy!' I commanded. Bones did as he was told, looking a little sheepish but pleased with himself – his tail still wagging nineteen to the dozen. 'You know Ernesto doesn't like it when you carry on so!'

Ernesto backed away, dabbing at his brow with his handkerchief. '*Dios mío*,' he muttered.

'Sorry,' I said. 'He's just rather fond of you.'

'It's quite all right, miss,' he said, but he still looked a little in shock. It happened any time I let Bones near him, but he was still not used to it. He turned and began going through the files in the cabinet behind him.

Ernesto was rather afraid of a lot of things, I had discovered. The list included spiders, sharp objects and, for some reason, pickles. Thankfully for the sake of his job, the one thing he didn't seem to be at all afraid of was death.

I went over to the window in the front of the shop that was currently housing a beautifully painted coffin decorated with immortelles – the everlasting flowers. I leaned across and put my business card in one of the window panels, balanced on the frame.

'What are you doing, Miss Violet?' Ernesto called from beside the cabinets.

'Nothing!'

Oliver gave me a look. Even Bones seemed to be peering at me suspiciously.

'What?' I whispered. 'Either Father will notice or he won't. I shall have to explain to him sooner or later.'

'And if he does?' Oliver asked.

I waved my hand dismissively. I would worry about that when it happened. 'Shouldn't you be out being his apprentice by now?'

Oliver spun round to look up at the clock that sat high on the back wall. 'Is it eight already?'

I nodded; although, to be precise, it was only five minutes to.

'Blast! I'd better run!' And, with that, he dashed out into the corridor.

Ernesto got back up, fanned himself and then sat down at the desk.

I crossed my fingers that Oliver wouldn't tell Father about my new business venture straight away, but I was fairly sure he wouldn't. We were firm friends, after all, and friends had to stick together. And, of course, I was going to rope him into it in any way that I could.

Even though things were going better for us financially, we were not out of the woods yet. We still only had one servant where once we had employed a whole staff. I realised now that we were lucky to have a roof over our heads, but even that would be under threat if Father couldn't repay all his debts. Perhaps if I could make a bit of money on the side it would help Mother and Father.

I opened the front door of the shop and stepped out into the bustling street, Bones trotting behind me. I couldn't help but smile at the sight of my card in the window. This was a new beginning. I had set the bait: now to wait and see what mysteries would fall into my trap.

CHAPTER TWO

I had a long wait. Mysteries, it seemed, weren't as widely available as I had hoped.

I busied myself, helping out round the house and the business whenever Mother wasn't making me practise ditties on the piano or try on woollen petticoats. But my mind was with that little card in the window.

I'd had a taste of investigating – the exhilarating rush of hunting for clues, following Bones's nose and foiling a murderer – and I wanted more. I knew better than anyone that life was for living. The dead lived in whispers, cobwebbed and rattling. I could be bold and bright and alive, and I intended to be so to the full extent of my ability.

But how could I when adventure refused to knock at my door?

I was pondering this a week or so later when I was straightening the flowers in the window display for the ninetieth time. Ernesto was taking lunch, and Bones was sprawled on the floor in a patch of light, motes of dust spilling over him. Suddenly his ears pricked up and, sure enough, in moments the shop door opened.

It was a lady, a relatively young one, with long black hair. I immediately noticed her style of dress, which was unusual and elaborate, folded at the front like a coat but made from delicate silk in the Chinese fashion. The second thing I noticed was that her garments were a brilliant peacock blue and gold – which was even more unusual. Rarely did anyone set foot in our shop who wasn't wearing black.

'Good afternoon. May I be of assistance?' I asked, repeating what I had heard Father and Ernesto say many times. I was about to call for them, but the lady stopped me in my tracks.

'Are you Miss Violet Veil?' she asked, the hint of an accent in her voice.

I paused, speechless for a second. 'Um – well, yes, I am indeed!'

'You are . . . not what I expected,' she said.

'Oh well –' I blinked – 'I am small for my age.' That wasn't precisely true, but I hoped it would make her think I was older. 'Besides, I am qualified. You know of the Seven Gates Murders?'

'Yes,' she said, recognition dawning on her face. It had been the big news in all the papers – my father's conviction, and then the unmasking of the real culprit.

'That was me.' I stopped, realising I perhaps ought to clarify. 'Or, um, rather, I solved the mystery. You might have seen my name mentioned?'

She nodded. 'I thought it was familiar when I saw your sign in the window. I am Miss Li and I live in Turner Square. It is good to meet you. May we discuss?'

'Of course,' I replied coolly. In my mind, I had considerably less confidence. I had been so excited for someone to respond to my advertisement, yet I had completely failed to plan what to do if it actually happened.

Bones was circling us, wagging his tail. I knew that meant he thought Miss Li was safe. He would be all growling and hackles raised if he sensed any threat. I glanced towards the corridor that led from the shop to our house. Ernesto was presumably out the back somewhere. Father was busy in the funeral parlour, and Oliver was helping him. No one would be any the wiser.

I hurried over to the main desk. 'Let's sit at, um, my desk,' I said, quickly tipping over the little brass sign that read **Edgar D. Veil, Undertaker**.

She looked around, seeming a little uncertain, but then took a seat in front of me. 'Thank you,' she said quietly. Bones padded over and squeezed under the desk by my feet.

I pulled out a piece of notepaper and a pencil from Father's tray. 'You have a mystery that requires investigating?' I asked eagerly. 'Is it a murder? A kidnapping?'

The woman raised her eyebrows.

I cleared my throat, realising I was pushing my luck. *Idiot*, I chastised myself. *She would go to the police for such matters.*

'A lost . . . pet?' I tried again.

'No,' she said finally. 'It is something . . . stranger. I was not sure where to turn.' She took a deep breath. 'I found this.' She reached into the top of her gown and pulled out a golden necklace.

I peered a little closer at it – it was beautiful, shaped almost like a lock with intricate flowers carved on to a blue background. Glittering beads in different shapes hung down from it. 'You found it?' I asked. I wasn't sure that this was a mystery. What exactly did she want from me? 'Do you . . . want me to look for the owner?'

'No, Miss Veil,' she said. 'It's mine. It was lost. I lost it on purpose.'

Now the necklace wasn't the only thing that was lost. I was right off the edge of the map.

'I'm sorry,' I said, lowering the pencil, 'but what is the mystery here?'

She took the necklace off and dropped it on to the desk with a clatter. 'These are usually for protection, for boys, but my father was given this as a child and then he had no sons to pass it on to. He made me wear it, but I do not think he really wanted to protect me. He was . . .' she paused, searching for the words, 'cruel and strict. I crossed many seas to get away from him, but he followed. When he died a few months ago, I didn't hesitate to . . . throw it away.'

'This must be valuable,' I said, more to myself than anything, picking it up and running it through my hands. It certainly looked and felt like real gold.

Miss Li nodded. 'My sister was furious with me, but to me it was a – a symbol of him, and of all the hurt he had caused, and I wanted to be rid of it. But then . . . there was this prophecy.'

I felt Bones stirring under the table – and, if I'd had

greyhound ears, I felt sure they would have pricked up too. I was still lost, but this sounded interesting. 'A prophecy?'

Miss Li waved her hand. 'My sister, Zhen, she has recently married a man. His name is Barnaby Campbell and he works at the bank in Havisham. He takes her to the theatre nearby, the Grecian. Do you know it?'

'I've heard of it in passing,' I said, which was true. I had never been. I often begged Mother to take me to the theatre, but beyond a viewing of *Swan Lake* one Christmas she always turned me down.

Miss Li fiddled with the braiding on her gown for a moment before continuing. 'There is a performer there. She calls herself Lady Athena. She tells fortunes. And they say she can —' she lowered her voice — '*speak with the dead.*'

I frowned at that. I had heard the dead, and they weren't good conversationalists. Usually all they gave me was a feeling, or fragments of words. It was something I mostly kept quiet, and I hadn't ever met anyone else — that I knew of — who could sense them. I had heard of mediums, of course, and of the seances that took place in parlours and halls, but there was little chance of my parents ever letting me near such things. I had read some of the books and pamphlets Father had on the matter, but he'd always told me that he believed such people to be a pack of frauds. Did this Lady Athena truly share my power, or was she a fraud too?

I felt a low rumbling growl from Bones by my feet, and reached down to stroke him. That was a warning, but I was unsure of what.

'But . . .' I began. 'How does this relate to the necklace?'

'Lady Athena,' Miss Li said, 'read my sister's fortune with the help of her "spirit guide". And she told Zhen that I would find this necklace. And, the very next day, it appeared on my nightstand, as if it had never left.'

My attention was starting to drift again. It seemed this wasn't the thrilling mystery I'd been hoping for – and I didn't have long before Father or Ernesto came back and caught me up to no good at the desk. 'Perhaps you just forgot where you'd left it,' I said. 'Or a servant found it and put it back.'

But Miss Li leaned forward and fixed me with a very serious gaze. 'That is quite impossible. You see, I . . .' She squeezed her hand into a fist. 'I threw the necklace into my father's grave.'

CHAPTER THREE

Once I had picked my jaw up from the floor, I knew I needed to ask Miss Li further questions. This was suddenly very interesting.

'Someone dug out the necklace?' I asked. 'A *grave robbery?*'

'That is the strange thing,' she said as if there weren't anything particularly strange about what she'd just said. 'His grave was not disturbed. I made myself go back there and look. But the earth was untouched.'

My mind raced. This detective business required far

more quick thinking than I had imagined. What were the right questions to ask? For a moment, I thought of Detective Inspector Holbrook – the surly and intimidating police inspector who had arrested my father last year. He had told me in no uncertain terms that I was *not a detective*. I bit my lip. If I were to prove him wrong, I had to work on my skills.

So this necklace had been in Miss Li's father's grave and now it was here. And the soil remained intact. Was it a fake, perhaps? A copy?

I stared down at it. It certainly looked genuine enough. And surely she would be very familiar with her own necklace. It was elaborate and unusual – not something that would be easy to come by in Britain. 'You're certain this is the real thing?'

She nodded. 'I spent years of my life with it round my neck. It has a distinctive mark on the back. Here.' She pointed.

'And who else knew about you throwing it away? Only your sister?' I asked.

She flushed a little. 'And all the others that were at the funeral.'

Aha. From the way she spoke, it sounded as though she may have made something of a public spectacle out of her actions.

'I just want to know how . . . how this Lady Athena knew about it,' she said.

'You don't believe she has powers?' I was relieved that she seemed to share my scepticism on the matter.

'I don't—' Miss Li stopped and shook her head. 'I don't know. Perhaps. What I do know is that my sister spends all her money on these performances. And now the theatre is asking for investors. The return of the necklace has made her belief very firm. I am just . . . so worried about her.' Miss Li's forehead creased as she stared down at the desk.

'Don't worry,' I said with renewed fervour. 'I'll do what I can to help you, Miss Li. We can get to the bottom of this!'

Her face lit up. 'You are sure? I cannot pay very much. Most of my father's wealth passed to my sister. He didn't approve of me. If he had had a son, we would not have got a penny.'

I honestly hadn't the faintest idea what I would charge anyone. What was a mystery worth?

'Please don't worry about payment for now, madam. I shall, um, consult my associates and get back to you when we know more.' I pointed at the necklace. 'May I keep this for now?'

'Yes,' she said with surprisingly little consideration. 'Take it.'

I nodded and tucked it away safely in my dress.

She hastily wrote her address down on the notepad that sat on the desk, tore it off and handed it to me. 'Thank you, Miss Veil,' she said with an air of relief as she stood up. 'Thank you for your time.'

Once I'd led her out of the door, I looked down at Bones, who was padding round me expectantly. 'Well, what do you say, boy? Are we on the case?'

He barked his agreement, and I rubbed my hands together with glee. 'Right,' I said. 'That's one associate consulted. Now for the other.' I ran out of the back of the shop, my footsteps bouncy with the promise of adventure. 'Oliver!'

★ ★ ★

I found Oliver exiting the funeral parlour, where I could hear Father and Ernesto talking about arrangements in the background.

Oliver wiped the sweat from his brow with a handkerchief and then stuffed it away in his pocket. This was probably a good idea as Bones had now jumped up and was enthusiastically licking his face.

'Do you have a moment?' I asked, keeping my voice low as I pushed Bones back down. 'It's important!'

Oliver rubbed his hands on his overalls. 'Your pa said

I could go for lunch. I was looking forward to one of Maddy's roast-beef sandwiches . . .'

'Never mind that!' I grabbed his arm. 'Food can wait. We have an investigation to discuss.'

I dragged the reluctant Oliver out through the kitchen, luckily escaping the notice of Maddy, our maidservant, who was busy with the sandwiches. We still had not yet been able to replace our cook, so those duties currently fell to Mother, Maddy and occasionally me if they were able to rope me into it.

I opened the back door and Bones raced out ahead of me, through our yard and into the cemetery.

Seven Gates Cemetery spread out from the back of our house. We didn't own it, but we had some responsibility for it, and most of Father's funerals took place in its twin chapels. That meant we were allowed a gate into it, while the rest of the place was walled off and locked at night to deter grave robbers. In my heart, though, the cemetery was ours.

Spring was well and truly making itself at home that day. I loved the cemetery in every season, but spring was particularly impressive. Although the place had been built relatively recently compared to some of the ancient churchyards, it was still the oldest of the city's cemeteries. A happy consequence of this was that flowers planted in decades past had taken root and begun to spread. Spring always arrived with a white carpet of snowdrops, and then daffodils, bluebells and primroses followed.

Bones frolicked among the sea of yellow daffodils that were gently waving in the breeze, while a cacophony of birds sang at him from the trees. I dragged Oliver over to my favourite bench under the oak tree.

'What is it, Violet?' he asked. He suddenly went wide-eyed. 'Not another murder?'

'No, no,' I said quickly. 'But a mystery nonetheless. We finally have a case!' I clapped my hands. My friend looked less enthusiastic. 'Don't worry – I'm sure it's perfectly safe.'

'Knowing you,' he replied, 'I'm sure it perfectly ain't. Go on, then, what is it?'

I ignored his jibe. 'A lady came to me in the shop, a Miss Li. It's –' I paused, wondering how to explain what I'd just been told – 'a little complicated. Long story short, there's a medium at the Grecian Theatre. She's been telling people's fortunes. And Miss Li had this necklace that her father made her wear, but she got rid of it.' I pulled out the amulet and dangled it in front of him.

'What's the fortune-teller got to do with this?' Oliver asked, wrinkling his nose. He wasn't really paying attention, I could tell. He was watching Bones, who had just got himself covered in pollen and was sneezing.

I poked him in the arm. 'You'll learn if you actually listen! This fortune-teller– Lady Athena her name is, apparently – told Miss Li's sister that the necklace would come back. And then she suddenly found it.'

'Hmm. What's strange about that?'

I stood up, ready for my dramatic flourish. 'Because she threw it in *her father's grave.*'

That got his attention. He snapped his gaze back to me and the necklace, forgetting the overzealous dog. 'You what?'

'Exactly. It reappeared, and the grave wasn't even touched. A real mystery.' I rubbed my hands together with glee. 'And there's more. Her sister has become completely convinced by this spiritualist lady, and might be about to invest in the theatre. Miss Li is really worried that something fishy is going on. She wants to find out how and why this prophecy came true. And that's where we come in!'

'Where you come in, you mean,' he said, raising an eyebrow at me. '*Violet Veil Investigations*, your card said. That means I don't have to get involved.'

'Oh, come on now!' I stamped my foot in the grass. 'We're a team.' I couldn't help but notice that he sat up a little straighter when I said that, as if he were pleased. 'I need you. Last year, you asked me to investigate for you. Now I need *you* to help *me* investigate. I don't want to do this alone!'

It bruised my pride a little to say that, but it was true. I was convinced that I was the brains of the operation, but Oliver was the heart and soul. He always made me feel braver than I really was.

He stared back at me, a short pause that felt like for ever. 'All right. I'll help you. When I've got time in between apprenticing, that is.'

Bones chose that moment to start barking and chasing after a squirrel. He was an essential part of the operation too – I could sense the dead, but Bones seemed to have a special intuition of his own. We had often followed his nose in the case of the Seven Gates Murders. Right then, though, his special intuition was apparently only telling him to chase squirrels.

I shook my head and turned back to Oliver. 'Thank you,' I said with relief. 'Now we just have to think about how we're going to do this. I think we need to get into one of those performances and see what this Lady Athena is doing – work out what she's up to. But I have no idea how! I'm not sure I can afford a ticket, and I don't think there's any chance of Mother and Father letting me go.'

'Wait,' Oliver said suddenly. 'Did you say the *Grecian* Theatre?'

'That's the one,' I replied.

He jumped up. 'I know someone who works there,' he said. 'My friend Archie. Ain't seen him for ages, not since he stopped shoeshining an' got a proper job. But we were good pals.'

'Really?' Oliver didn't mention his past life very often and that included his friends.

He nodded. 'I reckon Archie could get us inside. Leave it with me.'

I grinned at him. 'Oliver, you're brilliant.'

'If we solve this . . .' He paused. 'Will I get my name on the business card?'

'I'll think about it,' I said with a wink.

I hoped this *Lady Athena*, whoever she really was, was ready for us. Because we were certainly ready for her.

CHAPTER FOUR

The next day, Oliver disappeared before his break for lunch. I waited at the piano and reluctantly practised my major scales. If it were possible to play the piano sarcastically, I would have done so.

A little while later, he returned with a big grin on his face. 'Archie said he'd show us round,' he said.

'Well, what are we waiting for?' I jumped up from the piano stool 'Let's be off!'

He gave me a bemused look, one I was becoming very familiar with. 'Some of us have work to be doing, Violet.'

'I only don't because they won't *let* me,' I huffed, shutting the piano lid a little too heavily and making Bones jump. 'That's why I'm creating my own work. Come on – ask Father if he'll let you off for the afternoon.'

Oliver sighed. 'All right. But only because I know there's no one in at the moment.' He sniffed. 'Besides, you're lucky that your pa is a good man. Plenty of masters would give me a thrashing for even asking.'

It was true that Father was good to him, but I knew that there was a fair amount of guilt and horror involved. My father held himself responsible for the fact that Oliver had been almost sent to his grave when he was merely deeply unconscious and not, in fact, dead.

Oliver hurried away to the funeral parlour to ask, while I ran to the back door to get Bones's lead. Luckily, Mother and Maddy were busy upstairs, so there was no one to interrogate me about what I was up to.

Oliver returned, looking happy but a little flustered. 'He told me I could go in a couple of hours,' he said. 'Wait.' He stopped and patted Bones. 'You're bringing the dog?'

'Of course,' I shot back. 'Bones is an essential part of the operation.'

Oliver frowned. 'Ain't theatres for fancy folk, though? Don't think they let dogs in.'

'I'll think of something,' I said, putting the lead in my

pocket for later. I was sure I would. I was quickly developing a way of talking myself into places.

Once Oliver was finished and allowed to leave, we headed to the front of the house, to the shop. Ernesto was sitting behind the desk as usual. He looked up, and I noticed there was some relief in his expression as he realised that Bones was on a lead and not about to jump up at him again. 'Afternoon, Miss Violet.'

'Afternoon, Ernesto,' I said. 'We're just going to run some errands for Father.'

'All-all right,' he stuttered, still staring at Bones with twitching eyelids. 'Goodbye then.'

I hadn't been expecting it to be quite that easy, but I supposed Ernesto was more worried about the dog than whatever it was we were up to.

'Right,' I said as soon as we were out of the shop door. 'To the theatre!'

* * *

The Grecian Theatre was a fair walk away, just outside Seven Gates borough and into Havisham, in a district with some of the larger and more upmarket shops. I had passed it many times, but had never been inside. It had always seemed so grand, like a palace.

As I stood looking up at it, I could see it was, in fact,

rather tatty. There were cracks in the tall white columns and elaborate classical carvings that made up its frontage. The letter *E* was hanging askew on the end of the huge sign, and the windows all looked in need of a good clean.

The lowest level was plastered with posters bearing a drawing of a lady dressed in an unusual but glamorous manner – her hair loose, her dress long and flowing. The posters read:

THE GRECIAN THEATRE PRESENTS:

A NIGHT OF TRUE WONDERMENT

THE MAGNIFICENT MEDIUM

Lady Athena

WILL FORETELL YOUR FUTURE

WITNESS THIS INCREDIBLE SPECTACLE

MYSTICAL SIGHTS NEVER BEFORE SEEN

HER SPIRIT GUIDE SHOWS YOU THE WAY TO YOUR DESTINY

"NOT TO BE MISSED" – *THE TIMES*

I read this aloud to Oliver, who followed along slowly with his finger. Bones stared up at the posters silently – probably wondering what all the fuss was about.

'Blimey,' Oliver said, shoving his hands back into his pockets. 'Sounds impressive.'

'I suppose,' I replied. 'All posters are like that, though. They all claim to have the best product or the most spectacular show on earth. We'll have to see for ourselves what all the fuss is about.'

'Archie told me to meet him by the stage door at the back,' Oliver said. 'Come on.'

We trotted round the building. There it dropped the pretence that it was some sort of elaborate Ancient Greek temple and turned into a mishmash of smoke-stained stone and hastily added extensions. I spotted a tiny unassuming red door, from which an equally tiny red-headed boy in a uniform was waving at us.

'Hullo, Arch,' Oliver said.

A grin spread across the boy's face. 'Welcome! Come one, come all!'

'There's only two of us,' I pointed out. 'And a dog.' Bones barked and sat back on his haunches.

Archie blinked at me. 'Hmm,' he said. 'You didn't say nothing about a dog, Ol.'

Oliver shrugged. 'Sorry. She insisted.'

'Well.' The boy ran a hand through his scruffy red hair. 'Mr Anastos loves dogs. He probably won't mind. Gotta be quick, though, the door manager's gone for a break.'

Bones's tongue lolled out and he began panting happily. I supposed that was a good sign.

At that point, I remembered my manners. 'Ahem, anyway, I'm Violet Veil. Of Veil Investigations.' I dug into my pocket and pulled out one of my home-made business cards, pressing it into his hand. 'You've probably heard of me.'

'Oliver told me you were a friend of his, miss,' the cheerful boy replied enthusiastically. 'You must be very important. Come inside! I'll show you around. Might even show you the ropes – the ones that draw back the curtains, that is.' He laughed at his own joke while we just stared at him. 'This way!'

He motioned for us to come inside, and we followed, Bones pulling on his lead – presumably with excitement at getting to visit a whole new place with a whole new variety of smells.

Archie led us through some rather dark and damp corridors. At the end of one there was a locked door, and after he quickly pulled a key from his pocket to open it we emerged into a slightly fancier corridor with plush carpeting. We soon came across a set of stairs that led down to a pair of double doors with glass windows. He held one open for us. 'After you!'

'Oh my,' I said. Oliver whistled quietly.

'Welcome, my friends, to the Grecian Theatre! The most grandest theatre in the world!' Archie cried, throwing his arms out wide. What Archie lacked in height, he certainly made up for in enthusiasm.

We had entered the empty lobby of the theatre. It was like nothing I had ever seen before.

The whole place was covered in plush red carpeting, and shiny white marble columns stretched up to a ceiling carved with classical scenes. There were two chandeliers, the candles unlit but the glass glittering. An enormous bar took up the middle of the room, decorated with a huge spray of red and yellow flowers. A bored-looking waiter stood behind it, polishing glasses. He barely glanced up at us.

The closer I looked, though, the more the cracks began to show. Parts of the carpet were faded and worn with age. A Greek statue to one side was missing her nose. Besides that, there was a huge stain in a corner of the ceiling that appeared to be some kind of water damage.

'Archie?' someone called.

The boy's face immediately lit up and somehow also flushed at the same time.

A girl was being pushed into the lobby in a wheelchair by an older boy. She looked about my age, him a little older – perhaps around Oliver's age. Both of them were beautiful, with dark eyes and black curls – the girl's long and the boy's short.

'Afternoon, sir, ma'am,' Archie said, bowing repeatedly. I wondered why he acted that way when they were not much older than him. 'A-anything I can do for you today? Archie Pennyworth, at your service!'

'Morning, Archie,' said the dark-haired boy in a friendly tone.

The girl looked around as they neared us. 'Hmm. I suppose the brass could be a little shinier?'

I held tight to Bones's lead to stop him jumping up at them, which he was clearly desperate to do.

Archie suddenly stood to attention like a soldier. 'Yes, Miss Anastos, miss! Right away, miss! You'll see your face in all this when I'm done!'

The girl kept a straight face as he ran back out of the doors we'd come through, only to break into laughter once he'd gone.

'You shouldn't tease him, Eleni,' the older boy said. 'You know he just wants to please everyone. Especially you.' At this point, he seemed to notice us. 'Hello there,' he said. 'You're a bit early . . .'

Bizarrely, I found myself tongue-tied. 'I . . . well . . . we're not . . .'

'We're here for an investigation,' Oliver said quickly. 'I'm Oliver. This is Violet. This is Bones the dog. He's, um, essential.'

'Pleased to meet you,' said the boy, stepping forward and shaking our hands. 'I'm Niko, and this is my sister, Eleni. Our parents own the theatre. Can we help you?' He didn't seem bothered by Bones's presence and gave him a quick scratch behind the ears. Bones wiggled and wagged his tail happily.

Eleni gave us a little wave. Then she leaned forward, curiosity in her expression. 'And what are you investigating, precisely? You're our age, are you not?'

I realised a little too late that perhaps Oliver shouldn't have told the truth. But, if we were going to get anywhere, having some help from this pair could be vital. They clearly held a little sway at the theatre, and that would certainly come in handy.

And, for some reason that I couldn't explain, I trusted Niko and Eleni. I wanted to make friends with them. Perhaps it was that I so rarely got to meet anyone my own age, but there was something more than that as well. I felt drawn to them, and Bones seemed to trust them – which was very important in my book. And so the truth came out.

'I'm the one who solved the Seven Gates Murders, as you might have seen in the newspapers.'

The siblings' eyes went wide and they glanced at each other. Clearly that rang a bell.

Oliver pointed at himself and Bones.

'And they helped,' I added hastily. 'Well, following that success I've started my own detective agency. My client has asked us to investigate a mysterious matter involving Lady Athena. We were hoping to have a look around,' I said. 'And perhaps watch her performance?' I added hopefully.

'A mystery, eh?' Eleni said, lighting up. 'I do love a good mystery.'

Niko smiled, all crinkles round his deep brown eyes. 'You won't have to wait long,' he said. 'She's on tonight. Come on – we'll show you around . . .'

CHAPTER FIVE

We followed the pair over to what looked like a huge iron cage. 'Oh!' I exclaimed aloud. 'A lift! I've never been in one.' I had seen them occasionally on rare trips to the bigger department stores in Havisham's shopping district, but Mother had always called them 'infernal contraptions' and refused to set foot inside. Harper's Mourning Warehouse, where we purchased most of our clothes, didn't have one, much to her relief.

'I ain't never even seen one before,' said Oliver, running

his fingers over the metal as Bones sniffed the thing curiously. 'This new?'

'Oh yes,' Niko said. He looked up at it with pride as he slid back the metal gate that covered the door. 'We were able to have this installed recently for Eleni. It's brilliant, isn't it?'

'All this for me,' Eleni said with an exaggerated sigh, patting the arms of her wheelchair. 'I used to be a cross-country runner, you know. Until the terrible crocodile accident.' Niko rolled his eyes at her, and hers glinted back. 'I feel bad for Niko, having to push me everywhere.'

'Well, I feel responsible,' he said jokingly as he wheeled the chair inside the lift and turned it so that Eleni was facing us again. 'It was my crocodile, after all.'

I peered into the black-and-white box. I wasn't sure that it was big enough for four people and a dog, but Niko waved us in. 'You'll fit – don't worry.'

I couldn't help noticing the gap in the floor through which only blackness could be glimpsed – the long drop to the bottom.

Bones, ignoring my hesitation, pulled ahead of me and went to rest his head on Eleni's lap, over the frills of her blue skirt. She giggled and stroked him. I squeezed in beside Niko, feeling a little uncomfortable with how close I was. I could feel the warmth of his arm next to mine.

I looked up to see Oliver still standing in the corridor. 'Don't like small spaces much,' he said, shuffling uncomfortably.

'Oh, don't be a baby,' I said. 'You'll be fine.' I reached out and pulled him inside.

'Shut the doors, would you?' Niko asked.

Oliver, still looking uncertain, stretched out to pull the metal gate and the lift door closed. Niko grinned and pressed a button on the side wall, and the whole thing gave a mighty jolt and began to lurch upwards.

My stomach felt as though it were about to fall out. Oliver looked green, and Bones was whining. It was certainly a strange sensation. Niko, however, was still grinning at me, clearly enjoying himself.

When we reached the higher level, the whole thing juddered to a halt. Oliver opened the doors again and stumbled out on to the thick carpet in the manner of a seasick sailor who is desperately relieved to be back on dry land. The rest of us followed, Bones wobbling gratefully.

'You get used to it,' Eleni said. 'It's been a blessing. Much easier to get around the place now. I can walk a little bit with a stick, but stairs are my downfall.'

I hoped she didn't mean that literally.

We followed them until we came to another bar on our

left, and a pair of double doors to the right that were being held wide open.

'So here is the auditorium,' Niko said casually, as if it were nothing. But it was *something*, that was certain.

To begin with, it was enormous. We had entered from the back, and row after row of plush red seats stretched down from where we stood, eagerly awaiting an audience. In the centre, enormous red-and-gold curtains hung down, and I heard the echoed voices of the stagehands bustling around behind them. The stage was also framed by some of the most incredible painted carvings I had ever seen. A beautiful creamy white was the background for the shining scenes of Ancient Greece – I saw figures I was familiar with from books, like Icarus and Daedalus with their wax wings, the king of the gods, Zeus, with his thunderbolts, and Persephone holding the pomegranate that Hades used to trap her as queen of the underworld. There were hints of starry gold and a blue the colour of the clearest sky.

Compared to the rest of the place, this had clearly had money spent on it recently. There were the odd few chipped pieces of cornice or worn seat back, but the painting looked freshly redone.

Oliver was staring around in awe. Even Bones seemed impressed.

'Pick up your jaw, Oliver,' I teased, but I was sure I looked as stunned as he did.

'Never been in a theatre, neither,' he said in a hushed voice, as if we were standing in some grand cathedral. 'Cor, this is fancy.'

'Thank you,' Eleni said to him, sounding pleased. 'Mama and Baba have worked really hard on it. It's an old place, you see. Needs a lot of upkeep.'

I turned and gazed upward. Three balconies encircled the rear of the room, going up to the heavens. I wondered what it would be like to stand at the very top, with only a low brass railing to keep you from going over. And in the centre of the ceiling hung the most enormous chandelier I'd ever laid eyes on, glittering with endless glass.

'Never seen anything like it,' said Oliver in the same awed tone.

I smiled and ran my fingers over one of the seats in front of me. It was velvet, furry and soft. The thought of sitting in it and watching a show sent a shivery thrill down my spine.

'Niko, what you said earlier . . .' I started. 'Did you mean we would be able to watch Lady Athena's performance? I don't have very much money for tickets . . .'

'It's sold out anyway,' he said with a shrug. 'But . . . we actually have a box, for the family.' He pointed to one of the little inset balconies near the front of the stage. 'You're welcome to use it.'

Now I was definitely looking stunned. Oliver elbowed me. 'Pick up *your* jaw, Violet,' he teased back.

'Um, w-well,' I stammered. 'We couldn't possibly . . .'

'I insist,' said Niko.

'Thank you,' I replied, relieved. 'That would be wonderful. I'm sure it will be really helpful to our investigation.'

'You're welcome,' he said, that easy smile returning to his face.

I reined in Bones a little, who was urgently trying to sniff his way down the aisle. I had more questions for the siblings.

'So what does Lady Athena usually do in her performance?' I asked, handing Oliver Bones's lead so I could take out my notebook and pencil.

'Ah,' said Niko, rubbing his hands together, 'it's incredible. She has an ancient spirit guide named Achilles, and she can communicate with him from beyond the veil. He shows her the future.'

'Hmm,' I said. That didn't seem very likely to me. Ghosts were not the best communicators, nor in my experience did they have any concept of the future. In fact, quite the opposite. They were often stuck in the past, remembering how things had been when they were alive – although they could sometimes observe the present.

'She must be an impressive medium,' I said cautiously.

Eleni snorted. 'She's a snake is what she is.'

'You don't like her?' Oliver asked.

Eleni folded her arms. 'No. She's full of herself. Just this afternoon we saw her throwing her lunch back at Archie because her cucumber sandwiches weren't sliced in the right way and it would *upset her cosmic balance.*' She rolled her eyes.

'Come now, she's a performer, that's all,' said Niko amiably. 'And a successful one at that. You know how much good she's done for the theatre.'

Eleni sighed. 'I miss *plays*.' She looked up at Oliver and me. 'I want to be a playwright, you know. Like Shakespeare.' She got a faraway, dreamy twinkle in her eye as she spoke. 'Murder, mystery, mayhem, comedy, tragedy . . . Plays have it all.'

'What happened to the plays?' Oliver asked her.

'All we seem to have these days are these novelty acts,' she said sadly. 'That's what people want to see, apparently. It's *Lady Athena* most nights, perhaps the mime or a ballet if we're really lucky. But we haven't put on a real play in so long.'

'Have you written one?' I asked, fascinated. I liked the idea of writing, and rather fancied myself as a Gothic novelist, but it was not something I'd ever tried.

'She's written several,' said Niko. 'They're brilliant, truly.'

'Oh shush,' she said with a blush and a smile. 'I showed Father my latest script a few weeks ago. It was called *The Mirror Murder*. I thought it was my best one yet. He just shrugged and said there was no room for it in the programme.' The light seemed to go out in her eyes.

I felt sorry for her – I could understand the feeling of your dreams being pushed aside for what others wanted. But with my detective hat on (I didn't actually have a detective hat, but was beginning to think I should get one) I noted Eleni's dislike of Lady Athena. I was getting a picture of someone who did not appear to be very trustworthy. It seemed entirely likely that this medium was a fraud.

But if that were so – how could she possibly have known about Miss Li's necklace? I patted the gold chain where it lay in my pocket. There was a lot more we needed to find out.

'How long until the performance?' I asked, looking up.

Niko checked his watch. 'Half an hour until doors open.'

Oliver was starting to look very uncertain. 'We have to get back for supper, don't we, Violet? Your ma will be furious if we're not.'

I bit my lip, wrestling with my conscience. He was right, of course. But watching this performance was not only crucial to our investigation, it was also something I dearly wanted to do. It was exactly the sort of exciting experience that I had been longing to partake in during my long hours of domestic tasks and dull embroidery.

Bones trotted over and pushed his head into my side, and suddenly I had an idea. 'Aha! I can make use of you, boy,' I said.

I tore a page out of the back of my notebook and hastily scribbled a note:

Dearest Mother and Father,
Very sorry but Oliver and I have been detained on important business at the Grecian Theatre.
We will be back by bedtime, I promise.
Violet

'Take this home, boy,' I instructed Bones. 'Understand?' I folded the note and tucked it into his collar. He barked and swished his tail, which I assumed was a yes.

'Can he do that?' Eleni asked. 'Clever dog.'

'Well, I hope so.' I patted him on the head. 'He always knows his way around.'

Archie suddenly appeared behind me, polishing cloth in hand, almost making me jump out of my skin. 'Do you want me to take your dog outside, miss?' he chirped.

'Oh, um, yes, please,' I said, handing him the lead.

'Come on, boy,' Archie said. 'We'll see if Irving can find you some scraps on the way!'

The two of them trotted off together out of the back of the auditorium. For someone who had seemed unsure about the dog at first, Archie now looked like he wanted the two of them to be the best of friends.

'Let's wait out by the bar,' Niko said. 'The seats are comfortable, and I can fetch us some drinks.'

'Drinks?' I asked, suddenly feeling rather *un*comfortable. Did he mean alcohol? Father allowed us some of the rum punch on Christmas Day, but that was all.

'Oh yes, a round of neat whisky for us all,' he said, but I quickly picked up on his teasing tone. 'I was thinking more along the lines of a lemonade each,' he said. 'My treat.'

Now it was Oliver's turn to look shocked. 'For free?'

Niko shrugged. 'It doesn't cost us anything. Irving lets us have them.'

I didn't understand why they were being so kind, but perhaps they were lonely. I felt rather the same way. I hated to admit it, but I had been so starved for companionship that I'd befriended a boy wandering a rain-soaked graveyard who had recently come back from the dead.

'It's no trouble anyway,' said Eleni, waving her hand. 'You're our guests, and we never get to talk to anyone our own age these days.' She put her hand beside her mouth and added in a stage whisper, 'And, if you can dig up some gossip about Lady Athena, I'm all for it.'

Niko rolled his eyes. 'You're insufferable, sister. Show some gratitude.'

'You can't make me, brother,' she replied, looking up at him and sticking her tongue out.

I grinned at them both. I wanted so badly to impress them, and I felt sure that solving this impossible mystery would be just the way to do it.

CHAPTER SIX

We chatted to Eleni and Niko while we sipped our lemonade. The drink was perfect – sharp and sweet and even a little fizzy.

'That's the best thing I've ever tasted,' Oliver said.

'You should try Mama's lamb *kleftiko*,' Eleni replied. 'Or her stuffed vine leaves. Or anything Mama makes, really.'

The Anastos siblings told us some of the history of the theatre – how it had been built years ago during the fashion for classical revival, but was slowly falling into disrepair. Their parents had bought it after falling in love with the place and its ties to their Greek roots (and fairly cheaply for a whole theatre, Eleni said), and had been restoring it to its former glory. There had been a while when their situation was difficult but, thanks to Lady Athena's popularity, things were looking up.

'We could do *better*, though,' Eleni insisted, slamming her hand on the table in a delightfully unladylike fashion. 'If they would just let me put on my plays—'

She was interrupted by a commotion as the first guests flooded into the room. They must have begun letting people inside for the performance. The crowd swarmed round us, gathering about the bar. A friendly buzz of noise surrounded our table.

'Do excuse me,' said a middle-aged lady with an enormous bustle under the endless folds of her green skirt as she tried to get past Eleni's wheelchair. She stopped and looked down her pinched nose at the girl.

'Oh, my darling,' she said in a simpering tone of voice, 'whatever has happened to you?'

'It's the bubonic plague, I'm afraid,' Eleni said sadly. 'Highly contagious. I can show you if you like?' She motioned rolling up her sleeve.

The woman made a horrified face, and quite literally

bustled away as fast as possible. Eleni and Niko burst out laughing.

'Do you get questions of that sort all the time?' I asked. 'It must be exhausting.'

'Yes. Sometimes people even move my chair without asking, as if I'm a piece of furniture!' Eleni exclaimed. 'But I do think laughter is the best medicine.' She grinned.

'Not true,' Niko said. 'If it were, you would have been cured when Pietro the Magnificent Mime did his walking-on-air act and fell into the orchestra pit.'

She cackled. 'That *was* unbelievably amusing. He was fine, by the way,' she added quickly. The acrobats had left their mat down there.'

'Nikolaos, Eleni?' a warm, lilting voice asked from behind us. 'Who's this, *paidiá*?'

'It's *Niko*,' Niko mumbled, with a good-natured eye roll.

Eleni's face had lit up. 'Oh, Mama, this is Violet and Oliver. They've come to watch the show. We were just giving them a tour.'

I turned to see a woman who looked just like an older version of Eleni – a bright smile, curling and plaited deep brown hair and the same dark eyes, just with a few more lines in the corners. She was wearing a rich-red gown with an intricate beaded edging, such a beautiful colour that it made me feel rather envious that I was almost always dressed in black.

'Good to meet you,' she said. 'It will be very nice for these two to make some friends their own age.' She smiled. 'I am Maria Anastos. A warm welcome to the Grecian Theatre!'

She shuffled round the table, where she made a fuss of straightening Niko's collar and then bent down to give Eleni two kisses on the cheek. 'Are you feeling all right, *agapi mou*?' she said to her daughter, who nodded in response. 'I must rush, or the show will not go on!' She slipped away into the crowd.

Niko smiled and adjusted his collar to be artfully crumpled again. 'That's Mama. She runs the show, really. She loves the theatrics. Baba prefers looking after the building. This old place is his passion. He'll be somewhere backstage, I expect.'

The commotion around us grew louder. I saw that the doors to the stalls had been opened, and the excited crowds began flowing out of the bar and into the auditorium.

'Come on,' said Niko, getting to his feet. 'I'll take you to our box.'

* * *

I realised as Niko unlocked the door and opened it for us that the box was surprisingly small. There were only two seats in there, individual red-velvet chairs. 'Oh,' I said, trying not to show my disappointment. 'Where will you two sit?' I didn't really want the Anastos siblings to leave us. I knew I had to focus on the investigation into Lady Athena, but in that moment this was drowned out by my urge for friendship.

'Oh, don't worry about it,' said Niko, waving his free hand while the other rested on Eleni's chair. 'We've seen Lady Athena plenty of times. We live here, remember?'

'More than enough,' said Eleni cheekily, but with an edge of bitterness. 'We'll meet you again after, if you don't have to rush home.'

Oliver peered in. 'You sure this is all right?' He kept self-consciously brushing his jacket, even though it had been recently scrubbed for him by Maddy and had no trace of dirt on it.

'Positive,' Niko replied.

'Thank you,' I said with feeling, though I still felt that tinge of longing for them to stay.

Oliver and I stepped inside the box, and shuffled around to take our seats.

'It's packed,' he observed.

The place was filling up fast and roaring with conversation.

We were on the lower level, the closest to the stage, though we couldn't see anything behind the enormous gold-fringed curtain that hung over it.

'People really believe in this Lady Athena,' I said, looking out over the chattering crowds. 'Either that or they just enjoy the spectacle.'

'Is it going to be . . . spooky?' Oliver asked, and I felt him shiver a little beside me.

'We can only hope.' I grinned and rubbed my hands together with glee.

I heard the doors close at the rear of the auditorium, and then the lights went out. There were gasps and even a scream. Oliver looked around, puzzled. I too wondered for a moment if something had gone wrong, but when I turned back to the stage the curtains were solemnly parting.

'Not to worry, my dear,' I heard a gruff-voiced man say to his companion from somewhere nearby. 'It's all part of it.'

'But no one can see my gown now!' she whined.

I suppressed a chuckle. The Grecian Theatre certainly seemed to be a place where people went to show off to the finest of society.

When the curtains completed their slow parting, there was a far-off rumble like thunder, and smoke began to billow from the sides of the stage, the sharp smell of it hitting my nose. From where we were sitting, I could make out people working in the wings, but they were all in black and moved like shadows. The atmosphere was eerie, and it sent a thrill down my spine.

A thunderclap rang out, and suddenly there was a tall man on the stage, a spotlight illuminating him like a moonbeam. He wore a top hat and tails, and he had a dark beard clinging to his strong chin. He reminded me a little bit of Father, but with a sharper, more angular face, and eyes that looked as though they held secrets.

'Ladies and gentlemen,' he said in a booming voice, 'I welcome you on this fine evening to a spectacular event. One that will take you beyond the realms of the possible.' He paused, and I was amazed to find the audience was now silent, hanging on his every word. 'Tonight, my friends, you will bear witness as Lady Athena draws back the veil and reveals the mysteries that lie hidden there, guided by the spirits of the ancients.'

'Are there ghosts here now?' Oliver whispered nervously in my ear.

I closed my eyes and reached out with my unearthly senses. The huge space appeared black and silent within my mind. No ghostly glow, no whispers, no cold breath on the back of my neck. I shook my head. But, if Lady

Athena could truly summon ghosts, perhaps they would not yet be with us.

'I must warn you,' the mysterious man on stage continued, 'that my lady's prophecies are most powerful. She is the greatest fortune-teller since the oracle at Delphi, mark my words. And the path to such greatness takes her beyond the realm of the living, to speak with the dead. This, my friends, is the *only* way to circumnavigate the sands of time, to truly know what lies in the future. It is most dangerous. There is much to be feared.'

I didn't like the way he kept calling us friends. Something about this man seemed distinctly unfriendly.

'Thus,' he said, 'only one of you will receive a prophecy tonight. But as you will know –' he smiled, looking like a cat about to devour a mouse – 'my lady's reputation precedes her. She can only speak the truth. It is known that what she tells us will come to pass.'

There was a murmur of what I took to be agreement and intrigue. It seemed what Miss Li had told me about Lady Athena's following was true. People really believed in her. Only one reading, though . . .

I immediately decided I had to volunteer. It would get me closer to her, and I'd truly be able to sense what was going on. And, well, I had to admit I was rather excited at the prospect of knowing what lay in my future.

Now there was a sound like rainfall, and the smoke began to billow out once more. The man wheeled round dramatically, and then looked back at us. 'Aha,' he said in a practised manner. 'My lady is ready to join us. Remember to keep your wits about you. The barrier . . . to the spirit world . . . is about to be broken.' He turned, almost casually this time, and disappeared into the smoke at the back of the stage, as all went dark once again.

The orchestra in the pit struck up an ominous score.

Another thunderclap, and – I couldn't quite believe my eyes – the lady herself was illuminated as she descended from the heavens, arms stretched out. She floated down towards the stage amid the smoke. As it began to clear a little, I could make out a small set that surrounded her. There was some sort of wardrobe carved of a dark walnut, a table covered with a velvet cloth and two seats beside it. Sitting on the table was a crystal ball, elegantly perched on a shiny bronze stand.

There was also a gilt mirror, fairly long and slim, standing to one side. It was facing away from everyone except one of the chairs – presumably only Lady Athena could look into it. We were able to see part of the glass from where we sat.

She was a sight to behold, there was little doubt in that. She had honey-coloured hair that she wore long, in waves that draped round her. A loose, flowing white gown covered her, intricately decorated with blue beads all the way along the neckline and down the tie that went round the waist. A beaded blue snake circled one arm. She certainly looked as though she had stepped out of a classical painting.

The crowd held their breath as her bare feet touched the ground. She stared into the middle distance, before her eyes snapped forward.

'Good evening,' she said in a soft voice with a hint of an unusual accent that I couldn't place. I thought perhaps it was trying to be Greek, but it didn't sound anything like the lilt in Mrs Anastos's voice. 'I am the Lady Athena. I welcome you all, living and dead.'

She slowly sat down in one of the chairs. 'Who will step forward for a reading?' she asked.

This is it, I thought. *This is my chance.*

So I jumped up from my seat – only to be met by the sight of every single person in the audience doing the same.

CHAPTER SEVEN

The uproar in the packed theatre was enormous. Everyone was clamouring to be chosen, some of them waving their hands in the air like school-children.

The only person who wasn't standing, I noticed, was Oliver. He was looking up at me as if I were mad, and gripping on to his chair tightly. Perhaps he was worried I was about to force him to volunteer as well.

Lady Athena barely seemed affected by the roaring crowd. She simply stared. And then she slowly raised her arms. It was as if a spell had fallen over the audience as the silence rippled in.

Pick me, I thought as loudly as I could. *Pick me!*

Lady Athena's head tipped on one side, her honey-coloured hair cascading over her shoulders. Then she closed her eyes. After a few moments, she spoke. 'I'm getting a name. Mrs . . . Baker? No.' She bobbed her head, eyes still closed, looking rather like an owl. '*Mrs Barker*,' she said definitively.

'Ooh!' A lady in the front row jumped to her feet. She was fairly old, with cotton-wool hair and thick spectacles. 'That's me!'

My hopes crashed and I flopped back into my seat, defeated. A fog of mumbles and groans rose up from the rest of the audience, but I could have sworn I heard Oliver breathe a sigh of relief. I gave him a questioning look.

'I thought you were about to jump down there,' he whispered.

For a lady approaching her older years, Mrs Barker was sprightly. In no time at all, she had bustled to the side of the stage and stood in the spotlight that shone down beside the steps below us, her black skirts swooshing as she went. She must have been a widow. I wondered if she wanted Lady Athena to communicate with her husband.

'Mrs Barker,' Lady Athena said in her singsong voice, 'what wisdom is it that you seek from beyond the veil?'

'It's my cat,' Mrs Barker said, loudly enough for most of the audience to hear. Well, that was a surprise. 'Mittens. He's been missing for nearly a year, from my home in Savill Street. I just want to know what's happened to him.' She sniffed. 'Will he return to me?'

'Very well,' said Lady Athena, nodding thoughtfully. 'Please take your seat, Mrs Barker. I will ask this of my spirit guide. To do this, I will have to be hidden from view, as the sights of the other realm are most dangerous to those who are unprepared.'

As Mrs Barker shuffled back to her seat, Lady Athena turned towards the huge wardrobe and pulled out two long white strips of cloth from somewhere on her person.

'A volunteer, please?' she asked. 'I must be bound before I enter.'

Another rush of hands, and she chose a man from a few rows back with a silk cravat, who introduced himself as Mr Winston. He looked flushed with pride as he climbed the steps.

'My eyes and hands,' she instructed, and he tied the cloths round them. 'Make sure the knots are tight so that I will be unable to move.'

The man nodded, satisfied with his work, and then returned to his seat.

Lady Athena stood as still as a statue, blinded and hands behind her back, and the enormous doors of the cabinet flew open.

I leaned over the balcony and craned my neck to see what was inside, but all I could make out was a dark void. Oliver pulled me back to my seat. I brushed him off.

Smoke and mist poured out on to the stage once more. I watched as Lady Athena faced the wardrobe and then appeared to take a deep breath, her shoulders lifting and falling. Then she stepped forward and disappeared inside, the dark doors closing behind her. The audience gasped and muttered.

'What is she doing?' Oliver hissed beside me.

'Shush,' I said, staring at the wardrobe, trying to work out what was going on myself. I almost expected some sort of dramatic swell of music, but for a minute there was nothing but silence.

Then there were sounds. Not music, though. Far from it. A curious knocking came from inside the wardrobe, getting louder and louder. Then some strange, unearthly, far-off cries. The whole wardrobe started to shake as if in an earthquake. How was this happening?

I almost couldn't take my eyes off it, but I had to if I

was going to properly search for ghostly activity. I forced myself to close them, gripping the rail of the balcony with my hands, and reached out with my senses. This time I did feel something. At the edges of my thoughts, there was a faint glow, a slight whisper. But from the rattling wardrobe on the stage? Nothing.

Somehow that didn't make it any less unsettling. I opened my eyes to see the doors bursting open as the mysterious noises stopped.

The stage lights illuminated Lady Athena as she appeared to almost glide from the wardrobe, still bound with the white cloths.

Mr Winston took himself back upon the stage and carefully examined the knots. 'Tight as ever!' he proclaimed to a round of applause. He unpicked them and freed her, letting the bindings fall to the floor.

'Thank you, sir,' said Lady Athena.

Her eyes remained closed as he went back to his seat, but slowly she opened them again. The crowd went quiet, the air heavy with anticipation.

'Mrs Barker,' she said, 'I have taken a glimpse into your future. The sights that I have seen are beyond human understanding, but, with the help of my spirit guide, Achilles, I can offer you this wisdom.'

Mrs Barker stood up, the eagerness radiating off her.

Oliver began nudging me urgently.

'What is it?' I hissed.

He pointed at the golden mirror. Sure enough, there was something there. It looked like some sort of message had appeared, but I was too far away and not quite at the right angle to read it.

I did notice, though, that Lady Athena was staring at it.

'Your beloved companion,' she said, and I noticed she deliberately didn't say *cat* as if she perhaps thought this a bit silly, 'is still among the living, for his spirit has not gone to the other side.'

'Oh, thank goodness,' said Mrs Barker. There was a murmur of approval from the crowd.

'He will cross your threshold again,' Lady Athena continued. 'Tomorrow . . . After midnight. You must leave your door open and your gates unlocked, to welcome him home.'

Another ripple of murmurs. I made a mental note of her words. We would have to check if this prediction came true.

'Thank you, thank you,' Mrs Barker replied, dabbing at her eyes with her handkerchief. 'Bless you, my lady.'

I highly doubted that Lady Athena was truly the lady of anywhere. But something about her was so . . . regal. The way she carried herself was pure elegance.

'Now,' she said, gripping everyone's attention once again, 'I will pass on messages from your loved ones . . .'

★ ★ ★

What followed was an enthralling performance during which the medium spoke words that had apparently been told to her by her Ancient Greek ghost. Audience members were shocked and emotional every time, hands over their mouths as they nodded tearfully.

At the end of the hour, Lady Athena bid us all farewell. 'And until next time . . .' she said, 'may the spirits guide you.'

There was a rumble of thunder, the lights went down for a moment – and she seemed to drop out of sight. I almost couldn't believe my eyes. How had she done that?

'That was a heap of rubbish, wasn't it?' said Oliver as we watched the audience bustle out of their seats, the air ablaze with chatter.

Just like that, the spell was broken. I blinked at him for a moment before I found myself back in reality. 'You're right,' I said. 'I couldn't sense a single ghost. But . . . it was certainly convincing.'

The way she had spoken for the dead – I had almost thought it to be real, even though it was not the way I experienced their voices. I wondered if she had truly known the details of the people she was talking about, or if she had just been reading her believers' reactions.

The colour was slowly returning to Oliver's face. 'I didn't like it,' he said. 'Too strange.'

'I can't explain everything that she was doing,' I said, images of Lady Athena's bizarre act and her magic mirror floating through my mind. 'But I suppose we shall find out whether her prediction comes true.'

We exited the box and headed back towards the bar, where I was hoping we would run into Niko and Eleni again. Instead, I was in for something of a surprise as our path led us towards someone who looked almost exactly like Miss Li.

I quickly realised that this must be her sister, the one who was being brought to the performances by her husband. Sure enough, she was clinging to the arm of a tall man in an elegant suit with ruffled blond hair under his hat and a bristly moustache. What did Miss Li say their surname was?

'Mr and Mrs . . . Campbell?' I tried as we approached them.

'Hello there,' said the man. 'Do we know you?'

Oliver glanced at me anxiously. He was clearly wondering what on earth I was doing, as usual.

'Oh, um, good evening,' I said with a small curtsey (lest Mother's chastising voice begin echoing in my ears). 'I'm an acquaintance of your sister,' I said, gesturing to Mrs Campbell, formerly the elder Miss Li, who was looking at me with a similar expression to Oliver. 'I'm Violet, and this is my friend Oliver.'

'Charmed,' said Mr Campbell, nodding at us both. 'Barnaby Campbell.' I noted that he didn't introduce his wife. 'Wasn't that a magnificent show?'

Oliver shrugged. I tried to look enthusiastic. 'Oh yes, wonderful.'

'Lady Athena is just marvellous,' he said with a smile.

His wife joined him, nodding. 'She is very good. I am a huge admirer.'

'Do you come here often?' I asked, even though I already knew the answer.

'Wouldn't ever miss it,' said Barnaby. 'Her powers are beyond compare. She truly communes with the spirits and sees visions of the future. It has been proven time and time again!'

'It is fascinating,' I admitted, although my fascination lay in whether or not any of it was real.

Zhen Campbell smiled politely. 'We must be going now,' she said. 'It is nice to meet you both. Please give my regards to my sister.'

Barnaby tipped his hat, and the two of them walked away.

'Is that the time?' Oliver exclaimed, and I turned to see him staring at a clock on the wall. 'We have to get back or your ma and pa will—'

'Be furious – I know,' I finished. 'But we sent Bones with a note, didn't we? I'm sure we can squeeze in a little more before they close up the theatre for the night. Can we find the Anastos siblings?' I asked hopefully. 'Or Archie?'

He stared back at me, his eyes searching mine. 'What are you plotting, Violet?'

'Just a smidge more investigation,' I replied. 'I think it's time I interviewed some ghosts.'

Chapter Eight

We found Archie standing in a doorway, bowing enthusiastically to the clientele as they left the auditorium.

'Archie,' I said with a sugared voice, 'would you mind escorting us somewhere quiet backstage or upstairs for a minute? I just need to take a moment to, um, gather my sensibilities.'

'Oh, of course, miss,' said Archie. 'Follow me.'

'What's that supposed to mean?' Oliver hissed in my ear as we trailed after the boy.

'I haven't the foggiest,' I whispered. It was just something I'd read in novels. It had worked, though, so I wasn't going to complain.

Archie led us back through a few more heavy doors and into the rabbit warren of corridors that made up the backstage area of the theatre.

'There's a quiet parlour in here,' he said when we reached one of the many doors. He gave a gentle rap on the wood, but the silence suggested there was no one inside. 'It's the retiring room. It's where we have to take ladies who faint.'

'Does that happen a lot?' Oliver asked.

'Oh aye,' Archie said as he reached into his pocket for the key and clicked it into the lock. 'Especially when Lady Athena is performing.'

Oliver raised his eyebrows, but I could see what Archie was getting at. It was a rather spooky and otherworldly performance. And if she predicted something shocking in your future? Why, that could give anyone a funny turn. I thought it was a little silly, though. I knew most ladies were not as delicate as they or society pretended them to be.

'Thank you, Archie,' I said, looking round at the room – a rather plain affair with a few chaise longues and some dreary paintings. 'This will do nicely. Give us some time, will you?'

And, with a move that certainly would have shocked my mother or probably any other person in polite society, I pulled Oliver into the room and shut the door behind us.

Archie, thankfully, seemed perennially unbothered by anything. 'Right you are, miss,' I heard him say from the other side.

'You think there are ghosts in here?' Oliver asked. 'But you said you couldn't feel anything in the theatre, didn't you?'

'Ghosts generally prefer quiet, I think,' I said. 'Well, it's either that or busy places just drown out my senses too much.'

With my abilities, so much was guesswork. I had never been able to even voice my thoughts aloud until I met Oliver, and it was a relief to be able to do so.

'But . . . ain't they all out in the graveyard?' He sat down on a chaise longue and crossed his legs.

'Well, do you remember what I said about ghosts being like . . . echoes? Ripples in the stream? It seems as though sometimes when they've died in dramatic circumstances, or they have unfinished business, the souls linger round their place of death.' As I spoke, I closed my eyes and trailed my fingers across the raised patterns on the wallpaper. 'Sometimes they are drawn to an object or a person, rather than their earthly remains.'

'An' you think there'll be some ghosts here,' he said.

I shrugged. 'It's worth a try, isn't it? Now hush a minute.'

As Oliver went still, I closed my eyes and reached out with my second sense. 'Is anyone there?' I whispered.

There was a sound like the rustle of a rising curtain, and then a chill descended over me. I began to hear a crackly deep voice, like a record playing on a phonograph.

Thou canst not say I did it, the voice said. *Never shake thy gory locks at me.*

What did that mean? 'H-hello,' I said, a tickle in my throat. 'Are you a spirit?'

Aye, and a bold one, that dare look on that which might appal the devil.

The words sent a shiver down my spine. But there was something familiar about them. I was sure I'd heard them before.

'What leaves you lingering here, and not at your final resting place?'

Blood hath been shed ere now, i' the olden time, the voice came back.

I tried my best to interpret that. 'You were killed, murdered . . . long ago?'

Aye, and since too, murders have been perform'd, it said.

'More than one murder in this place's history?' I wondered aloud. 'A ripe spot for ghosts, then.'

'Blimey,' I heard Oliver mutter.

'Spirit –' I tried again – 'has anyone else communicated with you?'

A chill breeze swept through the windowless room.

If charnel houses and our graves must send those that we bury back, our monuments shall be the maws of kites, the ghost said.

'Um, very well,' I said, although I wasn't at all certain what that meant. It was dreadfully familiar, though. Perhaps I needed to be more specific. 'The medium, Lady Athena. Does she truly speak to you? Does she have any connection to the dead?'

A gust of that ghostly wind blew so hard that I could have sworn I felt my hair rush out behind me.

Avaunt! the crackling voice boomed, suddenly with an edge of fury to it. *And quit my sight! Let the earth hide thee!*

'*Macbeth!*' I said aloud suddenly as the realisation hit me. 'You're quoting from Shakespeare!' That was why I recognised the words the ghost was speaking. *The Complete Works of Shakespeare* was one of my father's prized possessions.

And then I promptly clapped my hand over my mouth because, if there was one word you weren't supposed to say in a theatre, it was *Macbeth*. *The Scottish play*, you were meant to call it. Dreadfully bad luck was said to befall those who spoke the name.

Suddenly everything went silent.

'Spirit?' I called.

Nothing. No more Shakespeare, no more chill breeze. I opened one eye to find Oliver looking back at me, his face a picture of horror.

'My goodness,' I said. 'Actors are so . . . theatrical.'

Oliver didn't speak for a moment. 'I . . . I . . .'

'What?' I asked, suddenly suspicious. 'Did you hear something?'

He frowned. 'I don't know. I thought I could, maybe. But your hair . . . it *moved*, Violet.'

'That was real?' I asked. 'I felt that.' This was most unusual. People rarely noticed any of the ghostly things that I did. 'It was probably just a draught from somewhere.'

'Hmm.' Oliver stood up and shivered. 'What did the ghost say? You said it was . . . quoting *M—*'

'Don't say it!' I shot back quickly. 'I remembered it's supposed to be cursed – you can't name it in a theatre!'

'Oh no,' Oliver said, suddenly looking more concerned. He wasn't particularly superstitious, but he was perpetually more worried about everything than I was.

'It could have been a load of nonsense,' I said, 'but he certainly seemed furious when I asked about Lady

Athena. I don't think she's popular with the spectral residents.'

He sighed and rubbed his scar. 'I suppose that makes sense. But come on – we must be getting back now, or . . .'

'I know, I know,' I said. 'You may spare me the lecture. We're leaving.'

★ ★ ★

Much to my disappointment, we didn't encounter the Anastos siblings again as we left. Archie accompanied us to the front doors. I was somehow surprised to find that it was night-time outside, after the warm and bright lights of the theatre.

'See you again soon!' Archie cried after us, with yet more enthusiastic waving.

'I hope so,' I said with what was probably a bit of a devious grin, as Oliver and I hurried away under the darkening skies.

'Bye, Arch,' Oliver called back.

There was much more of this mystery to unravel, and the Grecian Theatre was deeply entangled in it. And Lady Athena . . . would her latest prophecy come true as well? That was next on our list of things to investigate. I pulled my black gloves on and rubbed my hands together in anticipation.

We rushed back through the streets, Oliver having reminded me that we needed to keep a wary eye out for rogue drunkards and pickpockets. I jumped every time someone stepped out of an alley or leered at us from a pub doorway. I had become keenly aware that Bones was not by my side. Usually his presence afforded me a good deal of protection whenever we went out 'gallivanting', as Mother had often called it when she scolded me.

I glanced at Oliver, who was blowing on his hands to keep them warm in the cold night air. In that moment, I was very grateful not to be alone.

'What do you think?' I asked, on a quiet stretch of street bathed in the orange glow of the gas lamps. 'About Lady Athena?'

He shrugged. 'I reckon she's a fraud. Maybe the ghosts are fed up with her pretending that she's speaking to them. But then that don't explain how she's predicting these things an' getting them right.'

'Hmm,' I replied, 'indeed. And many people believe in her. You heard what Mr and Mrs Campbell said. They were praising her to the high heavens!'

Oliver shook his head sadly. 'No wonder they want to spend all their money on her. They've been sucked in right and proper.'

We turned the corner to our street, and I immediately knew that something was wrong.

Sitting outside the front door, his tail wagging and something clearly clutched in his mouth, was Bones.

Uh-oh. My lungs tightened and my footsteps quickened as we approached the black-draped front of our shop. *My note.*

'Um . . .' said Oliver. 'Is that . . .?'

I didn't answer. Bones must have dislodged it from his collar and retrieved it with his teeth.

Bones jumped up and put his paws on my shoulders, and I gently pulled the note from his mouth. How long had he been sitting there? Poor boy.

I turned and pushed on the door handle, which swung open. 'Hello?' I called cautiously as Oliver and I stepped through the doorway, only to see my father stand up from behind his desk. He did not look happy.

'Violet,' he said, 'you are – and I don't know how many times I've had to say this – in very big trouble.'

CHAPTER NINE

I watched as the nervous figure of Ernesto appeared behind my father.

'We're home now, Father,' I said with more confidence than I really had. 'There's nothing to worry about.'

He removed his spectacles and rubbed his temples in a gesture of exasperation.

'You have quite spectacularly missed the point, Violet. I can see that you're home *now*. What I would like to know is *where have you been?*'

'I, um . . .' I stumbled over the words, looking down at my shoes. 'We were . . . investigating an important matter.'

He narrowed his eyes at me. 'Really, now. Ernesto here told me that you said you were running errands for *me*.'

Sorry, Ernesto mouthed from behind him.

Father put his spectacles back on and turned to Oliver, his voice gaining an extra air of disappointment, as though Oliver had been appointed the sensible member of our duo. 'You too, Oliver? Why didn't you drag her back home?'

Oliver shrugged apologetically. 'Can't drag her anywhere she don't want to be dragged, sir.'

Father tilted his head in agreement as if this were a fair point.

'And she did send a note,' Oliver added, pointing down at Bones, 'with the dog.'

I unfolded the piece of paper, which was only slightly damp and had a few teeth marks. 'See! It says we're at the Grecian Theatre and will be back by bedtime.'

'That's all very well, but you are holding the note,' Father said, implying that I was simple.

'I realise that,' I said. 'Bones didn't come inside, obviously.'

Ernesto held up his hand in a somewhat wobbly fashion.

'I am afraid that was my fault. I saw the dog, but I, I did not want to let him in the shop . . .' He glanced at Father. 'I'm sorry, sir.'

Drat. I'd forgotten to account for Ernesto's fear of dogs. I'd thought Bones would be able to get into the house somehow. I supposed the back gate to the garden was shut, and our fence was very tall.

'No, no, you're quite all right, Ernesto,' Father said, patting him on the shoulder. 'The dog shouldn't be in here anyway. You've stayed late enough as it is. You can head home now.'

Ernesto nodded gratefully and hurried to the back room to get his things.

'And –' Father tipped his hands skywards – 'Violet, that is ridiculous. You can't rely on *the dog* to bring us messages. What if he'd run somewhere completely different?'

'He wouldn't,' I insisted, patting Bones on the head. His tongue lolled out happily. 'He knows where he's going.' Bones was special, and I knew it, even if my parents didn't.

'*For goodness' sake*, Violet,' Father said, banging his hand on the desk and sending a shudder through my skeleton. 'Listen to me for a moment. The important thing here is that you can't go running about without telling us. Your mother has been beside herself with worry. What if something were to happen to you?'

'I'm not going anywhere alone,' I argued. 'I was with Oliver and Bones.'

'I'll keep her safe as I can, sir,' Oliver chimed in, and I was pleased to hear him siding with me. Perhaps he had caught the investigating bug too.

'It was an important matter,' I insisted before Father could get another word in edgeways. I thought it might well be time to tell the truth. 'A case, in fact. I've been . . . hired. As a detective.'

From Father's expression, you might have thought I'd just told him that I was transforming into a fish.

We waited for his response, but he simply sat down heavily on his chair. Bones padded over and curled up on the floor beside him, probably relieved to be back in the warm.

'Someone . . . *hired* . . . *you*?' he said finally. 'For money?'

'Maybe,' I responded. I still wasn't certain about that part.

He exhaled as he stared into the middle distance. 'What is this case, precisely?'

I shuffled uncomfortably before explaining. 'Um, a lady called Miss Li came here. She asked me to look into the dealings of Lady Athena, the medium at the Grecian Theatre, who made an impossible prediction about Miss

Li's necklace that came true, and now our client is suspicious . . .'

'*Your client?*' Father looked up at me. 'You must be aware that this sounds ridiculous, Violet.'

That shook me into silence for a moment. But I soon realised that the best defence was sitting right in front of me.

I stepped closer to the desk.

'We saved your life,' I said quietly, waving at Oliver and Bones, 'by solving a mystery, did we not?'

Father tapped his fountain pen gently on the desk, and I waited with bated breath for his answer. Eventually he looked up, his features softening. 'That you did, darling. But it was dangerous and reckless. You know your mother was in a terrible state.'

'But you're here today!' I insisted. 'Dangerous and reckless it may have been, but we did it. We brought you back home to us.'

'*You* might not be here with us if the Black Widow had had her way,' Father said gravely. I felt a chill at his words. 'Murder and mystery are a perilous business. That's why I leave such matters to the police.'

'The police didn't uncover the truth,' I reminded him. '*I did*. I proved that I can do it. If you just give me a chance, I shall prove myself again. And if I don't, well –'

I shrugged – 'then I'll go back to needlework and flower arranging. And I'll be done with it.'

Perhaps that was a lie. I wasn't sure if I could give up the mystery business now that I knew how exhilarating and dangerous it could be. It had the adventure I craved. Then again, if I couldn't solve this case, what kind of detective was I?

Father exhaled. He chewed the end of his pen.

'*Please*,' I begged.

We couldn't stop now. We had to know what was really going on. *I* had to escape the box I'd been put in, or I'd be stuck being seen as nothing but a decorative object for the rest of my life.

He dropped the pen on to the dark wood. 'All right,' he said finally. 'I suppose you've given the lady your word so you must see this through.'

I turned and grinned at Oliver, who gave me a thumbs up.

'But –' Father held up a finger – 'I want you to tell us precisely where you're going before you run off anywhere. And I want you home before nightfall. No night-time jaunts, you hear me?'

I nodded in quick agreement. 'Yes, yes.'

'Oliver,' he added, 'you stay by her side. Keep her out of trouble.'

'Yes, sir,' Oliver said, giving a probably inappropriate salute.

Father pointed down at Bones. 'You too.' Bones licked his finger. 'And you can go straight to bed,' he told me. 'Supper has been cleared away already.'

'All right,' I said with more enthusiasm than I should have. 'Thank you for your understanding, Father.'

I hurried out of the shop and into our hallway. I heard Bones's footsteps on the tiles as he clattered after me, followed by Oliver's steady tread. I stopped at the stairs, waiting for my friend to catch up.

'What're you so cheerful about?' Oliver asked. 'I think that bad luck from the theatre followed us home.'

I jumped up and down on the bottom step, sending Bones dashing to the top of the stairs. 'But he said I can carry on my detective work! Veil Investigations lives!'

He raised an eyebrow at me.

'And you'll be investigating alongside me, of course,' I added, waving airily.

'Right,' he said. 'But you've been punished. Bed with no supper, no going out at night . . . '

My stomach was growling a little. 'Sneak me a piece of bread, would you?'

Oliver nodded. 'Course. But, if we can't go out at night, how are we gonna investigate this cat business? Lady

Athena told that old lady her cat would return at midnight tomorrow.'

'Drat!' I punched my hand in an unladylike gesture. 'I didn't think of that.'

'How about we go there the day after? Find out if the cat really came back?' He leaned against the wall, arms folded.

I sighed. 'No chance of catching anyone in the act there. But I think that's what we shall have to do. Perhaps we'll be able to ask Mrs Barker some questions, and take a look at the scene.'

I really didn't want to break the rules that I'd just agreed to, not when I was so close to my father letting me take a step down the path I dearly desired to travel on. 'The last thing we want is for Father to lock me in the house for the rest of my days.'

'Indeed, miss.' Oliver still reverted to calling me 'miss' sometimes, no matter how much I reminded him that I preferred him to use my name.

I grinned. 'So we take a look at what happens with this cat, and if it returns we'll work out how Lady Athena did it. Then we'll simply prove that she's a fraud, and get the answers Miss Li is looking for. How hard can it be?'

CHAPTER TEN

Two days later, as we stood in the pouring rain at one end of Savill Street, I began to regret my words.

'She definitely didn't say which house she lived in?' I asked as I backed against the wall under the porch of a tall home, Bones shivering against my legs. I hadn't brought an umbrella, and the spring had sprung a downpour upon us.

'No, an' she didn't draw Lady Athena a map, neither,' Oliver said, rolling his eyes as the water dripped off his face.

I prodded him. 'All right. All right!' I took a deep breath. 'What sort of detective would I be if I can't find where someone lives on a street? We'll work it out. Come along.'

I had told my parents that we would be going out for the day to work on the case – Mother was not best pleased, but Father was a man of his word, and so here we were. I had to prove to him that solving the Seven Gates Murders and catching the Black Widow hadn't been a fluke, that I was capable of much more.

Stepping out on to Savill Street, I found it was lined with fairly modern and well-kept houses, with brick frontages, striking stone porches and pocket-handkerchief front gardens. Red rooftops stretched away into the distance, topped with tall chimneys puffing out smoke.

'Bones, keep an eye out for cats,' I called. He gave me a knowing look that I suspect was telling me that was something he always did, and trotted on ahead.

I peered at each house in turn, looking for any clues. One letterbox bore the name Carter, another Arkwright. One front garden had a small yapping spaniel who tried unsuccessfully to leap over the wall at Bones. One door had a sign above reading *Miss Angela's Lodging House for Respectable Young Ladies*. None of these were promising.

Just as I was about to declare the whole thing hopeless, Bones stopped at the end of the row, sniffing at a black iron gate. I hurried over to him.

'What's he spotted?' Oliver asked.

'Oh,' I said, approaching the gate. 'Well.'

Attached to the railing with a sad piece of string was part of a sopping-wet piece of paper, the top of which clearly read MISSING CAT, the bottom either torn or fallen away.

Oliver and I exchanged a glance. 'Has to be the place,' he said.

I lifted the latch and let us in. There were some steps leading down the side, which presumably went to the back garden. We avoided those and instead darted up to the front entrance, where a small porch sheltered us from the deluge. The sound of the rain on the tiles was deafening.

'I say we talk to Mrs Barker first, and find out if the cat has returned, then take a look around,' I muttered, thinking aloud as I looked up at the ornate bell.

'WHAT?' shouted Oliver, putting a hand to his ear.

'I SAID, I SAY WE . . . Oh, never mind.' I rang the bell, and knocked, too, for good measure. Bones hung back, seeming a little wary.

Presently, the door opened and Mrs Barker appeared – with a fluffy tabby cat in her arms.

'Good morning,' she said. She looked a little dishevelled and her lined cheeks were tear-stained, but she was smiling widely.

'Mrs Barker?' I asked. 'You found your cat?'

She waved us in. 'Come into the hallway a moment, dearies. I can't hear a blessed thing over this rain!'

Oliver and I gratefully stepped inside and dripped on to the tiles, but Bones wouldn't come in. He stayed at the door, a low growl rumbling in his throat.

'Whatever is the matter with you?' I asked him. But Bones simply sat on his haunches and refused to move. 'All right, have it your way,' I told him. 'You wait there.' I pulled the door to and we turned to Mrs Barker, who was still smiling and petting her cat. The cat looked unimpressed.

'Do I know you children?' Mrs Barker asked, peering over her glasses at us.

'Um, no, ma'am,' I said. 'But we heard about your cat. At the Grecian Theatre.'

'An' we saw the sign on your gate,' Oliver added. 'Thought you might need some help looking for him.'

That was quick thinking on his part. It certainly sounded more plausible than the fact that we were trying to determine the accuracy of the missing cat prophecy.

'Ah yes,' said Mrs Barker, 'but Mittens has returned!'

The cat wriggled in her arms and tried to jump away, but she kept a tight hold on him. 'I couldn't believe it. I said to my Jonathan that I was so relieved Mittens would be coming home, and he told me I was going batty. But look, here he is! I left the back door open for him and he came in at the stroke of midnight! Just as Lady Athena said. She really is a miracle.'

'This is your Mittens, ma'am?' Oliver asked. He reached to stroke the cat, but it hissed at him and finally succeeded in jumping from Mrs Barker's arms and running away.

'Oh yes,' she said, still smiling at the cat's retreating tail. 'He's feeling a little out of sorts, I think – probably in shock, poor thing. Isn't he a beautiful boy? I had a wonderfully detailed drawing of him made up for the posters.' She pointed to the parlour, and I peered in to see a framed drawing of a fluffy tabby cat above the fireplace. Oliver raised an eyebrow.

'We'd best be getting back, then,' I said, 'and getting dry.'

'Indeed, dearie, you don't want to catch your death,' said Mrs Barker.

'If you don't need any more help, that is,' Oliver added.

'Oh, I'm quite all right,' she said with a wave of her hand. 'I have my Mittens to keep me company again.

Thank you, children.' She turned round and looked behind her. 'Where's he got to? Mittens?' She bustled away towards the back of the house, seeming to forget that we were still standing there.

Oliver nudged me. 'We should look out the back,' he said.

'Precisely what I was thinking,' I said. I hoped the rain hadn't washed away any evidence. 'Come on.'

'Bye, Mrs Barker!' Oliver shouted in the direction of the old lady, but there was no reply.

I opened the front door again, the sound of the rain growing louder once more. Bones was still there, circling nervously, and he greeted me as we stood under the porch.

'Hmm,' I said, scratching his damp snout. 'You aren't a fan of that cat, are you, boy?' He gave a quiet whine.

'Maybe he's got suspicions,' Oliver said loudly over the rain. 'Did you hear what she said about the poster?'

I nodded. 'A detailed picture! One that anyone could have seen.' If they were looking to, say, fake the return of a missing cat to fulfil an invented prophecy. 'I suggest we examine the scene of the crime.'

I took a step forward, but Oliver grabbed my arm. 'She'll see us sneaking around! Or someone else will! How are you gonna explain that? They'll call the bobbies on us . . .'

'Mrs Barker lives alone,' I said, waving up at the house. 'That cat is all she's got – I'm certain of it.'

'Servants?' Oliver said. 'Neighbours?'

'If anyone starts poking their nose in, I'm certain I shall think of something. Come on, Bones, let's go,' I commanded, pointing him towards the steps that led down to the back door and lower garden.

The three of us headed out into the downpour – Bones awkwardly stumbling ahead, me picking up my skirts and tackling the steep and slippery steps quickly while Oliver clung to the railings.

Bones immediately went to the back door and began sniffing around. A patio of stone slabs surrounded it – no evidence there, but Bones was certainly picking up something. The lawn grass was fairly long, and I fancied that it perhaps looked a little flattened in places, as if someone had walked across it.

'Are you getting a scent, boy?' I called to him over the rain. 'Can you trace it?' Whether he followed my instruction or merely his own nose, I didn't know, but he began tracking whatever he was picking up across the garden. He stopped at the flowerbed by the low back wall and barked.

Oliver jogged over, with me right behind him– and we soon saw what Bones had spotted. At the back of the flowerbed was a rather squashed bush, and beside it a set of footprints.

'Good work, boy!' I said, giving Bones a pat. He wagged his tail and wobbled with enthusiasm.

The rain would soon turn the prints to indistinguishable mud, but at that moment it was clear that someone had jumped over the wall, and recently. Now I was getting a better feeling about this case – it looked like someone really *was* behind Lady Athena's prophecies coming true. And not a spectre or a poltergeist, either, but a real flesh-and-blood person – with shoes.

I peered over the other side of the wall, where a few more of the footprints could be seen leading away, and tellingly there was not a single cat pawprint.

Oliver stood next to the marks in the soil. 'Bit bigger than mine,' he said, looking down at his scuffed boots. 'Not massive, though!'

'Probably an adult, then?' I grinned. This was our first step to proving that fraud was being committed. 'This was no magic or miracle,' I said with satisfaction.

'Is it ever?' Oliver asked.

'Remember that time you "died" and were resurrected?' I retorted.

'Good point,' he said, grinning back at me.

Suddenly I saw that Bones was staring up at the wall

to our right that bordered the neighbour's garden. Unfortunately, I noticed this too late.

'Oi!' came a voice, gruff and angry. 'What are you up to?'

A bald-headed man peered over the wall, his bristly eyebrows and beard framing a frown.

I stopped still, heart pounding.

'Now would be the time to think of something!' Oliver said.

Bones was quicker than me. He turned, took a run up and jumped the back wall, his scrabbling feet hitting the ground before he raced away. He had the right idea.

'Run!' was all I could say.

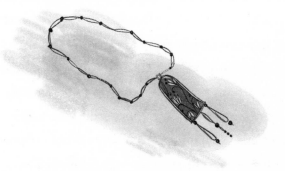

CHAPTER ELEVEN

We hurried along to the Grecian Theatre, eager to get away from the angry man and to share news of our findings. The three of us were soaked to the skin, and let me tell you that my heavy black dress and woollen petticoat were not light and breezy at the best of times, let alone when sopping wet. Bones at least didn't seem to mind.

'I've had enough of jumping walls and fences for a lifetime,' said Oliver grumpily. 'I nearly lost my cap.'

'Oh, stop moaning,' I told him. 'We got away scot-free.'

'By the skin of our teeth,' he said as he adjusted his hat, pulling the back of it down over the scar on his scalp. 'That bloke could have hopped over an' pummelled us.'

'Well, he didn't,' I said. 'And now we're fine. Albeit damp.'

But the rain suddenly cleared up as quickly as it had begun, the sun peeking timidly through the clouds once again, and Oliver and I breathed a sigh of relief. I tried to wring out some of the water from my clothes over a patch of grass, which gained me a number of judgmental looks from snooty passers-by with umbrellas.

'Ugh,' I moaned, 'we shall have to go into the theatre looking like drowned rats.'

'Didn't think you were that bothered about appearances, Violet,' Oliver muttered.

'I'm not,' I insisted with a huff.

Truth be told, I wasn't usually concerned with dressing to impress, or at least not as much as Mother wanted me to be. But when it came to Niko and Eleni . . . well, that was a different matter. I so desperately craved their approval.

Speaking of the Anastos siblings, I was pleased when we neared the theatre and spotted them right outside. Niko was pasting a **SOLD OUT** sign over one of the Lady Athena posters, while Eleni watched from her chair, arms folded.

'A little higher,' she said.

'That would cover up her face,' said Niko.

'Oh no,' Eleni said with a hint of gleeful sarcasm. 'How *terrible*.'

Oliver waved at them as we climbed the steps. 'Afternoon,' he said.

Bones ducked under the covered walkway and shook all the water off his fur, thankfully missing the rest of us.

Niko turned, dripping brush still in his hand. 'Oh hello! Violet and Oliver, wasn't it?'

'Yes,' I said with a small smile, trying not to be too pleased about the fact that he'd remembered my name. 'And we have news about our investigation. Can we come inside?'

'Oh, of course,' he said, placing his brush back in its bucket. 'Be our guest.'

'Tell me you have something that will put *Lady Athena* in her place,' Eleni added, making it clear that she thought the name was rather too much.

'I think we do indeed,' I replied.

Niko took the handles of Eleni's chair, hanging his bucket over one of them, and pushed it back inside the grand entranceway. It creaked a little as it went. 'Remind me to oil this thing,' he muttered.

The vast foyer was empty and quiet, besides a man

working in the ticket booth who was currently engaged in counting coins.

We stopped by a bench, upholstered in the same threadbare red velvet that was so prominent throughout the theatre, and I sat down on it.

'My apologies for dripping,' I said, 'but it can't really be helped.'

Eleni laughed, and her laugh was bright and sunny. She patted Bones as he once again nestled up against her. 'Tell us all,' she said.

'Well, at Lady Athena's performance, her prophecy was that a lady named Mrs Barker's missing cat would return at midnight yesterday. And, um, we unfortunately couldn't go at midnight to check, due to, um . . . circumstances.'

'Violet was forbidden from going out late,' Oliver added helpfully.

'Shush,' I said, blushing. 'That's not important. What's important is that we went there this morning and, well, firstly Bones was very unsure of the cat. It didn't seem that enamoured with its beloved owner, either.'

'Mrs Barker said the cat came in the back door at midnight just like Lady Athena predicted it would,' Oliver continued, 'so we checked the garden an' there were footprints. Someone had clearly jumped over the wall an' chucked the cat in through the door.'

Eleni's mouth dropped open. 'So you're saying someone sneaked in and tossed this Mrs Barker a *feline imposter*? How deliciously dramatic.'

'I think they might well have done,' I said. 'She seemed convinced, but who knows? It's certain that the cat didn't return on its own, though. There were no pawprints behind the wall, only human ones.'

Niko tucked a dark curl behind his ear and unhooked his bucket. 'I suppose Lady Athena didn't say the cat would get back by itself, did she? Perhaps it was a thief who felt remorse and returned it.'

'After this long?' I asked.

He shrugged. 'It doesn't seem very damning on its own.'

Hmm. Perhaps he had a point. I felt a little deflated.

'Well, I think it does,' Eleni chimed in, putting the wind back in my sails. 'It's most suspicious. We ought to go and talk to her.'

Just as I was about to express my gratitude, we were interrupted by a short man with a balding head of wispy dark hair, and a moustache on a face that was as friendly and open as one could get. He pushed through the double doors and came striding into the room.

'Hello, children!' he boomed, his voice bigger than it ought to be. 'Who are your friends today?'

'Baba,' Eleni said with a smile, 'this is Violet and Oliver. They were just . . .'

I gave a quick shake of my head. I wasn't sure that I wanted their father to know exactly what I was up to – especially if I were actually about to discredit one of his main acts.

'. . . telling us how much they love the theatre,' she finished without a flicker.

The man shook our hands with great vigour. 'Good, good,' he said. 'I'm Georgios Anastos. Welcome!' He put his hand to the side of his mouth. 'I love this old place too. That is why I throw all my money away on it. Don't tell my wife.' He winked.

Eleni and Niko gave each other sideways glances that suggested they'd heard this before.

'She already knows,' Eleni said in a stage whisper.

'Niko, my boy,' said Mr Anastos, pretending he hadn't heard, 'we need you backstage. Can I borrow you from your friends?'

'Of course,' said Niko quickly.

'You're abandoning me?' Eleni teased. She put a hand to her forehead. 'I shall just wither away and die here, I suppose.'

'We can help you!' I offered.

Niko raised an eyebrow. 'Are you sure?'

'Course,' Oliver said. 'It's no bother.'

'Bye for now, then,' said Niko, a twinkle in his eye.

'Just keep the dog off the seats,' said Mr Anastos, a hint of amusement in his voice. He patted Bones, who wagged his tail happily. Mr Anastos waved and led his son away towards the back of the theatre.

Eleni huffed and wheeled her chair to turn away from them. 'Come on,' she said. 'Someone take the reins –' she gestured to the handles behind her – 'and let's go and find Lady Athena.'

★ ★ ★

Eleni directed us through the twists and turns that led to the dressing rooms backstage as Oliver pushed her wheelchair. Bones trotted along beside us. But, as we went further down a corridor, a commotion became apparent.

Someone was having an argument. I heard shouting and banging, and then we all stopped dead in our tracks as a door bearing the nameplate LADY ATHENA flew open and a man stumbled out backwards.

' . . . and yet you have no problem taking all our work!' he said, brushing himself off. 'You charlatans! You . . . scoundrels!' He shouted this last part to the door, which had been unceremoniously slammed in his face.

'What on earth . . .?' I whispered. Oliver raised an eyebrow at me.

'Terence?' Eleni called out. 'What's the matter?'

But the man ignored her and simply stormed past us, practically elbowing Oliver out of the way in the narrow hallway. Bones growled as he passed.

'Who was that?' Oliver asked.

'Terence Clearwater,' Eleni explained. 'He's an actor, and usually the hero in a lot of our plays. He has a heart of gold, but he can be rather hot-headed.'

'I can see that,' I said. 'And it would seem he has an issue with our medium.'

Eleni waved us towards the dressing-room door. 'Let's find out what she has to say.'

We moved on and I knocked hastily on the dark red wood. Bones pushed against my legs. He was always keen to see who was on the other side of a door.

For a moment, I could hear some hurried muttering coming from within the dressing room, and then all went silent. Presently, the door swung open to reveal the man we had previously seen onstage – with the dark beard, the angular cheekbones and the top hat.

'The Lady Athena is charging her energies,' he said as if this explained anything.

'Oh, come off it, Jacob,' Eleni said. 'Can we come in? We'd just like a few words with the *lady*.'

It amused me that Eleni seemed incapable of describing Lady Athena as a 'lady' without the word dripping with scorn.

The man's eyes travelled over the four of us – which must have been an odd sight, I had to admit. I thought he was perhaps doing some calculations as to what would happen if he were rude to the theatre owner's daughter.

'Very well,' he said with a sharp nod. He looked at Oliver and me. 'I haven't made your acquaintance, have I? Mr Hyde, Lady Athena's manager, at your service.'

'I'm Violet, and this is Oliver,' I said. 'We're friends of Eleni and Niko.' I didn't know if that were even true yet, but it certainly felt good to say it.

Bones, however, was not feeling so friendly. He had started quivering and a growl began rumbling in his throat as he looked up at Jacob Hyde.

'Shush, boy,' I hissed.

'Come in,' Mr Hyde said, standing back with an outstretched arm. 'The dog stays outside.'

I frowned. 'All right. Bones, stay.' He whined in protest, but sat down and dutifully waited as I walked into the dressing room with Oliver and Eleni following.

The first thing that struck me upon entering was the smell of incense, so strong that it was like an explosion at a perfume factory. It reminded me of church.

The second thing I noticed was how dark it was. There was not a single window in the room: the place was lit by a few dribbling candles casting flickering shadows over the framed posters for Lady Athena's performances.

And lastly . . . there were the skulls.

CHAPTER TWELVE

I had spent a lot of time around the dead. Skulls, however, I was not so used to. Especially when they were staring back at me from multiple directions.

They were sitting round the room, several of them on the dressing table where Lady Athena was currently perched in a plush chair. She was already wearing her stage outfit. Something shimmered in the mirror behind her, but it was gone when I blinked.

Oliver shuddered at the grim bony visages. 'Are those real?' he asked quietly.

I gave him a worried look in response. They certainly bore a close resemblance to the real thing.

An odd tingling sensation went through me, the kind I felt when I was close to ghostly presences. Perhaps they *were* real. Oliver appeared deeply unsettled by the room, too, and kept glancing around and fidgeting.

'Well,' Eleni said, putting her hands demurely in her lap, 'hello, your *ladyship*.'

I fancied that I saw a flicker of annoyance in Lady Athena's face, but she was good at concealing it. 'My dear Eleni. Have you consulted your astrological charts lately?'

'You know, I keep forgetting to,' Eleni said without a trace of sarcasm. *Oh*, she was good too. 'What a shame.'

Mr Hyde walked round us and stood beside Lady Athena's tall chair, his arm resting on the back. 'You have something to ask?'

'Yes,' said Eleni. 'These two are investigating a story for . . . the newspaper.'

I cleared my throat. 'Nice to meet you, Lady Athena. We wanted to, um . . .'

It suddenly hit me that I was woefully unprepared for this interview. What was I supposed to say?

Oliver, on the other hand, seemed to shake off his fear and come to life. I think perhaps he remembered his Jack

Danger persona – the rogue newspaper journalist who asked tricky questions.

'You were just having an argument with that actor,' he said. 'What was that about?'

With that, he pulled out the pencil that always seemed to be tucked behind his ear. He didn't even have his notebook to write in, but he twiddled the pencil round his fingers in a way that perhaps betrayed his underlying anxiety.

'Rather young to be reporters, aren't you?' said Mr Hyde, frowning.

'I'm short for my age,' said Oliver, which made me grin. I remembered telling him to use that excuse last year.

Mr Hyde gave an exasperated sigh and rolled his eyes. 'That man is bothersome. He keeps harassing my wife.'

For a moment, I wondered who his wife was, but then I realised what he meant – our Mr Hyde was Lady Athena's husband. So they really were in this together.

'Whyever would he do that?' asked Eleni, although she didn't seem as shocked as her words might imply.

Mr Hyde waved his hand. 'Terence doesn't believe in Athena's talents.' Beside him, she stared forlornly at the floor. 'And, more to the point, he thinks we are taking up his space at this theatre. Pah! We have the most successful show by a mile. Perhaps the actors ought to try harder.'

Eleni narrowed her eyes at this, but said nothing.

'He does trouble me so,' said Lady Athena, raising her pale eyes and touching her husband's hand with her own. 'His energies are negative.'

I didn't know what that meant, and I wasn't sure I wanted to ask. I had to make sure we remembered the matter at hand. I nudged Oliver, who seemed to be better at questioning.

'Um, ma'am, your vision about the cat . . .' he began.

'Ah yes,' she said. 'It returned, I presume?' She reached over and patted one of her gloomy skulls in a most disconcerting way. 'Achilles is never wrong.'

That was supposed to be the name of her spirit guide, wasn't it?

'The cat did indeed appear at its mistress's door,' I explained carefully, 'but there was something peculiar about it. It didn't seem to be the same animal. And, to add to that, there were footprints leading from the back wall as if a person had deliberately placed the cat in the lady's home.'

To her credit, Lady Athena looked genuinely baffled, while her husband simply blinked. 'What?' she asked in a meek voice. 'That's rather strange. I . . . Achilles didn't mention anything about that.'

Mr Hyde folded his arms. 'Well, the cat appeared just as Athena predicted. I say her record is untainted. Is that all?'

'And if it's not the same cat?'

The man stared back at me from under the brim of his hat. 'Can you truly prove it is not? Does it not appear the same?'

'Well, um . . .' I looked at Oliver, who was still twiddling his pencil.

He shrugged. 'I suppose.'

'Good,' said Mr Hyde. 'Now, if you'll excuse us, our lady needs rest. When she gets a headache, she must have a clear room and a stick of incense to recover. Goodbye.'

I thought that perhaps the strong incense was more likely to give her a headache than to cure it, but that was beside the point. Mr Hyde wanted us out, and I wasn't prepared to argue with such a tall and strong-looking man – even taller with his top hat.

'Fair enough,' said Eleni. 'Oliver, can you take me back out?'

'Course,' said Oliver, and the three of us retreated – with me having to get the door because Mr Hyde did not offer to open it. He stayed beside his wife, who was stroking the top of the mysterious skull and staring into the middle distance.

As we left, Bones jumped up with excitement. I petted him absent-mindedly. 'That was strange,' I muttered as I pulled the door shut behind us.

'Rather,' Eleni agreed as we moved away from the dressing room. 'She seemed surprised by what you said, didn't she? But then she is a good actress, much as she pretends not to be.'

I stopped further down the corridor, once I was certain that they couldn't hear us. 'I think she really was surprised. Mr Hyde, on the other hand – he defended her too quickly. Are you thinking what I'm thinking?'

The other two looked at me blankly. As did Bones, although that was normal.

'It's him!' I said. 'Mr Hyde. He has to be the one orchestrating this. He carries out her prophecies for her; she makes money; both of them win.'

'I suppose he's certainly invested,' said Eleni. 'He stands to gain a lot from her popularity.'

'Precisely,' I replied with a triumphant smile.

'I dunno,' said Oliver, shifting on the spot. 'She was definitely shocked when you told her about the cat.' Bones's ears pricked up. 'If she's a fraud, wouldn't she know what her own husband was up to?'

'And he didn't exactly have a well-prepared defence,' Eleni added, propping her chin on a gloved hand, 'which you might expect if he really were the culprit. He just said we couldn't prove it was a different cat.'

I frowned. 'Hmm. I still think he's the most obvious suspect. We have to keep an eye on them both.' An idea suddenly came to me. 'Eleni, you can be our girl on the inside!'

'Ooh,' she said, sitting up a little straighter in her chair and rubbing her fingertips together. 'Do tell . . .'

'If you report to us what Lady Athena's new prophecies are, we can look into them – see if they're coming true. You and Niko could watch the pair while they're in the theatre, and we can stake out the scene in the field.' I had to admit I was using vocabulary I'd picked up from adventure books that I'd stolen from Father's shelves. 'As long as it's during the day, that is . . .'

Drat. I had a feeling this new rule was really going to get in our way. *Unless* . . .

'We're not allowed out of the theatre at night, either,' Eleni sighed, quashing my idea. 'Not that I'd manage it anyway,' she added. 'I'm usually in a deep sleep, or tossing and turning with aches and pains.'

I put a sympathetic hand on her shoulder, and she tapped it with her own.

'Day-time investigation it is, then,' I said, a little defeated. But I hoped that could still get us somewhere. 'We may not be able to catch Mr Hyde in the act, but we can probably build a good case.'

'I just don't think you can be so sure, Violet,' Oliver said. 'My gut thinks it ain't him.'

'Forget your gut, Oliver,' I told him. 'Use your brain.' He gave me a sullen look.

'Perhaps you're just hungry,' Eleni added helpfully. 'Take me in the direction of the bar, and I'll see if we can find some food . . .'

Bones barked in agreement. Food it was.

* * *

We went home from the theatre that afternoon filled with sandwiches and a new sense of purpose. Or at least I was feeling purposeful. I had given Eleni my address in case she needed to contact us with any information. Oliver was still dragging his feet.

'I don't think you should jump straight to blaming Mr Hyde,' he said as we neared the corner of our road, Bones snuffling through the spring blossoms that had fallen to the ground.

'Oh, come on,' I said. 'Apart from the evidence, he just looks like a villain, does he not?'

Oliver stopped on the wet pavement. 'An' I look like a street boy, don't I? An' you look like a dainty girl.'

I glared at him.

'My point is people are a lot more than what they look like on the outside.'

'*Hmm,*' I said. He did have a point. 'I suppose.'

I carried on walking in case Bones got too far ahead of us and give Ernesto a fright at the shop again.

'His name, though! Mr Hyde! Do you suppose he's read Stevenson?'

Now Oliver's expression was blank. 'What?'

'*The Strange Case of Dr Jekyll and Mr Hyde,*' I said. 'You must have heard of it.'

He shrugged. 'Nope.'

'It's a Penny Dreadful,' I told him.

We reached the shop window, and I tried to pretend that Bones wasn't cocking his leg against the wall by pointedly looking away for a few seconds.

'The kind Father buys secretly and Thomas is always trying to read, even though he's not allowed. It's about a man with an evil alter ego named Mr Hyde.'

'Well, unless your man named himself, it's probably just a coincidence,' Oliver said, taking his hands from his pockets to open the door.

Suddenly I noticed through the window that there

were customers inside. 'Wait, we should grab Bones's collar—'

I wasn't quick enough. Bones went bounding into the undertaker's shop, dizzy with excitement.

There were only a *few* screams.

Chapter thirteen

I went to bed that night with a cup of hot cocoa, and only a slight ringing in my ears from Ernesto's screaming. Thankfully, he recovered from his ordeal. Mother had let him lie on the chaise longue in the parlour with a damp cloth over his eyes to calm down. Bones had been given a thorough telling-off, and was now lying shamefaced on my bedroom rug with his head on his paws.

Alongside the cocoa I held my notebook. I rested it on my lap and stared into the flames of the fire that Maddy had lit for me in the hearth. I dipped my pen in the inkpot on my nightstand: it was time to write some case notes.

CASE NOTES

Being an investigation into the curious prophecies of Lady Athena at the Grecian Theatre by Veil Investigations

Incidents:

The impossible re-emergence of Miss Li's necklace from her father's grave

The return of Mrs Barker's cat who had been missing for nearly a year

Future prophecies will be reported on by Eleni Anastos

Suspects:

1. Lady Athena. Stands to gain much from her prophecies coming true, but seemed surprised when we confronted her with evidence that the cat did not return of its own accord.

2. Mr Hyde. Also stands to gain as the husband of Lady Athena. Acted suspiciously.

3. Mr Anastos? As owner of the theatre, he also benefits from Lady Athena's popularity.

I paused after writing that. I didn't particularly want to accuse Mr Anastos of anything. He had seemed so friendly. And what would that mean for Niko and Eleni? I had only recently been through the traumatic experience of having my own father falsely accused of a crime. For their sake, I really hoped he wasn't involved.

On the rug, Bones sheepishly coughed up a piece from the bottom of Ernesto's trousers.

I sighed, abandoned my notebook and pen on the nightstand and rolled over to go to sleep.

★ ★ ★

The next week, we received a telegram from Eleni, delivered by the telegram boy on his shiny bicycle. It read:

```
Have news of Lady Athena. Meet at
11 a.m. tomorrow at the Grecian? — E
```

I smiled down at it. It was rare that I got so much as a letter from anyone, let alone a telegram.

'Who is it from?' Ernesto asked. He tried to read it over my shoulder.

'A friend,' I replied with a small smile, secreting the piece of paper away in my pocket. I hoped whatever this news was it might mean that we could move forward with the investigation. The chance to see Eleni and Niko again was a welcome bonus. I just hoped whatever it was wouldn't point towards their father.

And so, the following morning, we found ourselves back in front of the imposing frontage of the Grecian Theatre. Eleven bells rang out from a nearby church – we were right on time.

Bones bounded up the steps to the windowed doors as if he were right at home. As if on cue, the door was opened by Niko. 'Morning,' he called out to Oliver and me while Bones skirted round his legs. 'Come on in.'

I smiled back at him. 'Good morning,' I replied. Oliver, I noticed, looked rather sulky.

We went into the empty and echoing foyer where we found Eleni sitting in her wheelchair beside a bench, her expression bright with excitement. I took a seat next to Niko. Oliver stood holding on to Bones, lest the dog should decide he wanted to chew Eleni's dress next.

Eleni rubbed her hands together. 'I have much to report,' she said.

'Do go ahead,' I said. I assumed from her demeanour that she thought she had something potentially incriminating against her nemesis.

'So Lady Athena has made four prophecies since we last spoke. The first was that a man would receive a letter from his dead wife.'

Oliver frowned.

'That's . . . quite a claim,' I said. 'Tell me you've seen this letter?'

'Fortunately, I have,' said Eleni. 'The poor man is one of Lady Athena's . . . disciples. He comes to every performance, hoping to receive a message from his wife. So the next night he came in, proudly waving this letter, tears in his eyes.'

'What did it say?' Oliver asked, his tone flat. I wasn't sure if he were disturbed or sceptical.

'I am at peace . . . I miss you dearly . . . we will be together again in death . . . That sort of thing,' said Eleni, waving her hand dismissively. 'He said the handwriting was just like hers.'

'I took a look,' said Niko. 'He had another letter that she'd written to him before she passed, and it seemed authentic.'

Eleni squinted. 'Or someone is talented at forgery. Anyway, the next prophecy was that a woman named Mrs Lambert would receive a gift of a large sum of money in the post.'

'Lucky her,' Oliver said, raising an eyebrow. 'Wish I'd had that one. Did she get it?'

'I thought the same. And indeed she did,' said Niko with enthusiasm. 'She was telling everyone as soon as it happened. It was a miracle.'

'Anyone could have sent that,' I pointed out. 'It doesn't seem particularly supernatural.'

'Precisely,' Eleni snapped, glaring at her brother.

Niko ignored her. 'And the third was that Mr Henley would be visited by a ghost outside his window on the eve of his uncle's demise. That one hasn't happened yet.

I spoke to him and he said it was not for a fortnight. But is that enough of a supernatural nature for you?'

Eleni did not look impressed. 'You know as well as I do that a ghost is made from a white sheet and smoke and mirrors.'

For a moment, I considered protesting that ghosts were real, but I didn't think that would help the situation. There definitely seemed to be tension between the siblings.

Oliver stroked Bones's head thoughtfully, clearly considering what we'd just been told. 'Are most of these people regular customers?' he asked.

'Yes, I believe so,' said Eleni.

Hmm. I took note of that. If they were people who regularly attended, that would make it easier for Lady Athena, or perhaps more likely her husband, to find out information about them.

'Now this last one is for you,' Eleni said. 'You live beside the cemetery, don't you?'

Bones's ears pricked up, as did mine.

'Oh no,' said Oliver, his face going whiter than usual. 'Don't tell me there's gonna be skeletons walking about or something.'

Eleni laughed. 'No, unfortunately. There is a recent memorial to a girl there, named . . . Caroline Spring, I believe?'

I nodded. 'That sounds familiar. Is it an angel statue?'

'Yes,' she replied. 'And, according to Lady Athena, a wreath of white lilies will appear on it, as a message from Caroline in heaven.'

I jumped up. 'We have to go and look!'

'Let us know what you find,' said Eleni, and Niko smiled in agreement.

'Thank you for this,' I said, taking Eleni's hands and squeezing them. 'Perhaps it will lead us closer to the truth.'

Bones began circling on the spot, eager to get going. 'Come on, boy,' I said. 'It's time for your favourite. A walk in the cemetery . . .'

* * *

Back within the walls of Seven Gates Cemetery, surrounded by a sea of stones, it didn't take me long to remember where the grave of Caroline Spring was. It was down one of the tree-lined avenues, a fairly recent addition in white marble. The angel was memorable as, unlike many of the others in the cemetery that stood pointed skywards, this one was laid down atop the tomb – eyes closed in eternal sleep.

As we got closer, Bones ran over to it and began sniffing around. And there, on the angel's head, was a wreath of white lilies.

Oliver gasped and pointed at it. 'Look!'

But, as I got closer and picked it up, I noticed something immediately. Women were expected to be familiar with flowers, and years of having to help my family create floral arrangements for funerals had finally paid off in that I had very firm knowledge of what a lily looked like.

'Those aren't lilies,' I said with both confidence and confusion.

'What?' Oliver said, leaning closer.

'I think they're rhododendron flowers,' I explained. 'I don't think this was a supernatural feat. I think this was put together by someone who couldn't tell their flowers apart. Perhaps a man, who was never taught such things.'

Oliver and I looked at each other. 'Mr Hyde?' we said in unison.

It could be another clue. I had noted down everything Eleni told us, but none of it seemed to point to any particular culprit. A man with an involvement in the theatre – that didn't particularly narrow it down.

What I felt certain of was that I wanted to attend a performance again. To see if I could work out what Lady Athena and her husband were *really* up to. But, being forbidden from going there at night, when would I ever get the chance?

CHAPTER FOURTEEN

The following Thursday, I was flicking through Father's morning paper as I ate breakfast, when something caught my eye.

SPECIAL MATINEE PERFORMANCE BY A CLAIRVOYANT

THE 'LADY ATHENA' TO PERFORM HER MYSTICAL ACT FOR MAYOR

At 4 p.m. tomorrow afternoon, there will be a special matinee performance at the Grecian Theatre in the borough of Havisham. The mayor of the city of Mordon will be in attendance, as will many other guests of importance. 'Lady Athena' is a spiritualist of some apparent psychic talent, who tells fortunes and is gaining great popularity with sold-out performances each week. Theatre owner Georgios Anastos commented: 'This is a spectacular show that must not be missed!'

I almost choked on my porridge. This was our chance!

'Oliver! Father!' I called out. I picked up the paper and dashed along the corridor. 'Bones, find them!'

I followed Bones's nose and found the pair of them fixing up a coffin.

'Have you seen this?' I asked, brandishing the newspaper.

Father peered over his glasses at me. 'Yes,' he said. 'I see one every morning.'

I glared at him. This was not the time for silliness. 'I meant the story.' I tapped the page with my finger. 'It says there will be a show by Lady Athena at four p.m. tomorrow!'

Oliver popped up from behind the workbench with a nail between his teeth, as Bones ran over to sniff the coffin, perhaps remembering the time I'd filled one with apples. 'Oh!'

Father looked back and forth between us. 'Am I missing the significance of this?'

'You said I can investigate if I'm home by nightfall, did you not? So we can go to this one. Please let us, Father!' I clasped my hands together, begging.

He patted his pockets and pulled out his slim leather diary. 'We have a funeral to furnish tomorrow,' he said. 'But if we are finished by then . . .' He stared at the ceiling. 'I suppose you can go. Don't tell your mother, though. I'm sure she thinks it unsavoury.'

'Yes!' I did a little dance with the newspaper. Oliver grinned at me and Father just shook his head. He always had that look of *what on earth is my daughter up to this time?* about him.

'But are the performances not always sold out?' Father asked, putting his diary away and picking his polishing cloth back up. 'And I don't know that I can spare the money for tickets.'

'I know the right people,' I said with a smile.

★ ★ ★

And so the next afternoon found Oliver, Bones and me outside the Grecian Theatre. Well, in fact, some way away from it because the entrance was swarming with people.

With some horror, I realised, as we pushed our way forward, that many of them were journalists, bearing notebooks and the occasional camera on a tripod. With even more horror, I realised that I recognised some of them from when my father had been arrested on suspicion of murder.

I spotted some of the audience members we'd seen before too. Mr Campbell and Zhen stood deep in discussion with the lady who had been complaining that her dress would not be seen in the dark – this time in an even more extravagant green velvet number. Many ladies appeared to be wearing their largest and most impressive hats, topped with bows and feathers and in one case an *entire stuffed bird*. That made me wince as we shuffled past, but I had to admit that the blue-and-green sheen was beautiful.

We reached a column and I grabbed hold of it for dear life. Oliver backed against it. 'Seems like Lady Athena is getting even more popular,' he said breathlessly. Bones whined and curled round our legs.

I hopped up on to the stone step beside the column, and was surprised to see the angry actor – Terence, wasn't it? – standing in the doorway, surrounded by journalists.

'. . . an honour to have the mayor visit us,' he was saying, 'but I wish His Worship would have graced one of our many wonderful plays.'

There was a murmur of discussion. One of the reporters waved his hand. 'Mr Clearwater – Tempest Smith here, *Weekly Bugle*.' I remembered his slicked-back hair and smarmy expression from when he'd come to report on my father's arrest. 'What do you think of Lady Athena's great success?'

Terence's expression turned sour. 'Quite frankly, my good sir, I think these novelty acts belong in music halls, and not in serious theatre.'

I heard the frantic scribble of pencil on paper as the reporters realised that this was some juicy gossip. I shot Oliver a glance, and he raised his eyebrows at me.

'It's ridiculous, honestly,' Terence continued. 'Many of us have honed our craft for years, performing *true art*, shaping the soul of the theatre.' He huffed. 'These people are little more than charlatans.'

At that moment, the doors of the theatre swung open, and Mr Anastos appeared. He hurried out and stood beside Terence.

'Terence,' he said. 'I think you should step back inside.'

Tempest Smith popped his hand up again. 'Wouldn't you say Lady Athena's many true prophecies speak for themselves?'

'They speak to fraudulence and *trickery*!' Terence exclaimed, making Bones jump. 'We must save the theatre from these charlatans!'

Mr Anastos patted him heavily on the shoulder. 'Terence,' he said again, in a warning tone.

At this point, Terence appeared to realise who was talking to him, and he turned round slowly. 'Sorry, George.'

His boss simply gestured inside, and Terence gave a curt nod before stepping back in.

I noticed Niko's and Eleni's concerned faces peering through the glass doors.

Their father cleared his throat. 'Welcome, all, to the Grecian Theatre! Do not mind my friend here.' He gestured towards where Terence had gone. 'He is feeling tired and unwell.'

'Mr Anastos,' Tempest Smith piped up, 'what can you tell us about this event?'

'Oh, it is a great honour to have the wondrous, the *astounding* Lady Athena at our theatre. I tell you this: she will perform miracles. And we are so, so honoured to have the mayor himself at our great theatre. Now, I shall tell you a bit about the history of our building . . .'

It was at this point that I was tapped gently on the shoulder. I jumped, and realised that Niko had somehow crept out and was now standing beside me. He must have spotted us. 'Come with me,' he whispered, tilting his head towards the doors.

I grinned, and the four of us crept into the lobby. Bones began sniffing round the ticket booth. Eleni was beside Terence, who had his head in his hands.

'I'm sorry,' I heard him mutter, though it was somewhat muffled. 'I just find this whole situation dreadful.' He lifted his head. 'Actors *are* the theatre, don't you agree?'

'You know I do,' she said with clear sympathy. 'I'm no fan of Lady Athena, either.'

His eyes shone as he looked at her. 'One day, Miss Anastos,' he said, 'you're going to write the greatest play of our time. I can feel it. You see the truth. It will serve you well.'

Eleni's cheeks flushed red. 'And you may have the starring role,' she said. 'As long as Baba doesn't ban you from the premises, that is.'

Terence sighed. 'I'll talk to him.'

Georgios Anastos chose that minute to walk in. He had the *I'm not angry, but disappointed* look that many fathers have perfected. 'A word please, Terence?'

With a sheepish half-smile in our direction, Terence took a deep breath and got to his feet to follow his employer.

Now that distraction was over, I waved a greeting to Eleni. Bones lifted his head and then bounded over to lick her hands, making her giggle again.

'Hello, everyone,' she said.

Niko exhaled and bit his lip. 'Terence is something of a liability, isn't he?' he said.

Eleni glared at her brother. 'He's hot-headed, but he's a good man. He just cares about the theatre, that's all.'

'We all do,' said Niko, rubbing his temple beneath the lock of dark hair that tumbled over it.

'Sometimes I wonder,' Eleni shot back. She tossed her curls. 'Anyway, what brings you two here?' she asked Oliver and me. 'More investigating?'

'We saw the headline in the paper about the special performance,' I explained. 'Father agreed to let me come because it's the afternoon.'

Oliver took off his cap and wrung it like a wet cloth. 'We were wondering if you might let us watch from your family box . . . thing, if that's all right?'

'Oh, absolutely,' Niko replied. I grinned at him and he gave Bones a pat on the head.

Eleni shuffled uncomfortably in her chair. 'I can't

believe the mayor has decided to come and see Lady Athena's act, of all things.'

'Excuse me.' Niko prodded her. 'It will be wonderful publicity, and you know it. You can see the crowds out there.' He motioned towards the doors where even from behind the glass you could hear everyone chattering.

Eleni waved her hand dismissively. 'It'll be the usual nonsense.'

'Oh, I don't know,' Niko replied. 'She assured me earlier that it will be a performance that we *won't* forget. Come on, I'll get Archie to take you two to the box . . .'

CHAPTER FIFTEEN

Despite the bright day outside, inside the theatre it still felt like night-time. The warm amber glow of the lights illuminated the place, but there were still deep shadows in the corners, where anything could be hiding. If it were ghosts, though, I still couldn't hear them.

We were back in the viewing box that belonged to the Anastos family, with the same red-velvet chairs and the wonderful view of the dark stage.

'Can I bring you anything, miss?' Archie asked. He had

already fetched a bone from the kitchens for the dog, who was now happily chomping away on the plush carpet.

'No, thank you, Archie,' I replied, unsure what sort of thing I would even be asking for. Fancy food and drinks, perhaps? But I certainly didn't have the money for those.

'All right. We hope you enjoy the –' he paused and stared into the middle distance as if reading his lines from a sheet – '*spectacular performance this afternoon with our special guest, His Worship the Lord Mayor.*' Then he grinned, looking pleased with himself, and bowed out of the tiny room.

Oliver gave me a look. 'I can't believe you talked me into this again,' he said, a hint of teasing in his voice.

'Oh shush, you,' I said. 'This could be vital for the investigation, and you know it.'

It wasn't long before the rest of the excited crowd of patrons and reporters flooded into the auditorium. From above, it was like a sea of expensive dresses and hats. Everyone wanted to look their best even more than ever now that the mayor was in attendance.

Once they had all shuffled into their seats, a booming voice called out: 'ALL RISE FOR HIS WORSHIP, THE LORD MAYOR!'

And everyone stood up again. I craned my neck to get a better look as the mayor made his way to his seat. I had never seen him before, but he appeared to be a rather ordinary-looking man wearing an enormous feathered hat and a golden chain that glinted in the light.

From then on, things proceeded much the same as they had before: the darkness, the thunderclap and Mr Hyde appearing onstage. This time he began, 'Ladies, gentlemen and distinguished guests . . .' And I thought – although perhaps I was imagining it – that he seemed rather perturbed.

The rest of his speech seemed to be the same, until he said: 'And, for this special event, my lady will be stretching her talents to their very limits by giving us not one, but *two* prophecies of the future.' He held out his hands as there was some nervous applause, and then the rain and the smoke began as before. 'Ah, the Lady Athena is ready to join us. Remember to keep your wits about you. The barrier to the spirit world is about to be broken.'

With that, Mr Hyde backed away into the darkness, and the show began.

Again the smoke, the music, the rumble of thunder, and Lady Athena appeared onstage.

'Good . . . afternoon,' she began as she walked forward. 'I am the Lady Athena. I welcome you all, living and dead.'

Was it just me, or was her voice wavering? She seemed

a bit uncertain, though whether that was simply because she was thrown off by the time of day, I couldn't be sure.

'I believe we have a special guest with us.'

There was a murmur as the crowd looked towards the mayor.

'Your Worship, I may have a message for you,' she said.

'Of course she does,' muttered Oliver sarcastically. I giggled and jabbed him in the ribs with my elbow.

'Will you step forward for me?' Lady Athena continued. The mayor nodded and got to his feet. 'Is there something you would like to know? A question you have for the future?'

The mayor cleared his throat. 'Ahem, well.'

He shuffled, looking rather uncomfortable at being put on the spot as the light burned down on him. I had a suspicion that he wanted to ask something like, 'Will I be elected mayor again?', but that was perhaps not best asked in front of an enormous crowd of citizens.

'Hmm. There is a race on at Lansdowne Racecourse this weekend, on which I have placed a bet. Will my horse win?'

Lady Athena considered this. 'Very well. I will consult the spirits, and see what they can tell us of your future.'

Once again, she stepped inside her mysterious, rattling

wardrobe. All eyes were on the stage. I heard gasps and worried whispers. The whole thing still set me on edge, though I could sense no ghosts. The *Macbeth* actor ghost had certainly seemed to have some anger towards her, though, so the spirits were at least aware that she was up to something.

When she finally emerged, her eyes glazed over, she spoke again. 'Your Worship, the spirits have assured me that you will have good fortune. Your horse will surely triumph at the race.'

The mayor gave a booming laugh. 'Wonderful!'

Lady Athena bowed as the audience clapped. But I knew they were all waiting for what came next – the chance to be chosen for their own prophecy.

'Who will step forward for a reading?' she asked.

This time, I wasn't surprised when everyone got to their feet to volunteer.

But what did surprise me was what happened next.

A strange expression came over Lady Athena's face. She wasn't gazing out into the crowd, but into her mirror. If I didn't know any better, I would say she looked as though she'd seen a ghost.

'No . . .' she said, just loud enough to hear. She put her hand over her mouth.

Bones suddenly sat up and growled, his treat all but

forgotten. He could sense something was wrong. Was this not part of the performance?

Slowly, the medium lowered her hand and raised her eyes towards the audience again. 'I have received a message,' she said.

I began to wish that I owned a pair of opera glasses. If only I could see what was really on that mirror. I tried to lean over the balcony, but Oliver pulled me back.

'It says,' she continued, her voice wavering. 'It says . . .'

She didn't seem able to speak. Instead, she merely turned the tall mirror to face us all. And there in huge, smudged, foggy letters was written:

THE PLAY IS DONE
ONE OF YOU WILL DIE TONIGHT

And then she collapsed on the stage, her billowing white dress swallowing her like a shroud.

CHAPTER SIXTEEN

Mr Hyde was the first to reach her. Suddenly his demeanour seemed entirely different – no longer stoic and suave, but panicked. He knelt down next to his wife.

'She's breathing!' he called out towards the stagehands, who were making their way towards her. 'Can you hear me, my love?'

Lady Athena stirred a little, but she didn't wake.

Mr Hyde scooped her up in his arms as if she weighed

nothing, and left the stage. 'I'm taking her to the dressing room!' he shouted.

The horrified silence of the crowd turned to murmurs as people relayed the message to those further back. And then there was uproar. Even Bones joined in, putting his paws up on the balcony and barking.

'Oh my *goodness*,' the lady in the box beside ours said with a gasp. I saw some ladies begin to sob or fan themselves dramatically.

I stood up. 'Oliver, we have to stop this!'

He looked back at me, pale-faced. 'How? It didn't even say who's gonna die.'

'Then we'll have to work it out,' I replied.

I could feel the rising panic in my chest. If this message were real, then whoever was making these prophecies come true was going to take a step in a very, very wrong direction. *Murder*.

'Quick. We need to find the others!'

I pulled open the door, hitched up my skirts and raced down the corridor, Oliver and Bones quickly following behind. Some guests were already beginning to leave their seats and wander out into the hallway, looking dazed. They didn't even seem to notice the fact that we had a dog with us, which must have been rather unusual.

'Bones!' I called, turning to him. 'Eleni and Niko, where are they?'

He paused, put his nose to the ground and then headed for the stairs. I shared a quick glance with Oliver, and then we followed. Bones's nose was never wrong.

At the bottom, Bones stopped again on the floor of the lobby, tail in the air, and then he bounded away towards backstage.

'Wait, stop!' someone called out as we ran towards the private areas of the theatre. But a barman with a tray of drinks came out of the door just as Bones got there, and he slipped through. The man spun away just in time, and Oliver and I dashed past.

'Sorry!' I shouted over my shoulder.

Bones skidded to a halt when he came to the dressing-room corridor, and I soon spotted why – Eleni and Niko were outside Lady Athena's door, worried expressions painted on their faces.

Maria, their mother, came storming out, her hands in the air. 'She is out cold,' she said. 'Mr Hyde is with her. This is madness! Madness! Threats, in our theatre?' She leaned back against the wall. 'I'm going to faint myself.'

'Go and sit down, Mama,' Niko said, putting his hand on her shoulder. 'She will be all right. She's just in shock, that's all.'

Maria shook her head rapidly. 'I need to find your baba. He will know what to do.' She hurried away.

The siblings noticed the three of us coming down the corridor.

'Violet!' Eleni called. 'There you are!'

I stopped in front of them, panting almost as much as Bones. 'We saw what happened from the box.'

'What are we gonna do?' Oliver asked. 'Is it a real threat?'

'We have to assume it is,' I replied, my mind racing. 'Everything Lady Athena has predicted so far has come true. Someone is in danger and we have to work out who . . . before it's too late.'

'*They* have to be the ones behind this,' Eleni hissed, pointing at the dressing room. 'She makes it all up – surely she knows what she's saying?'

'It could be,' said Niko, shuffling uncomfortably. 'But then why would she faint?'

Eleni threw her hands in the air. 'I don't know! Probably to put on a good show! People will be talking about this for weeks.'

'If it *is* them, if they made up the threat themselves,' Oliver whispered, 'how can we stop them?'

Bones was sniffing round the door. A door, I suddenly realised, that someone had hastily unlocked and left the key in the hole, right where we could reach it. Without even thinking twice, I went over and locked the door.

'Violet!' Oliver exclaimed, looking at me with horror. 'You can't!'

'Have you got a better idea?' I asked, keeping my voice low, knowing he didn't have an answer. 'If we keep them in here, they can't hurt anyone. And, if anyone does get hurt, it rules them off the suspect list!'

'What if they need to come out?' he shot back. 'For food or water, or the lavatory, or, or, a doctor! You can't just lock people in a room.'

'One of us should stay here,' I hissed back. 'In case they need help.'

'I can do that,' Niko said with a small wave of his hand to volunteer. 'I'll keep an eye on them.'

'Violet, no . . .' Oliver pleaded again, but I wasn't going to listen. Locking those two in their room could save someone's life. It had to be done.

'All right, Niko,' I said, 'but be careful. If they really are behind this, you could be in danger. If they break out of the room, you should run and get someone.'

'Right.' He nodded.

'Let's move away from here, head towards the front of house,' Eleni said, 'so we can work this out. We don't want them to hear,' she added with a tip of her head.

That was a good plan, I thought. We needed to be able to talk at a normal volume again.

'Take me with you, would you?'

★ ★ ★

The three of us (and Bones) stopped by the threadbare bench in the foyer and perched upon it. Around us, guests were still making their way out. It was a sea of baffled faces with waves of gossip and concern.

'I'm sure Baba will be trying to get to the bottom of this,' Eleni said, 'but perhaps we can get there faster. Remind me what the threat said? Mama told us so quickly. She was in *such* a panic.'

I gulped. 'It said, *The play is done. One of you will die tonight.*' I stroked Bones's soft head over and over, trying to calm myself so that I could think properly. His dark eyes gleamed as he stared up at me with concern.

'So someone in the audience is gonna get killed?' Oliver asked, the fear etched in his tight brows and worried frown.

'Perhaps not,' I said. 'It could be anyone in the theatre, couldn't it?'

Eleni tapped her fingers on the arms of her chair. 'I think the first part is the key. *The play is done.* It could just mean someone's life is over, but . . . the play? Could that not confirm that it will be someone connected to the theatre?'

'Someone who's threatening Lady Athena's business?' Oliver asked with a worried glance at Eleni.

The words hit me with a horrifying realisation. I jumped up, sending Bones darting away. 'Terence!' I cried, ignoring the shocked expressions of the final stragglers from the audience. 'It could be Terence!'

Eleni went pale. 'Oh no,' she whispered. 'Oh no . . . Oh *heavens*, you could be right. He denounced Lady Athena in front of everyone earlier, and all the reporters . . .'

'Where is he?' I asked, the panic rising in my chest.

'He was with Baba earlier,' she said. 'I think Baba called an emergency meeting backstage, and Mama went off to find him.'

'We have to go an' check,' Oliver said.

Our eyes met, and we all nodded desperately.

Oliver quickly turned Eleni's chair and we clattered back towards the auditorium. Several ladies made indignant noises as they had to jump aside for three people, a wheelchair and a dog racing past them. Eleni called out directions as we barged through the bar once again and out into the back corridors.

I heard the commotion before we wrenched open the final door. It was a minor relief to find Mr Anastos standing on a pile of crates in the area behind the stage, with many of the theatre's workers assembled in front of him. I took a quick glance round the vast room. It was packed with scaffolding, ladders, ropes and huge pieces of painted scenery. Bones began sniffing hopefully at a prop that looked like a very realistic shaggy dog.

'I know you're all very concerned!' he was calling out. 'Please, everyone, calm down! I'm sure this is some sort of mistake.'

'Lady Athena doesn't make mistakes!' someone yelled. There was a grumble of angry agreement.

'Well, if it *is* true –' Mr Anastos ran a hand over his face – 'it might not be a threat of murder. We don't know this.'

'It could *just* be a terrible accident,' another voice said sarcastically. This was met with another ripple of mutters.

'We're in danger!'

'You have to do something.'

'Please, sir!'

Mr Anastos patted the air with his hands as if that would help. 'Everyone, please! We must not panic. We will all look out for each other, no?'

When yet more angry shouting came in response, Eleni muttered, 'I've had enough of this.' She pushed herself up in her chair until she was shakily standing, and waved her hand in the air. 'BABA! BABA!'

Everyone paused and turned to stare at her, the crowd parting between her and her father. Some of their jaws dropped open and their eyes went wide in amazement.

'Oh, a miracle, I'm cured,' she said, rolling her eyes.

'Eleni?' Mr Anastos said, peering through the crowd. 'Are you all right, *agapi mou*? Is Niko with you?'

'He's safe,' she called back, sinking down into her chair with relief. 'But where is Terence, Baba? We think he might be in trouble.'

'Terence?' He blinked. 'Oh, he went home.'

Bones barked, and I looked down at him. He had become restless, shuffling in circles. He knew something was wrong. This was bad. *Very* bad.

'We need to send someone to his house!' Eleni cried. 'Quick!' She looked back at us. 'Violet and Oliver, can you go?'

'Where does he live?' I asked, the words almost getting stuck in my throat.

'Round the corner,' she said. 'I can explain—'

Mr Anastos jumped down from the crates and waded his way through the murmuring crowd. I saw Archie sitting on the floor, looking fearful, while a maid tried to comfort him.

'Everyone stick together,' Mr Anastos ordered. 'Eleni, you stay here with your mama, all right?'

Eleni nodded sombrely, and I saw the fear in her eyes.

He stopped in front of us. 'I will find Terence,' he said. 'I can't send you children alone. Just . . . just in case. He lives on Whitehall Road.'

'We'll come with you,' said Oliver, and Bones barked his agreement. We had to get there, and fast.

★ ★ ★

We all went as swiftly as we could. Bones sped ahead, his tail trailing low. Mr Anastos walked with big, quick strides, and Oliver and I hurried along behind. But, as soon as we turned the corner on to the quiet road lined with brick terraces, my heart sank like a shipwreck.

There was a police wagon, and a roped-off gate, and there on the pavement stood Inspector Holbrook.

We were too late.

CHAPTER SEVENTEEN

I t was Father who taught me how to piece together a story.

One long, hot summer, the groundskeeper had been laid up in bed with a swollen ankle and so the cemetery grass grew tall and yellowed, waving in the gentle breeze. Crickets chirped and bees buzzed in every direction. Father took me out while he attempted to hack some of the overgrowth back. I am sure the appearance of a fellow dressed all in black and wielding a scythe was not at all concerning to the cemetery's visitors.

He sat me down in the shade of Mr Applewood's chest tomb while he worked. With little else to do, I stared at the gravestones around me. 'This one's broken,' I said to Father, pointing at a column that looked as though the top half had slid away. A stone anchor rested on the bottom, with intricate beaded designs hanging from it.

He stopped and dropped the scythe in the grass, then wiped his brow with a handkerchief. 'Oh no,' he said. 'It's made that way.'

'Why?' I asked, wrinkling my nose.

He crouched down beside me. 'A gravestone is a story, Violet. It leaves our mark on the world. John Bloom's family chose the column to say that his life was cut short. And it's a strong symbol, for the head of a family. What else does it say?'

I squinted at the inscription.

IN LOVING MEMORY OF
CAPTAIN JOHN CHRISTOPHER BLOOM
1845–1880

WITH SORROW GREAT WE SAY TO
THEE OUR SON IS SETTING OUT TO
SEA HE LIETH HERE, HIS SHIP BELOW
BUT WHERE IS FOR THE LORD TO KNOW

'A ship's captain,' I said. 'That's why he has an anchor.'

Father nodded. 'He was well loved and respected. I can tell you that because I arranged his funeral.' He reached his hand towards the stone. 'But always think about what you can see. Use your senses. The craftsmanship on the stone, the neatly planted flowers, the immortelles and the poem show that people cared for him, but –' he paused – 'it also shows wealth. A status symbol. There are people as noble as kings with nothing to mark their resting place. Remember that.'

In that moment, I didn't really understand what he meant – perhaps I would later. But there was something else I wanted to know the answer to. I hopped up and shuffled over to the grand memorial.

'Where is your ship, Mister Captain John?' I asked.

Father chuckled. 'I don't think you'll get an answer, my dear.'

I cocked my head on one side for a minute and then turned back to my father. 'He says it's wrecked off the coast of Ireland. He says he's glad he made it back here because the crabs wouldn't be good conversationalists.' I paused. 'Now he's laughing.'

Father stood up and ruffled my hair. 'You are a most peculiar child, Miss Veil,' he said.

I smiled. I had learned a lesson. Senses told a story. I just had one more sense than most people.

★ ★ ★

That day, as we stood opposite Terence's house, I had already pieced the story together.

The presence of the police meant that the worst had likely happened. By the side of the road, Inspector Holbrook was comforting an older lady who was sniffling into her handkerchief. A neighbour, probably, who had heard a commotion and sent for the policemen, given that she was outside the house. If Terence had suffered something natural like a heart attack, it would not have been noticed so quickly.

The front door was open, but it didn't look as though it had been forced. Terence had probably opened it willingly, let the culprit inside. Someone he knew, or someone who was merely convincing? Either way, it was a terrible mistake, and the last he would ever make.

And the worst part was I could feel it. Bones was whining and sticking close to my legs. There in my veins I felt the cold chill of a recent death, saw the hints of grey ghostly fog creeping round the door. But the newly dead took a while to settle, and I wasn't likely to find any answers from the spirit world yet.

Beside me, Oliver shuddered. I felt tears prick at the corners of my eyes.

There was one piece I was missing, though, and unfortunately it was the most important one.

Who was the culprit?

If Mr Hyde and Lady Athena remained locked in their room, then they were innocent, and I was running out of suspects.

Mr Anastos approached the gate slowly. I watched as Inspector Holbrook put his hand on his shoulder, spoke calmly to him. He sank back against the wall in disbelief.

I brushed away my tears angrily. This wasn't *fair*. We worked it out. We should have been there on time.

It was at this point that Inspector Holbrook looked up and spotted us.

Uh-oh.

He marched across the street. Bones tried unsuccessfully to hide behind my legs.

'Miss Veil,' he called out. 'Mister Oats. Why do I find you lurking at my crime scene yet again?'

I gulped. 'It's not . . . we're not . . .'

'Investigating?' the gruff inspector asked. 'I should hope not. You did plenty of that last year. Tell me why you're here.'

Oliver launched into an explanation before I could stop him. 'We came from the Grecian Theatre, sir. We saw Terence shouting at the reporters earlier, and then Lady Athena said someone was going to die in her show, and we thought we ought to run and check on him, and—'

'Slow down, boy,' Inspector Holbrook said. He pulled out his notebook. 'You're saying this Lady . . . Athena *predicted* that Mr Clearwater would die?'

'Is he . . .?' I asked, even though I knew the answer in my heart.

The inspector nodded slowly.

I breathed out, a cold, shuddery breath. 'Well, no, not exactly,' I explained as Bones pushed his nose into my hand to comfort me. 'There was a message on her mirror.'

I relayed what had happened, watched his pencil scratch down the details.

'Well, I'll be blowed,' he said, rubbing his bristly moustache. It wasn't often that I'd ever seen him look surprised or confused, but now he was displaying signs of both. Then he seemed to snap back to the present. 'You two, get off home. This is no place for children to be hanging about. We'll call your father if we have need of his services.'

'But Mr Anastos,' I said, pointing at the theatre owner, who was staring blankly at the sky. 'He's in shock. He was friends with Terence.'

'Don't you worry about that,' Inspector Holbrook replied. 'I'll walk him back. It seems we have questions to ask at the theatre. Now both of you, *home*, and not a word to any reporters, do you hear me?'

'Yes, sir,' Oliver and I mumbled in unison. Bones barked.

With the inspector watching us very carefully, we turned in the direction of home and began walking in silence except for our shaky breaths and our feet hitting the cobbles.

The grey fog wouldn't leave my mind, and my heart still hurt as it pounded. A man was gone from this world for ever. Oh heavens, if we had only got there sooner.

I dug my nails into the palms of my hands. Whoever was responsible for this . . . they had gone too far. They had taken a life. There was no going back from that. I swore to myself, there and then, that we would catch them – and we were going to make them pay.

CHAPTER EIGHTEEN

The following days passed in a blur. I scarcely wanted to leave my room. Bones lay on my bed, his shining eyes staring at me with concern. I had cried all my tears when explaining what had happened to my parents, and now there were no more left to shed. Miss Li's golden necklace hung on my nightstand, taunting me with unanswered questions.

I knew that I shouldn't, but I could not stop blaming myself for what had happened to Terence Clearwater. In my head, I rewrote the events of that afternoon so that

Oliver and I had arrived just in time and caught the murderer red-handed, Bones probably dragging them out by their trousers.

But who knew if that was even possible? I hadn't the faintest idea how the message appeared on Lady Athena's magic mirror, but how long had it been there? Perhaps the murderer had waited outside Terence's house all day. Even if we had worked out who was being threatened, there was nothing to say that we really could have reached him before it was too late.

Father had indeed been contacted, and plans for Terence's funeral were underway. It all felt so bleak and hopeless. Oliver tried to comfort me, and Thomas had even let me cuddle his favourite teddy bear, but it didn't help. I knew I wanted to stop the murderer, but could I?

My investigation fever had turned into investigation malaise. It was like a misty bog that I had wandered into and could not find my way out of, no matter how hard I tried.

★ ★ ★

One day, Father managed to rouse me from my sorrows with the promise of some real work to do. He set me in the back of the shop working through the inventory lists, while Ernesto met grieving relatives and Oliver helped out the back. It was rather dull, but being trusted with a proper task was rare and it at least meant my mind was occupied with something other than guilt and despair.

'Please can the dog stay outside, Miss Violet?' Ernesto begged. 'He bothers the customers.'

I reluctantly agreed, although I knew Ernesto was the one really being bothered. Bones seemed rather grumpy about it, but he bounded out of the gate into the cemetery and was off chasing rabbits back into their holes within minutes.

I was browsing a copy of the Norman Brothers' trade catalogue – and considering ordering some more brass bar handles for coffins – when I heard someone enter.

'Good morning, ma'am,' said Ernesto. 'How may we be of assistance?'

'I was looking for Miss Violet?' a voice with a soft Chinese accent said.

I jumped up and hurried over. 'Miss Li! Welcome!'

'Oh?' said Ernesto, his eyes moving slowly back and forth between me and the elegant lady in peacock blue and gold. 'Is this a . . . friend of yours?'

'Um, my *client*, in fact,' I said. 'I'm investigating a case for her.'

Ernesto raised his eyebrows, but thankfully didn't say

anything. Miss Li tipped her head at him politely. She was holding a newspaper under one arm.

'Can you give us a moment?' I asked with a little desperation. 'To talk about the case?'

Ernesto shuffled a bit and straightened his tie. 'Well, hmm, I suppose so. You will call me if anyone comes about a funeral?'

'Yes, of course!' I said.

'All right, then,' he replied, sounding positively unsure. He backed away slowly and then turned to head through the hallway to the funeral parlour.

'I'm so sorry, Miss Li,' I said, 'I have to – um – share my premises. Won't you take a seat?'

She sat down, and I noticed she was a little unsteady. 'I saw the news,' she said, her brow furrowed with concern. She placed the paper down on the desk in front of me.

ACTOR'S MURDER FORETOLD BY FORTUNE-TELLER

SHOCKING PERFORMANCE PRECEDED REAL-LIFE CRIME

The Lady Athena's Wisdom also Predicts Mayor's Horse Triumph Against All Odds at the Races

I read the words, feeling hollow inside, and then looked up at Miss Li. She nervously tucked some dark strands of hair behind her ears.

'Ah,' was all I could say.

'I am . . . afraid, Miss Violet,' she began. 'Afraid for my sister and her husband. Before I was worried about their money. Now I think they might be in danger. Have you discovered . . . anything?'

I stared down at the knotted wood of the desk for a second, trying to find the right words. Silently, I cursed myself for not doing my job properly. Why had I moped for days when I could have been working on the case?

'It's rather complicated,' I said finally. 'We have some suspects and some leads. I found proof that Lady Athena's prophecies are neither magical nor spiritual, but that someone seems to be carrying them out on her behalf. Unfortunately,' I said with a sigh, 'we don't know who.'

'And it's not this Lady Athena herself?' Miss Li asked, crinkling her nose.

'I don't believe so,' I said. 'She was – *ahem* – detained when the murder took place, as was her husband. So it is unlikely to be either of them, unless they are working with a third party.'

Miss Li stared down at the desk for a moment, and

then her eyes looked back up at me. 'But it is all about Lady Athena, no?'

'What do you mean?' I asked.

Miss Li pulled over an inkpot and drew a little circle round it with an elegant finger. 'She is at the centre of all this, even if she is not responsible. She is the one making these claims – talking to the dead, telling fortunes. She is the one with the fame and the fortune.'

I nodded slowly, thinking. 'You're right. You're *right*! That could be the key to all of this!' I pictured the lock-shaped necklace in my mind as I spoke.

My client blinked at me.

I cleared my throat and tried to regain some professionalism, but a fire was being kindled in my chest. 'I believe I have some new avenues of investigation to pursue.'

'Oh?'

'Don't you worry,' I said, standing up. 'I will get to the bottom of this, Miss Li. For your sister. And for Terence.'

Miss Li continued to look confused, but her brow softened with a hint of relief. 'Thank you.' She stood up. 'Please let me know if you find anything.'

'I will,' I replied with a genuine smile. I was beginning to formulate a plan.

★ ★ ★

Later that afternoon, I was ruminating on my idea while I helped Mother and Maddy with the washing. Maddy was wringing out the clothes and we were pegging them on the line.

If you peered over our tall garden fence, you would see almost every line dripping with clothing as it blew in the gentle breeze – the difference was that there were plenty of bright colours and starched whites on the others, while ours was almost entirely black.

The death industry involved a surprising amount of laundry. Thankfully, Father was able to pay for a washing service for the business. But there was still the matter of all our household clothing.

I was balanced on a bucket with a wooden peg in my mouth, staring out at the cemetery. I could detect wispy shimmers of ghosts hovering in the air. On the edge of existence, as always – that was where I would find answers about Lady Athena, I was sure of it.

Mother chastised me. '*Violet*, stop daydreaming and hang up your dress, please.'

I sighed and hopped down on to the grass where Bones was lying and panting in the spring sun. 'I wasn't *daydreaming*. I was considering my investigation.'

'If you could try considering the washing,' she replied pointedly, 'that would be much appreciated.' She wiped her forehead.

It had been a strange life for my mother – having a period when she had staff to do everything around the house, and now being back to doing most of it herself. As I lived on the edges of existence, she lived on the edge of the social classes.

I folded my best dress – still pretty sopping despite Maddy's work with the mangle – and grabbed another peg from the bag to hang it up. Bones rolled away as the droplets of water fell on his head. 'It's really quite important,' I insisted. 'I must go to the theatre this afternoon. I—'

'The washing is important, Violet,' my mother said, coming up behind me and tutting as she straightened out the dress.

I turned to look at her. 'But this is a matter of life and death. It's not the same as . . .' I waved my hand. 'Washing and darning and cooking.'

I loathed my daily tasks with a passion. Most girls my age had a proper education these days, but my parents were rather old-fashioned and I had been left with a string of governesses, followed by nothing at all when we ran out of money. Thomas's education had been prioritised.

'Oh,' Mother said, her brows knitting. 'So you would live well without clothes and food, would you?'

'No, but—'

'No buts, Violet!'

She threw a peg down and it bounced off the bucket with a clang, making Bones jump up and race away. Maddy was pretending to take no notice, as she usually did when Mother and I argued.

'I know your disdain for women's work. You tell me frequently. And *I* tell you that you will learn the importance of it as soon as it is not being done. *It's dull,*' she said, suddenly doing a painfully accurate imitation of me. '*It's pointless. I don't get paid. I don't want to learn to sew.* You are preoccupied with death, but this is *life*, Violet.'

But is it really living? I thought to myself, but I was wise enough not to speak it aloud.

'Clothes need mending,' my mother continued, holding up a pair of stockings with a hole in. 'Babies need caring for. People need to eat. Houses need to be cleaned. It's hard work, but it's the most important work there is.'

I stared down at the pail full of washing for a moment until I could find the right words. 'I want a choice,' I said quietly. 'I want the choice to study and learn and have a profession. I want to solve this mystery.'

I looked up at Mother, and found she was staring at me, searching my eyes.

She chewed her lip a little, her expression softening. Then she reached out and stroked a lock of hair away from my face.

'Maybe you shall, my love. But, unless you want to do it in stained rags, I suggest you finish helping us with the washing first, hmm?'

Feeling dejected, I carried on in silence, my arms chilly with the water from the clothes. My mother had a point, as much as I would rather not have admitted it.

Eventually Bones started barking at the back gate, wanting to be let out into the cemetery. I went over to him, and he appeared concerned, cocking his head as he looked up at me, tail swooshing low.

'Never mind, boy,' I said quietly as I scratched him behind the ears. 'We shall be out investigating in no time.' I was itching to go now that my meeting with Miss Li had renewed my purpose.

I unhooked the gate and watched as Bones gratefully bounded out into the grass, dodging between the gravestones. On the breeze, I heard the faint ghosts giggle as he trotted round their feet.

I smiled. 'I think we shall be paying a visit to Lady Athena. And this time she'll speak the truth to me. I'll make sure of it.'

CHAPTER NINETEEN

That afternoon, when Oliver had finished his duties and I had done enough housework for Mother to release me, we headed for the theatre. Once again, Father had given me strict instructions to be back before dark, to which I had politely nodded along.

'What exactly are you plotting?' Oliver asked me, his arms straining as Bones pulled him along on the rope lead.

I tapped my nose. 'You'll see. I just need you to distract Mr Hyde and buy me some time with Lady Athena.'

'Do you think they know about you locking them in their dressing room?' he asked.

'I'm sure Niko let them out as soon as he realised they were not involved in the murder.'

Oliver snorted. 'You're sure?'

'Well, they're not still in there, are they? *Famous medium trapped in dressing room for a week* would have made the newspapers, don't you think?'

'Now you're being silly, Violet,' he said.

I stuck my tongue out at him. 'Just get Mr Hyde out of the picture, and I shall have a proper talk with her. Ladies only.'

Bones barked.

'Oh, and dogs.' My senses always seemed to be somehow amplified when Bones was around, and I was going to need all the help I could get.

When the theatre came into view, I saw that some black banners had been draped over the front entrance – in memory of Terence, no doubt. I felt a lump in my throat.

I hadn't seen Eleni and Niko since it happened. I hoped they were all right. I carried a sadness for them too, but beneath it was a touch of excitement as I thought of seeing them again. Suddenly my doomed investigation had returned to life.

'There's Archie,' said Oliver, waving down the alley that

led to the back doors. He was nearly pulled off his feet as Bones spotted his new best friend and went clattering over the cobbles, dragging Oliver behind him.

'Steady on, boy!' I called, picking up my skirts and running after them.

But Bones had already put his paws on Archie and was greeting him sloppily, evidently hoping for a treat.

Archie spluttered and laughed. 'Hullo, Bones!'

Oliver and I also greeted the theatre boy (a lot less messily) and I asked if he could help us. 'I just need a private moment with Lady Athena. It's an important matter.'

Archie looked puzzled. 'Well, I suppose . . .'

But we were interrupted by someone clearing their throat. I turned to see a large burly man in a fitted uniform similar to Archie's, who loomed in the doorway.

'Who are you lot?' he asked gruffly. 'You can't have your friends hanging about here, Archie.'

'Oh w-well, th-they're not . . .' Archie stammered, looking up at him. 'Well, they, they are my friends, sir, but . . .' He gently lowered Bones's paws from his shoulders, and Bones skulked back to his usual hiding place behind me.

Oliver suddenly straightened up. 'We're investigating Mr Terence Clearwater's murder.' He reached out and shook the big man's hand. 'Jack Danger, at your service,' he added. 'I'm a reporter an' private investigator. And this is my . . . sister.'

I fought the urge to roll my eyes. Archie just blinked in confusion.

The man looked a little bewildered, but he nodded in acknowledgement. 'I'm Barrett, the door manager,' he said. 'Dreadful thing, that was.'

'We were with Mr Anastos when he found out,' Oliver said sadly.

Now I was a little more impressed. It was rather quick thinking to use the name of Barrett's boss.

'We need to have a word with Lady Athena as part of the investigation. Believe me, sir, we want to make sure Mr Clearwater's murderer gets what's coming to them.'

'Ah,' Barrett said, and I was surprised to see him give a little sniff and cast his eyes heavenwards. Then he looked down at us again. 'Well. You can go in and talk to her, but then I want you straight back out, all right?

'Yes, sir,' Oliver said quickly.

'And the mutt stays outside.'

I huffed. 'He's not a mutt! He's a pure-bred greyhound, and he's extremely well behaved.'

The latter of those things was definitely a lie. As for whether Bones was pure-bred, I hadn't the slightest idea.

He could well be, although he was rather small, but given that I'd mysteriously found him wandering the cemetery I couldn't say for sure.

Archie was wringing his hands. 'He's a good boy, sir,' he squeaked, 'and Mr Anastos likes him.'

Barrett gave an exasperated sigh. 'All right, fine. But, if the dog starts chewing the scenery, he's out.'

'Thank you!' I said. Barrett stepped aside – like a mountain moving – and let us through the door.

'How do you know these people again?' I heard him ask Archie as we trotted into the corridor.

We did it, I was thinking to myself with a smug smile. But then I remembered the task ahead of me, and it was not going to be easy.

'Next time we should just go in through the front door,' I suggested. 'And call for Niko and Eleni.'

'Less fun, though,' said Oliver cheekily. He was enjoying his Jack Danger persona far too much.

I let Bones off his lead. He went on ahead of us and, without thinking, I followed him. Soon we were in the corridor outside Lady Athena's dressing room.

'Well done, boy,' I said, giving him a pat. I turned to Oliver. 'Do you think you can get Mr Hyde away for long enough?'

'I'll see what I can do,' he said, tipping his cap at me.

I remembered then that Mr Hyde had refused to let Bones in last time. *Hmm.* I bent down. 'Bones, can you hide round the corner? Come quick when I call you, mind.'

Bones blinked at me, and then trotted back down the corridor with his tail between his legs.

Oliver hesitated for a moment, and then knocked on the door. I was quite surprised that he wasn't protesting and telling me I was mad.

The door was quickly opened by a scowling Mr Hyde, and the strong incense smell wafted out. 'Yes?' he said. His eyes readjusted a bit lower to our heights. 'Oh, it's you two again. The lady is busy. Good day.' He went to close the door.

'Wait!' Oliver said, catching it with his foot. He pulled his notebook from his pocket. 'It's for the paper. We want to write a feature on you.'

Mr Hyde peered back out at us, one eyebrow raised. 'Me?'

'Oh yes, sir,' Oliver said. 'We're calling it, um, *The Great Mr Hyde: The Man Behind Lady Athena.*' He traced the outline of the imaginary article in the air with his fingers.

I thought I saw a flash of vanity in Mr Hyde's expression – perhaps Oliver had tapped into something there.

'Hmm. What newspaper did you say you were from again?'

'The . . . *Greyhound*,' said Oliver.

The tall man wrinkled his nose. 'I'm not familiar with that one. Not one of those ghastly gossip rags, is it?'

'Oh no, sir,' said Oliver, without hesitation. 'It's very serious. Full of words.'

I elbowed him discreetly to make him stop talking before he dug himself any further into a hole, but, to my surprise, Mr Hyde seemed to be convinced.

'And you're not prying about what happened to Terence?' he asked.

'Wouldn't dream of it, sir,' said Oliver. 'Just want to talk about yourself.'

'Hmm,' Mr Hyde said again finally. 'All right.' He turned back into the dark room. 'I shall return shortly, my dear.' Then he looked at Oliver. 'All right, let us go somewhere quiet where we may talk.'

'Splendid!' said Oliver with a convincing smile.

I watched the two of them walk away. What an odd pair. Then I whistled for Bones and unceremoniously barged into Lady Athena's dressing room.

This Lady Athena looked quite different from the previous versions I'd seen. For one, she was wearing a floral dressing gown and was halfway through smothering her face in cold cream. For another, she looked rather aghast when she spotted me in the mirror.

'Oh!' she exclaimed, nearly dropping her cream and fumbling to catch the glass bottle before it hit the floor.

I couldn't blame her. After all, a strange girl had just let herself in with a rather enthusiastic dog.

She turned round in her chair to look at me. 'Do I know you?' she asked in a slightly panicked voice, setting the face cream down next to one of her skulls. The candle beside it flickered. 'Oh, are you the girl who came in a while ago?'

'Yes,' I said, shutting the door behind me. Bones circled and then lay down at my feet. 'It's Violet Veil. Hello, Lady Athena. I'm investigating Mr Clearwater's murder, and I want to talk to you. About your powers.'

Something changed in her cream-covered expression – a smidge of concern that she tried to hide. 'Well? I am renowned for them.'

'You can talk to ghosts, can you?' I asked, folding my arms. I felt the hairs on the back of my neck stand up as I noticed something important. It seemed I was right – Bones being there had heightened my senses. 'You can see them?'

'Of course,' she snapped. 'You've been to my performances, I'm sure.'

'Then why can't you see that there's one right behind you?'

She spun round to look at her mirror. 'What? I . . .'

'No, you can't, can you?' I said, lowering my voice to a whisper. 'She's watching over your shoulder, in the mirror. A little faint, perhaps, but she's there.'

Below me Bones sniffed the air, his tail twisting with curiosity.

Lady Athena looked back and forth between the candlelit mirror and me. 'I can't see a thing,' she said, but I could hear the panic in her voice. 'Is this a jape?'

'She has kind eyes,' I whispered, watching the image as the shadows danced across it, 'brown curls in her hair and a yellow dress.' I peered a little closer at the image of the girl, one that I'd seen as only a mere shimmer when we'd first walked into the dressing room. 'With an M embroidered on it.'

Lady Athena had gone as white as snow. Her knuckles stood out as she gripped the arms of her luxurious chair. '*Stop it*,' she hissed. 'I don't know who told you, but . . .'

With a nod to Bones, I stepped closer to the dressing table and peered over Lady Athena's shoulder, feeling the warmth of the candles.

'Hello,' I said quietly to the ghost in the glass. 'Who are you?'

Mary, the voice tickled in my ear.

'Mary,' I repeated, and Lady Athena put her hand over

her mouth and stifled a sob. 'Why do you watch over Lady Athena?'

The ghost smiled timidly in the flickering reflection and then she replied.

'Wh-what . . . what did she say?' Lady Athena asked shakily.

I looked down at her, saw tears brimming in her eyes.

'She says she watches over you because you're her sister.'

I paused.

'*Olivia Jenkins.*'

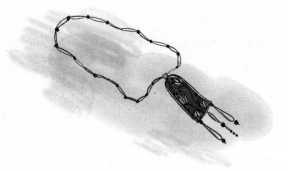

CHAPTER TWENTY

I pulled up a chair and sat down beside Lady Athena. Bones went over to a grate in the wall and started sniffing at it curiously.

Once the fraudulent medium had stopped crying and had dried her tears on her handkerchief, she spoke again.

'I don't know who you are,' she said in a low, shaky voice, 'or how you come to have this power. But . . .' She gulped. 'Nobody calls me by that name. Not any more. The only way you could know that is if . . . if . . .' She waved her handkerchief in the direction of the mirror.

'If Mary told me,' I finished gently.

Even knowing that Lady Athena was a fraud, I wanted to treat her with kindness. To lose a sister was deeply painful.

Bones seemed to sense my reaching out to her, and came back to put his nose in her lap. To my surprise, she didn't bat him away, but instead sat stroking his head while he closed his eyes.

Lady Athena stared into the glass, as if she could stare hard enough to make Mary appear. I could still see that shimmering vision, the girl with the kind eyes.

'She's happy,' I said, wanting to offer some reassurance. 'But . . .' I tilted my head to one side, concentrating a little harder to hear Mary's concerned whispers. 'I think she's worried for you. She senses danger.' I paused. 'Can you tell me what has really been going on? How did you end up in . . . all this?' I gestured round the room, at the sold-out performance posters and the candles and the skulls.

Lady Athena took a shuddering breath, and ran her fingers through her golden waves of hair. And then she spoke.

'My real name is Olivia, as you now know. I grew up with very little. We were lucky to have a roof over our heads, I suppose, but our home was cold and damp, and there were eight of us. We had to fight for food.'

Bones whined up at her and she scratched his ear. I listened intently – I knew that the better you were at listening, the more information people would volunteer.

'When Mary caught a sickness and, and –' she swallowed – 'passed away, I pretended that I could hear her voice. And my family believed me. Or at least I think they did. It seemed to bring them comfort.'

I nodded sadly.

'And then word began to spread. My grandma told people about my . . . talent. And people wanted to see it. My pa . . . he spotted an opportunity. He started asking for money, told people I could talk to their loved ones. I felt bad about it of course, but it made enough to feed our family.' She still didn't look at me, her eyes fixed on the mirror. 'I began to study other mediums, saw how successful they were.'

'You learned the tricks of the trade?'

'Oh yes,' she said with a small dry smile. She seemed pleased with herself, with what she'd achieved. 'First it was just in parlours: rapping on wood, and Ouija boards, and making ectoplasm out of muslin. Then I went to performances, and I would sneak backstage to learn about smoke and mirrors, and trapdoors, and spirit cabinets. How to read someone to know what they wanted to hear. How to research your believers so that you can seem to know impossible things.'

Her voice cracked a little, and I thought perhaps she was uncomfortable revealing the deepest secrets of her act. But I knew that she wasn't really talking to me. I had just opened the floodgates, the ones that had held fast since the death of her sister.

'And it became . . . all of this,' she said, now waving at the room just as I had. She finally looked back at me, her eyes sweeping across my dress. 'You look fairly well-to-do,' she said. 'I suppose you don't know what it's like. To have nothing, and then to find the path to everything before you.'

I started to speak, but then stopped myself. No matter the hardships our family had faced, it was far from having nothing. I was beginning to see that I had so much more than I'd ever known.

'I took that path,' she said. 'And it has paid me with reward after reward.'

She gestured down at herself, at her flowery dressing gown. 'Olivia Jenkins? Olivia Jenkins is a *nobody* from Sadler's Croft. Do you think the mayor would even know her name? Of course not. He wouldn't look at her twice if she brought him his tea and biscuits.'

I nodded. I knew what she meant. That was the sort of life that she would have if she let others choose for her.

She pushed Bones's nose gently aside and stood up,

crossing the room to where her stage dress hung on a wooden hanger. The white billowy material looked like what I imagined a Greek goddess would wear on her wedding day.

'When I put this dress on,' she continued, 'I am Lady Athena. My name is on everyone's lips.' She sighed as she ran the fabric through her fingers. 'I just want to be remembered. I don't want a pauper's grave. I want a statue. I want to have mattered.'

'You do matter,' I told her, frowning. 'You would matter if you were a maid.'

'Ha,' she said quietly. 'To you? Perhaps. To the world? A different story.'

'Everyone leaves their mark on this world,' I said, remembering something my father had once told me.

'Yes,' she said, smiling, suddenly bright with confidence. 'And my mark shall be as the most famous medium in history. You have seen that my predictions come true. I am the new oracle!'

'Wait,' I replied as Bones went back to sniffing the vent in the wall. Perhaps there was a rat in there. 'You admit to falsifying your ability to talk to ghosts, but not the predictions?'

She sat back in her chair, spreading her hands wide. 'I cannot explain it, Miss Violet. I receive the prophecies, and they are true. They appear in my mirror.'

I stood up. 'Do you swear it? Because we have evidence that someone is making them happen.' I still strongly suspected her husband, even though we knew he couldn't have killed Terence – at least not alone. 'Do you swear you don't know how it's happening?'

'I swear,' she said quietly. 'I swear on Mary's grave.'

There was a shimmer in the image in the mirror. I felt something tickle my ear. It seemed as though Mary were agreeing. She didn't appear to have any reason to doubt her sister's words.

'All right . . .' I said, looking over at Bones. He turned and his night-time eyes blinked back at me. He wasn't giving me a warning, either.

'I've told you everything,' Lady Athena said, a hint of desperation creeping into her voice. 'I have no reason to lie. But please, in return, keep my secrets. I will deny this conversation ever took place.'

That rather rubbed me up the wrong way. 'So you can keep deceiving people? Pretending to talk to their loved ones?'

'I'm giving people hope!' she shot back. 'Hope that there is more to this world than what we can see. You've witnessed how happy people are when I pass on messages from their loved ones!'

Her pretty lies, more like. I stood up, my fists clenched, sending Bones running back to me and into his defensive position. 'And I've seen Mr Anastos's face when his friend got murdered, just as in *your* prophecy! You're playing with fire, Miss *Olivia*, and other people are going to get burned!'

'Don't call me that—' Lady Athena started, but we were interrupted by the sound of the door crashing open.

We both looked round, Bones growling, his hackles raised.

'What is going on here?' Mr Hyde demanded.

★ ★ ★

There were a few heavy moments where no one spoke. I had no idea how much Mr Hyde knew of his wife's true nature and identity – but I suspected that, as he worked on her act, he must at least know the secrets behind it. Still, I didn't think blurting out, 'I scared your wife with the ghost of her sister to get her to reveal all of her darkest secrets,' was wise. I waited for Lady Athena to say something.

'Young Violet here was concerned,' she said eventually, when he folded his arms and gave us a flash of his steely gaze. 'About my prophecies. And the death of Terence.'

Mr Hyde gave a sigh, leaned back against the door and

pinched the bridge of his nose. 'I've been thinking about this, my darling, and we need to stop.'

'*What?*' both Lady Athena and I exclaimed, making Bones's ears prick up. That was the last thing I had expected him to say.

'I think this has become a dangerous game. We must stop the performances, at least until the murderer is found. What if we're the next target? You know someone tried to trap us in this room already.'

I spluttered and tried to hide it with a cough. Bones gave me a questioning look.

'This is our life, Jacob,' Lady Athena protested. 'This is my *destiny*. I cannot stop. It's important!'

'It's madness,' he said with a shake of his head. 'This is not the path we agreed upon,' he muttered.

I stood up. 'I ought to take my leave,' I told them, sensing that an argument was about to ensue. 'Come on, Bones.'

Luckily, Mr Hyde seemed to barely notice I was there. He crossed the room and took Lady Athena's hands. 'We need to discuss this immediately.'

But the medium was still looking at me.

'Don't forget what I said,' I told her. 'If you need guidance, perhaps you should talk to *my friend*.' I made a subtle gesture towards the mirror. 'She seems as though she has a good heart.'

Lady Athena blinked and gave me a barely perceptible nod.

In the mirror, I could have sworn that Mary's ghostly lips twitched into a smile.

CHAPTER TWENTY-ONE

Bones and I ran straight into Oliver in the corridor. 'Whoa, whoa,' he said, holding up his hands as I dodged him at the last second, while Bones nearly knocked him over. Every time Bones laid eyes on Oliver, his excitement was as though they had not seen each other for twenty years.

'What happened?' we both asked at the same time.

Oliver waved a hand to tell me to speak first, his other hand busy scratching Bones's head.

'I used some of my . . . *abilities*,' I said as quietly as I could. 'And Lady Athena confessed. A bit of a tragic tale, to be honest, but I do believe her. She told me that she came from nothing, and that her act is a deception that started as a product of her imagination, but she truly believes in the prophecies.'

'Really?' Oliver asked. 'Oh, I'd be surprised if she was ever poor. Lady Athena sounds like a toff's name to me.'

I noted that he was more shocked by her background than by her being a charlatan, or by the fact that she truly believed her fortune-telling was genuine.

'Her actual name is Olivia,' I explained.

'Oh!' Oliver grinned. 'That's a good name, that. Sounds familiar.'

I poked him in the ribs. 'I thought your name was *Jack Danger*, you rogue.'

'Well, Mr Hyde fell for it,' he said with a shrug.

'We ought to find Niko and Eleni,' I said, 'and let them know what we've discovered. Bones?' I put my hands on my knees, and he turned his face up to mine. 'Can you find them?'

He wagged his tail and turned, nose to the carpet, and began leading us along.

'Why do we need to tell them?' Oliver asked suddenly. 'It's our investigation.'

I waved a hand. 'True. But they're our men – our, um,

people – on the inside. We shan't get to the bottom of what's going on here without them. They ought to know this place inside out.'

Bones came to a stop in front of the next door and pawed at it.

Oliver gave a barely concealed sigh, pushed the heavy wooden door open and held it back for me to slip through. I wondered if I should question his reluctance, but it didn't seem like the time. I wanted to know what had happened during his discussion with Mr Hyde.

'What exactly did you talk to Lady Athena's husband about?' I asked as we walked out into the (thankfully empty at that moment) formal downstairs bar, which smelled strongly of alcohol and polish. 'He seemed rather flustered when he came back.'

'I poured on the charm, asked him about his success at being a manager an' running the show.' Oliver smiled. 'I was writing it all down in my notebook. He seemed a bit concerned about my handwriting. I told him it was that, um, whatchamacallit – shorthand? Where you write in squiggles all quick so that you can copy it out proper later.'

'Ha!' I laughed. 'That was rather clever. We'll make a real reporter of you yet. But what did you say that had him so rattled? He told Lady Athena she had to stop her performances at once. And this is their livelihood, not to mention their ticket to fame and fortune.'

Oliver didn't reply for a few moments, so I halted beside an ornate globe and searched his face intently.

He appeared a little embarrassed, his cheeks flushing. 'Um, I feel a bit sneaky. He was showing off about Lady Athena's prophecies, an' I asked him if he was afraid that the next prophecy might say that the murderer was coming after them too. I showed him my scar an' told him I knew what it was like to be murdered. He looked peaky an' said he had to go.'

I patted Oliver on the shoulder. 'Somewhat heavy-handed, but it worked.'

We followed Bones round the building into the grand part of the entrance hall with the statues and the staircases, and he began bounding up the stairs. Theatre staff were giving us some odd looks, but I often found that if you walked round a place with enough purpose people would assume you were meant to be there.

When we reached the next floor, Bones paused for a moment, nose to the ground. Then he carried on towards another set of stairs.

'Are you sure he knows where he's going?' Oliver asked, getting a tad breathless. 'I don't think we're even supposed to be up here.'

'Have a little more faith,' I replied as I hopped on to the stairs, these less ornate than the marble ones below. 'Bones hasn't led us wrong before, has he?'

The top floor of the theatre was rather pokey, and up there the cracks were really beginning to show. Quite literally, in fact – there were cracks in the walls and ceiling, and the ornate wallpaper was flaking off in places. The red carpet was worn and threadbare from decades of feet walking over it. I supposed the seats high up in the top circle were the cheapest, so not as much effort was put in to impress the patrons who chose them.

Bones stopped outside a heavy set of double doors in the hallway, which had a sign reading **PRIVATE** above and a little bell next to it. He looked at the door, head tilted to one side in bewilderment.

'Oh, we definitely ain't supposed to go in there,' Oliver said.

'I'll ring the bell,' I protested. 'We shan't be barging in. Whatever do you think of me?'

Oliver gave me a look that implied that was precisely the sort of thing he thought I'd do.

'Hmmph,' I said, and gave the bell a flick. It jingled daintily.

For a few moments, we waited, Oliver shuffling as he usually did – unable to keep still. *Always prepared to run,*

I thought. But then, just as I was beginning to wonder if anyone had heard, the door swung open to reveal Niko.

'Oh!' he said, eyebrows raised. 'Hello. I wasn't expecting you two. Uh, three, I suppose,' he added as Bones greeted him with a wet nose.

'Sorry,' I said quickly. Niko had a way of making me feel unusually flustered. 'We didn't mean to drop in unannounced, but there have been new developments and we wanted to speak to you and Eleni.'

'Aha.' He nodded, patting Bones gently. 'You'd better come in, then.'

'Do you . . . live up here?' Oliver asked, peering through the doorway. I could see a coat-rack and an umbrella stand just inside.

Niko waved us in. 'Oh yes, these are our living quarters. Eleni's in the kitchen.'

He took us in and opened another door that led to a hallway with doors and arches. Past one arch I could see a parlour with red chairs and a fireplace, but Bones was already making his way through another. Beyond this one was a rather nice dark wood kitchen with a stove and a table over by the window. Eleni was sitting in her chair beside it, staring outside, deep in thought. A lone pigeon was pecking along the stone ledge – and of course that caught Bones's attention.

The dog barked and went bounding over, jumping up to put his paws on the windowsill, sending the pigeon scattering and Eleni jerking upright in surprise.

'Ah!'

'Sorry!' I called, hurrying over to take hold of Bones's collar and pull him back down. 'Silly dog,' I chastised him. 'Um, hello, Eleni. Sorry about that.'

She blinked up at me. 'What are you doing here?' she asked. 'Not that I'm not pleased to see you, of course. I just . . . I rather thought . . .'

Niko leaned against the wall with his arms folded, while Oliver leaned against the opposite wall, mirroring him. 'We thought what happened had put you off the mystery game.'

'It isn't a game,' I insisted, pushing Bones's nose away from the window as he tried to investigate the pigeon's perch. Unperturbed, he wandered off, probably in search of a snack. 'And no, I'm still on the case.'

'He doesn't mean it like that,' Eleni replied. She smiled up at me. 'It really is good to have you back.' I felt a warmth spreading through my chest.

'That's the first time I've seen you smile since—' Niko began.

'I know, I know.' She waved a hand at him, gave a little sniff and wiped the corner of her eye. 'I've been in the depths of misery, quite frankly.'

I didn't blame her. I'd felt quite the same, and I hadn't even known Terence. She must have felt so dreadful that we hadn't stopped the killer in time.

'Well, I have something that might lift your spirits a little,' I told her carefully. She raised her eyebrows in a questioning manner. 'I have extracted a confession from Lady Athena. She truly is a fraud.'

I heard Niko splutter behind me, but Eleni's eyes brightened. 'Tell me more,' she said.

I explained some of what we knew – that Lady Athena's medium act was a fabrication, and a facade she'd been keeping up for some time, but that it appeared she genuinely believed that the prophecies were real.

Eleni picked at the stuffing in the cracked leather arms of her wheelchair while she listened. 'Goodness,' she said, wide-eyed, when I'd finished. 'I knew it! I knew there was something fishy about her.' She gave a short laugh. 'How on earth did you persuade her to tell you all of that?'

That gave me pause. Did I want to tell them the truth? I looked back at Oliver, who gave me a sort of *up to you?* gesture with upturned palms. Then I glanced at Bones, who was pawing at a biscuit tin, and frankly no help at all.

I took a deep breath. 'Lady Athena doesn't have the power to see ghosts. But I . . . do.'

CHAPTER TWENTY-TWO

'*Really?*' Eleni exclaimed.

'I, well . . .' I took a deep breath. 'I'm an undertaker's daughter. I spend a lot of time around the dead. Sometimes the borders between things are blurry . . .'

I was fidgeting my fingers. I knew I was dancing around the subject. I didn't want Eleni and Niko to think I was mad or dismiss me the way I'd always been dismissed when I was younger. I found that I cared more for their opinion than I usually did for the opinions of others.

I took another deep breath and started again. 'What I'm trying to say is that I can sense ghosts.'

I looked at their expressions. Eleni was blinking. Niko had raised an eyebrow.

'Like a medium?' he asked. 'You communicate with the dead?'

'Um . . . sometimes?' I said. 'It's rather more complicated than that. I might hear them speaking. I might see a hint of them. I might just feel cold or a tingle down the back of my neck . . .' I rubbed a spot above my collar self-consciously.

'Goodness,' said Eleni after a pause. She glanced at Oliver, who was remaining carefully silent. 'Did you know this?'

He nodded. 'I believe her,' he said simply. Then, as if realising he needed to explain further, he added: 'She knows odd things sometimes.'

Oh, Oliver. That was a funny way of putting it. I wondered if I'd just been imagining that he sometimes seemed to be detecting what I could.

While Eleni and Niko were looking at each other in puzzlement, I decided I might as well dig my grave deeper. 'I heard a ghost here, in the theatre. He was quoting from *Mac—* the Scottish play, you know? And it seemed that he was angry with Lady Athena. I suspected then that she was inventing her medium abilities.'

Eleni went a bit pale. 'Are you saying the theatre is haunted?'

Niko made a face at her. 'Did you not think of this when Lady Athena was drawing back the veil every night?'

She waved a hand at him. 'That was just a performance, you bore. I told you I never believed a word of it. Besides, I thought she claimed to be speaking to the afterlife, not bringing the ghosts here.'

Bones chose that moment to slink back and duck under the table. I tried to ignore the mysterious chewing sounds, and just hoped whatever he had wasn't expensive.

'Most places are a little haunted,' I explained. 'My hypothesis is that spirits have a sort of . . . anchor to something. Usually it's their body. Sometimes it's the place where they died. Sometimes it's another person or an object. And, well – Lady Athena is haunted.'

'Wait.' Niko leaned forward and unfolded his arms. 'I thought you said she was—'

'Making it up, yes. She is. I was able to see the ghost, and she wasn't. It's her sister, who died when she was only young. They must have had a strong connection and something of it remained. Her sister is watching over her.'

Eleni shivered in her chair.

'That's how I encouraged her to confess everything,' I said with a nonchalant shrug that was not at all how I felt.

'I can't believe it,' she said.

'It was quite simple, really.' I tried not to look at Oliver. I was sure he was rolling his eyes at me.

Eleni leaned forward and peered at me, as if my ghostly powers would suddenly reveal themselves. 'Are you . . . certain? It all sounds a little far-fetched, you must admit.'

'I believe you,' said Niko, visibly surprising all of us. 'What?' he asked. 'I think there's more to this world than we can see and understand. Lady Athena's prophecies, your . . . abilities.'

Eleni frowned. 'But if . . . Could you . . .' She took a shaky breath and traced a crack in the smooth wood of their table. 'Could you talk to Terence? Tell him we're sorry that we couldn't save him?'

My heart broke a little for her. 'I'm sorry,' I said quietly. 'I don't know. It's hard to talk to the recently deceased. And ghosts are like . . .'

'An echo,' said Oliver. 'Or a ripple.' He had obviously been paying attention when I'd told him.

I nodded. 'Some are strong and some are barely a whisper. And we don't know what his spirit would be anchored to, if it's here at all.'

Eleni looked crestfallen. 'I don't want him to be gone for ever,' she said quietly.

I reached out and put my hand on her arm. 'I can't

say I know what happens after someone dies,' I said. 'Perhaps their soul goes to heaven, or *beyond the veil* – perhaps they leave an echo behind here too. But that's not all. What did he leave you?'

The question came from something my father would say to grieving relatives. He knew grieving better than anyone.

Eleni sniffed and wiped a tear from her eye. 'I don't know. We weren't . . . related or . . .'

'I don't mean his second-best bed or anything like that,' I said gently. 'Tell me a memory of Terence. What did he teach you?'

She stared down at the table for a moment. 'He taught me most of what I know about playwriting. He used to lend me all his scripts, show me how they were put together. And then he would read my plays and write notes on them.' She gave a tiny painful laugh, her eyes still not meeting ours. 'Whenever I forgot to write stage directions, he would write in *exit, pursued by a bear*.'

Niko chuckled sadly.

I smiled at Eleni, her arm warm under my hand. 'Then don't you see? He is never gone. He's in every play that you write. He left you a gift, and you must use it.'

There were a few moments of heavy silence, and then slowly she smiled back. 'Thank you,' she whispered.

I thought I had better get back to the matter at hand. 'The thing is, Lady Athena's husband is trying to persuade her to stop, but I don't think even that will work. She believes what she prophesies is true, and she wants to go ahead with the performance.'

Eleni frowned. 'I wonder if this will convince Baba to stop her. He must see the truth now . . .'

Niko sighed.

'Um, Violet?' Oliver suddenly piped up.

'What is it?' I asked, turning to face him.

'Bones is spraying crumbs all over the carpet.'

I jumped up. 'I'm *very* sorry,' I said, reaching under the table to grab Bones's collar and drag him out. 'I think it's time that we exit, pursued by a dog . . .'

* * *

Oliver and I headed back down towards the lobby – me pulling along a sheepish Bones, who was still licking his lips.

'I think we need to talk to the boss,' Oliver said. 'If Lady Athena ain't stopping the show, then maybe he's the one to do it.'

'I think you're right,' I replied.

But, as we pushed through the doors, a commotion at the front desk became apparent. Bones began to growl.

It was Mrs Barker, holding a wicker basket from which a strained yowling could be heard. She was leaning over the counter, her rather old-fashioned bustle sticking out behind her.

'This is NOT my Mittens!' she was saying to the young man cowering in the ticket booth. 'Something's not right!'

'Mrs Barker?' I called. 'Oliver, hold Bones for a minute, will you?'

'Right,' he said, taking the dog from me.

I trotted over. Mrs Barker hadn't heard me. She was still ranting. 'I want that woman to explain herself to me!'

'Please, ma'am,' the young man pleaded. 'If you just calm down, I'm sure Mr Anastos will sort everything out . . .'

'Calm down?' She put the noisy basket on the counter. 'I'll calm down when she tells me what really happened to my Mittens!'

I tapped Mrs Barker gently on the shoulder, and she turned round to peer at me. 'Oh, hello again, dear. I'm rather in the middle of something . . .'

'You realised—' I stopped myself just in time. 'You think this is a different cat?'

'Oh, I couldn't be more certain. It's a monster!'

Just as she said that, a sharp-clawed paw shot out of one of the holes in the basket, sending me jumping backwards. I could still hear Bones growling, and when I glanced over Oliver was straining to hold on to him.

'See, the cat is a vicious beast!' Mrs Barker exclaimed. 'It tore my curtains to ribbons. To *ribbons*!'

I heard the doors to the rest of the theatre open and turned to see Mr Anastos, closely followed by Archie trotting along behind – who must have run to fetch him.

Mr Anastos was a little red-faced and out of breath. 'Madam,' he boomed. 'Archie tells me you are troubled?'

'More than a little troubled.' Mrs Barker sniffed. 'Your Lady Athena promised my cat would return to me. *This*,' she said, taking the basket from the counter and shoving it into Mr Anastos's arms, 'is not my cat!'

There was a hiss and Mr Anastos flinched. Bones barked. 'I'm sure this is a . . . misunderstanding . . .'

Mrs Barker folded her arms. She was clearly sharper than I had judged her. 'It is a charade is what it is! I paid good money to be spun a yarn! This is no magic. Someone has clearly brought this feral cat to me. As if it could replace my Mittens.'

'Please, please,' said Mr Anastos, gingerly lowering the basket to the floor. 'Perhaps the spirits made a mistake. I will refund you the money for your ticket, and you may choose a seat at any of our other performances.'

'Hmmph,' said Mrs Barker. 'And you can keep the cat

too. You shall be hearing from my Jonathan about this. He's a solicitor, you know. Good day to you, sir!'

And, with that, she marched out.

Mr Anastos stared down at the basket on the floor. 'Oh,' he said. And then he murmured a word in Greek that I didn't understand, but it sounded exasperated to say the least. He wiped his hand over his eyes.

He could have been a potential suspect in the conspiracy, but the shock on his face told a different story. I didn't believe he had any prior knowledge of this whole business. And, of course, he'd been with us when Terence's body was found, and we had seen his reaction then too.

Say something, Oliver mouthed at me as Bones's feet skittered on the floor with his determination to either get away from or bite the scary cat.

'Um, Mr Anastos, sir?'

He looked at me as if he hadn't realised I was there. 'Oh, Violet, hello. Please excuse me. I don't want a fuss. Everything is all right, no?' He turned to Archie, who was nervously twiddling his fingers. 'Find this a home, will you?' he said, picking up the basket and handing it to him.

I suspected Mr Anastos was concerned about Mrs Barker spreading the scandal to the press. But I feared that things were about to get much worse than *feline imposters*.

'Sir, I know Lady Athena's performance is important

to the theatre, but I think everyone is in danger. This cat is just the tip of the iceberg. I think someone is actually carrying out Lady Athena's prophecies. You saw what happened to Mr Clearwater!'

A deep furrow spread across his brow. 'God moves in mysterious ways . . .'

'But he doesn't go about distributing fake cats or murdering people,' I protested. 'There's a *person* doing this, I swear to you. I don't think it's Lady Athena, but –' I paused, thinking it better not to admit to locking her and her husband in their dressing room – 'it's *someone*. A crazed admirer, perhaps, or someone connected to the theatre—'

'*No*,' Mr Anastos said firmly. 'None of us would do this. I know everybody here. They are my family. And if it's an outsider? How can I control what they do?'

'You could stop the performance,' Oliver said from over by the doors.

Mr Anastos turned to him. 'I can't do that,' he said. 'She's our most popular act. You know my children – I do this for them.'

'But what if they're the ones in danger next?' I insisted. 'Or someone else here?'

He remained silent – the only noises being the distant yowling from the cat that Archie had left with, and Bones panting. 'I'll have the police send a constable,' he said eventually. 'They will keep an eye on things.'

'But—' I tried again.

He held up a finger. 'I will talk to the lady, and I will make sure she tells only good fortunes.'

Oliver raised an eyebrow. I think both of us were sceptical that Lady Athena could be told to do anything.

'Don't you worry, my dear,' Mr Anastos continued, his face lighting up once again with a ringmaster's grin. 'Everything will be fine. The Grecian Theatre has weathered many storms, and she will weather this one too. After all – the show must go on!'

CHAPTER TWENTY-THREE

I didn't share Mr Anastos's confidence that everything would be fine. Despite our best efforts, it seemed the performance would go ahead that evening, and I was filled with dread. Anything could happen.

And, of course, we had the issue that I was forbidden from going out at night. How was I supposed to investigate properly without being at the scene?

Oliver, Bones and I walked home under the cloudy sky, dejected. I had discovered Lady Athena's secret, yes, but

I felt no closer to knowing who was really behind the prophecies.

After we had eaten supper, I retired to my room with my notebook. It was time to update my case notes.

Incidents:

The impossible re-emergence of Miss Li's necklace from her father's grave

The return of Mrs Barker's cat who had been missing for many months

The receipt of a letter supposedly from a deceased wife

A large sum of money received in the post by Mrs Lambert

The prediction that Mr Henley would be visited by a ghost on the eve of his uncle's demise – we know not whether this took place

The memorial of Caroline Spring decorated
with a wreath of white lilies (which were,
in fact, rhododendrons)

The unexpected triumph of the mayor's horse
at Lansdowne Racecourse

The murder of actor Terence Clearwater

Suspects:

1. Lady Athena. Stands to gain much from her
prophecies coming true, but seemed surprised
when we confronted her with evidence that the
cat did not return of its own accord. She has
been lying about her medium powers, but seems
to truly believe her prophecies. Locked in
dressing room when murder took place.

2. Mr Hyde. Also stands to gain as the
husband and manager of Lady Athena.

Acted suspiciously. But seems to be concerned for his wife and wants her to stop performing. Locked in dressing room when murder took place.

3. Mr Anastos? As owner of the theatre, he also benefits from Lady Athena's popularity. Could he be behind the prophecies? But Mr Anastos seemed shocked by the cat incident and Terence Clearwater's murder. What about Mrs Anastos?

4. Someone else involved with the theatre? An actor?

Oliver knocked on my bedroom door, despite it being wide open. Bones jumped up from his spot beside the fireplace to greet him.

'Have you solved it yet?' Oliver asked, leaning against the frame.

I put my pen down and gave him a withering look. 'Don't be a dolt,' I said.

He shrugged. 'Maybe I just believe in you.'

'Perhaps you shouldn't,' I said, looking down at my notes and rubbing my hand over my eyes. 'I fear that we aren't getting anywhere.' I looked back up at him. 'Oliver, this is hopeless! I can't solve this from my bedroom. We need to go back to the theatre. Tonight.'

Oliver's eyes went wide. 'Oh no.' He held up his hands. 'Not again.'

I jumped up and went over to him, stepping over Bones who had settled down on the rug. We needed to be quiet if we didn't want to draw attention to ourselves.

'Whoever our villain is, things are escalating,' I hissed. 'If they've killed once, they could do it again. I shan't be sitting in my room waiting for it to happen! If the show must go on, we must go too.'

'What are you gonna do to stop a murderer?' Oliver asked.

'I stopped one before, did I not?' I shot back. I would have thought that the case of the Seven Gates Murders and the Black Widow was still fresh in his mind.

'WE stopped one,' he interrupted, but I waved his comment away.

'We won't be alone. There are two of us, and Bones, and Niko and Eleni . . .' I was already racking my brains for how we could pull off a daring escape operation. I returned to my dressing table, dipped my pen in ink and began scribbling some notes.

There was a pause, and then Oliver said from the doorway: 'I think you trust them too much.'

That shook me from my thoughts. 'Pardon?'

He shrugged. 'You trust them too much. They're part of the theatre, ain't they? They could be involved in this.'

I glared at him. 'They're our FRIENDS,' I insisted.

'Are they on your list of suspicious people?' he asked.

I looked down at my notes, even though I knew they weren't. 'No,' I said finally.

He said nothing, then, which was somehow worse. I could feel him judging me.

'Look,' I said, 'they're on our side. Right now, we need to think how we can leave without anyone noticing. Where is everyone?'

Oliver sighed and then held out his hands to count them off. 'Your pa is working in his office.' He put each finger down as he spoke. 'Thomas is in his bedroom. Maddy is in the kitchen, helping your ma wash up. Ernesto's gone home.'

I nodded. 'So we have a clear path out of the front door, if we're sneaky about it. Right. I say you go down there, make a show of yawning and tell Mother and Maddy you're going to retire to bed. Perhaps say you're not feeling well. Then we put on our finest clothes, tuck some rolled-up sheets in our beds, and we slip out to the theatre.'

'You really think that'll fool them?' he asked, screwing up his face. 'What about the dog?'

I looked down at Bones on the rug. He wagged his tail slowly and rolled over. 'Hmm. We could tell him to stay here.'

At that, Bones scrambled up and put his head in my lap desperately. It seemed he was objecting.

'On second thoughts, we might need him. And he's good protection.' I considered the dilemma for a moment. 'Tell them you're taking him to your room, perhaps. Mother might open my door to check on me, but she wouldn't open yours.'

Oliver shuffled and rubbed his hands together. 'All right. All right.'

'You're . . . really going along with this?' I asked, feeling a rush of excitement. 'You're not going to say, "Too dangerous, miss – we'll get in trouble, miss," and all that?'

'Oi, you insisted I don't call you miss, so I don't!' he said. But his anger seemed to have faded, and now there was a hint of a smile on his face. 'Well, it's true. It is dangerous an' I'm sure we're gonna get in trouble. But I think you're right. I think we have to get to the bottom of this before anyone else gets hurt. So it's worth it.'

I grinned at him. 'The game's afoot!'

'What have feet got to do with it?' he replied, staring down at his scuffed boots.

'I . . . never mind. Do what I told you, quickly and quietly now, and I shall meet you outside the front of the shop.'

'Right you are, miss,' Oliver said, tipping his hat and walking away with Bones by his side. I stuck my tongue out at the empty doorway.

★ ★ ★

I had seen all the fancy ladies dressed in their finest at the Grecian. Now it was my turn. I was sure Oliver was right, and we were very likely to get caught – but I thought that if this was to be my last venture to Lady Athena's performance then I was going to do it in style. Impressing the Anastos siblings was only part of my motivation. Bones was circling impatiently, as if he could sense my excitement.

Father's words echoed in my head: *I want you to tell us precisely where you're going before you run off anywhere. And I want you home before nightfall. No night-time jaunts, you hear me?*

It wasn't 'precisely' *night-time*, was it? It was merely the evening. And perhaps, if I left a letter explaining our whereabouts, I could reasonably protest that I had told them 'precisely' where I was going. As for being home by nightfall, well . . . I would have to hope he'd forgotten about that one.

I went to my wardrobe and picked out my nicest dress, one that had been purchased a few years ago when we'd been better off. I had grown a little big for it, but Mother had altered it for me recently and made a few adjustments that brought it more in line with the year's most fashionable silhouettes. She was rather talented when it came to sewing.

Rather than being plain black like most of my clothes, this dress was a deep velvet in the darkest blue, like the night sky. It had elegant sleeves, a beautiful brocade on the front and buttons embroidered with crowns.

Getting into it without any assistance was certainly going to be a challenge – thank goodness I was already wearing a corset. I did what probably looked like an extremely awkward dance round my room as I pulled it over my head and bent my arms into something of a ridiculous position to do it up.

It was longer than most of my dresses, which were knee-length. This was a more grown-up cut, closer to the floor. I was going to have to pick my skirts up when walking through the filthy streets because there was no chance of us getting a carriage.

I rifled through my drawers for a matching ribbon and tied up my hair, leaving some of my curls spilling down.

I smiled at myself in the mirror. Even when on the trail of a murderer, it was important to be well-turned-out.

I heard Oliver making a show of stomping upstairs to bed, with Bones clattering up behind him. So that was all going to plan. Now it was just the matter of actually sneaking from the house. I opened my bedroom door again to keep an eye out for Oliver. If we went separately, it would be less suspicious.

The grandfather clock in the hall downstairs began to chime, and not long after I saw Oliver and Bones slip past in the corridor as I laced on my shoes. Oliver could be surprisingly light on his feet when he wanted to be, as could Bones. Sometimes you wouldn't even know Bones was there until you spotted him slipping out of the room with a roast chicken leg in his mouth.

I took a deep breath, and patted the concealed pockets of my dress to check for my things – my coin purse, notebook, pencil and handkerchief. I was ready to follow them.

The clock had finished chiming, and I slipped out of my bedroom. *Creeeak* went one of the boards, and I froze in place until I was sure no one had noticed. Hopefully they would think it was just the house settling.

I continued on until I reached the bottom of the stairs, and had a few blissful seconds of triumph . . . until I heard footsteps approaching from the kitchen.

Chapter twenty-four

uick! I had to hide somewhere. If I ran back upstairs, it would be too noisy. My eyes darted round the room. The door to my left led to the dining room, and blessedly it was slightly ajar. It was my only choice – I pushed through it, just before my mother came into the hallway.

In a panic, I dived under the table, pulling the tablecloth back behind me. And now I was stuck.

'Bones?' I heard Mother say. 'Is that you?'

I held my breath, tried not to make a sound. Our old

green carpet was rough and scratchy on my hands – I hoped it was not going to stick to my velvet dress.

Footsteps came towards me and, peering from under the cloth, I could make out Mother's feet in her house slippers. I hoped the darkness of the room would hide me.

Don't lift up the tablecloth, I begged in my mind. *Don't lift up the . . .*

'Daft dog,' Mother said, and then she turned and left the room.

I breathed out.

I waited a little and, much to my relief, I heard the familiar sound of her pushing the treadle on her Singer sewing machine. That would help – she was distracted and the noise ought to cover my footsteps.

So then I moved quickly – I scrambled from under the table, brushed myself off and went to peer out of the door to the hallway. The coast was clear. Praying that Father or Maddy would stay where they were, I slipped down the hall as quietly as possible and went through into the back of the shop.

I found Oliver and Bones waiting for me by our next-door neighbour's house, just out of sight of the shop window.

'What took you so long?' Oliver demanded as Bones

ran up and pressed his nose into my hands. Oliver was wearing an old suit of my father's that he had been given. It was a little big, but still smarter than what he normally wore.

'I was nearly caught,' I explained. 'I had to hide under the table.'

'What?'

'Never mind – we must be off.'

I hurried away, holding up my skirts to keep them from touching the ground. It was time for the show, and the darkening skies overhead rumbled with the threat of rain.

★ ★ ★

The exterior of the Grecian Theatre was once again buzzing with people, and likewise my mind was buzzing with thoughts.

We were going to have to talk our way inside . . . and then what? I was beginning to regret having made such a rash decision. What would Lady Athena predict? I almost hoped she would be true to what Mr Anastos had hopefully made her promise and say something completely harmless, like it was going to rain, or that the shops would close at night. But I knew that saying trivial things like that would ruin the spectacle, and that was what Lady Athena's career thrived on.

Bones was already sniffing round the feet of some of the gentlemen waiting on the steps, who were either ignoring him or shooing him away. I turned to look for Oliver, and found him a little way behind me.

'Hurry up,' I hissed. 'They're about to let everyone in!'

He leaned against the wall, catching his breath and putting his hand to his head. 'Well, I . . . I don't have a watch, do I? And you made us late.'

We were interrupted by the doors swinging open. I spotted Archie standing to attention beside one of them as the crowds flooded in. I went up to the wall and slipped along until I reached him.

'Archie!' I hissed. 'Can we come in?'

He peered round the glass-panelled door at me. 'Miss Violet? I don't know – it's very busy tonight . . .'

As if to make his point, two women with bulging sleeves, bustles and wide-brimmed hats tried to fit through the doors at the same time, almost getting stuck. Archie watched in horror, clearly unsure whether he was supposed to help with this until, after some wiggling, the two ladies burst through into the lobby, both huffing at the indecency of it all.

Archie turned back to me, his face crinkled with worry. It probably didn't help that Bones was licking his shoes.

'Just let us in so we can talk to Niko and Eleni,' I begged. 'Look, we even dressed the part!'

Archie's head bobbed back and forth – presumably to see if anyone were watching – and then he quickly waved us in.

'Cheers, Arch!' Oliver said quickly.

'Don't mention it,' Archie replied. 'No really, don't mention it!'

But we were already trotting across the carpet. To my surprise, we spotted the Anastos siblings quickly as we went through the arches into the grand reception hall. They were over to one side, watching the audience flood in. I waved at them.

Niko smiled at me. 'Violet!' he exclaimed. 'You look wonderful!'

I curtseyed at him, trying not to blush. I wasn't used to acting ladylike. 'Thank you,' I said.

'And I'm also here,' said Oliver.

Eleni tried to hide her laughter while I jabbed Oliver in the arm. 'You both look smart,' she said. She glanced down at her own slightly faded peach-coloured dress. 'I should have worn something more extravagant.'

'But you don't like to watch Lady Athena's performances,' I pointed out.

'Oh no,' she said. 'But I do like to watch people. And

I'm curious as to what dramatic scenes may unfold this evening.'

As she said that, I noticed that Zhen, Miss Li's sister, was walking past us. Of course, Mr Campbell had told us that they never missed a performance. His wife was wearing a beautiful dress of yellow Chinese silk, but tailored in a more Western style. She smiled nervously at me and then wandered through the archway beside us in the direction of the lavatories. I wondered where her husband was.

But I was thrown from that thought by the next person that walked into the grand entrance hall: Inspector Holbrook.

'What are you doing here?' I exclaimed.

'A good evening to you too, Miss Veil,' the tall inspector said, tipping his hat at us as he strode over. 'I might ask the same of you.'

'Just an evening at the theatre,' I said, folding my arms. Bones had slunk behind Eleni's wheelchair – he wasn't a fan of the police.

'Without your parents or a chaperone?' Inspector Holbrook asked, raising an eyebrow. 'Do they know you're here?'

'Of course,' I said, silently cursing myself for lying. Lies rarely got anyone into *less* trouble.

'She's with us,' said Niko. 'Our parents own this theatre.'

Eleni nodded. 'She's our guest.'

The inspector looked down at Eleni. 'What happened to you?' he asked.

'I have a rare disease called none-of-your-business,' said Eleni, turning her nose up at him.

I tried to keep a straight face. 'So tell us, why *are* you here, Inspector?'

'To look out for trouble,' he said. 'And, if you're the cause of it, I shan't hesitate to send for your parents.'

'I shall be a model citizen as always,' I said. Oliver rolled his eyes.

Inspector Holbrook merely frowned at me, and strode away towards the auditorium.

'Father called him, I think,' Eleni explained.

Oliver nodded. 'He did say he was going to get the police to keep an eye on things. The Inspector must be interested because of the murder.'

'Well, I hope it helps,' I said, reaching behind Eleni's chair to pull Bones back out. 'There is still a murderer on the loose, and I'm afraid of what Lady Athena is going to say. That's why we're here. Would we perhaps be able to borrow your viewing box again?'

'Of course,' Niko said. 'I don't think Mama or Baba will be using it, either. They'll be supervising backstage.'

'Oh, *thank you*,' I exclaimed, clapping my hands together.

Niko looked up at a golden clock on the opposite wall. 'I had better run along,' he said suddenly. 'They'll want me to help.'

With a quick smile, he darted across the room. He was light on his feet, I noticed, dodging the guests easily. Bones tried to follow, but I kept tight hold of his collar.

'Ugh!' Eleni huffed, raising her hands. 'Why must my brother forget that I can't run after him?'

'Come with us,' I said. 'You can watch the performance.'

She sighed deeply. 'Normally, I would tell you that I would prefer to stick pins in my eyes. But, as I said before, I'm curious. If there's to be some excitement, I don't want to miss it. Would you mind pushing me?'

I grinned at her and then went round to take the wooden handles of her wheelchair. Oliver was still staring after Niko, just like Bones.

'Come on,' I said. 'Oliver and Bones, pull yourselves together. We must attend the performance.'

That unfortunately meant facing our old nemesis again – the lift. But we made it to the next level relatively unscathed and headed for the box. Eleni pulled out her key to let us in.

The three of us plus the dog crammed into it – Oliver

and me on the chairs, Eleni in between and Bones curled up on the floor.

Something about the atmosphere in the theatre already felt strange. I scanned the crowd and began to notice something: some of the men looked familiar, and were scribbling in their notebooks. *Reporters.* So Terence's death had caused a stir. And I was willing to bet that many of the whispering people in the stalls were hoping to witness further shocking spectacles. *The vultures,* as I called them. They were the sort of people who attended hangings.

I could see Inspector Holbrook sitting in the front row, and his useless officers Pickles and Williams stationed by the exit doors. I wasn't sure what good them being there would really do, unless the murderer decided to start attacking people in the middle of the auditorium.

I noticed there was no Mrs Barker this time – presumably she still hadn't forgiven Lady Athena. But I could see Zhen Campbell making her way to her seat.

When the lights went down, I felt a shiver go through me, and I knew it wasn't the prospect of ghostly activity, having firmly ruled out Lady Athena's supernatural abilities.

It was the usual routine with Mr Hyde, but even he looked on edge. 'Ladies and gentlemen, I welcome you on this fine evening . . .'

'See,' Eleni whispered, 'it gets mundane if you watch it all the time.' She yawned. 'I'm so tired of their nonsense.'

'Shush,' Oliver replied, 'we want to hear what happens.'

'Hmmph,' Eleni said, the two of them glaring at each other.

I rolled my eyes and looked back at the stage. Once Mr Hyde had finished his speech, looking rather uncomfortable the entire time, Lady Athena made her grand entrance to the sounds of the dramatic orchestral score and the rumbling thunder.

'Good evening,' she said, emerging from the smoke, and I noted that she showed no hint of concern as she introduced herself. 'I am the Lady Athena.'

It was as though Olivia Jenkins were putting on the role of Lady Athena like an overcoat, or perhaps a mask. There was that mysterious accent again. This mystique was all of her own making.

But it was about to be shattered.

'Who will step forward for a reading—' she began to say, but she was interrupted by a letter floating down from above her.

Every eye in the theatre followed that white envelope as it slowly fluttered down like a dove. For a moment, I wondered if this were part of the show, even though I hadn't seen it before. Perhaps, had things been different,

Lady Athena might have pretended it was, or even ignored it.

Instead, as it landed close to her feet, she took a few steps and reached down to pick it up. Mumbles of discussion bubbled up from the crowd as she opened it and in a shaking voice began to read.

'*Lady Athena, your husband will pay the ultimate price. Death comes for us all . . .*'

CHAPTER TWENTY-FIVE

Gasps and panic filled the room. I wondered if Lady Athena were going to faint again – but she just stood for a moment, staring at the letter under the harsh spotlight. And then she ran off into the wings, knocking her table as she went – sending her crystal ball rolling into the orchestra pit, where it landed in a tuba.

Inspector Holbrook jumped to his feet. He pointed up to the roof of the stage. 'Constables, up there now!' he ordered. 'Williams, with me, I will have Mr Hyde and Lady Athena taken to a secure location!'

Constable Pickles pushed open the exit door and ran.

I turned to Oliver and Eleni. 'We have to do something!'

Eleni's face was drawn with worry. 'I'm no fan of theirs,' she said, a hint of panic in her voice, 'but I don't want him to die! Not like Terence, not again!'

The clamour was growing down below as people stood up in their seats and shouted to each other. Bones was already scratching at the door of the box, trying to get out.

'The inspector said he's gonna protect him,' said Oliver. 'Perhaps we ought to just stay out of it.' He was gripping the arms of his seat tightly.

'Oliver, when have I ever stayed out of anything? Come on!' I got up and went to the door. 'It's Mr Hyde the murderer is after, not us. Let's go backstage and find out what's happening.'

'I agree,' said Eleni.

The three of us and the dog hurried to the lift, Eleni's wheelchair creaking through the corridors as we went. We had to wait for it to come all the way up before we could pile in.

'Can't this blasted thing go any faster?' I asked, trying to restrain myself from kicking the metal door.

'Welcome to my world,' said Eleni.

After what seemed like an age, the door opened and Oliver let us out. I pushed Eleni's chair as we headed backstage, dodging a few confused audience members and whispering staff as we went.

We came to a halt in the dressing-room corridor as we found our way blocked by the imposing figures of Inspector Holbrook and Constable Williams. They were standing beside Lady Athena's door.

'. . . keep the door locked and don't take your eyes off it,' Inspector Holbrook was saying. 'If the culprit is still in the building, we need to find him.'

'Understood,' said Williams, taking up his position.

'*See*,' I whispered to the others. 'Locking them in their dressing room *was* a good idea.'

'He's protecting them, though, not locking them in for sport,' Oliver shot back.

'It was to stop them in case they were the murderers!' I hissed.

Unfortunately, Inspector Holbrook had spotted us.

'You lot!' he boomed, marching over. Bones cowered behind Eleni's wheelchair. 'Go home and stay out of this!'

'I am home,' Eleni said. 'And they're my guests. If there's a crime taking place, we deserve to know what's happening.'

I nodded. 'You were impressed when I solved a mystery before, sir, so why not let us help you out now?'

The inspector raised an eyebrow. 'And I did you a

favour, then, did I not? Don't make me rethink my kindness to you. If you treat murder like a game, Miss Veil, you are sure to lose.'

I glared back at him. It was true that he had saved us from trouble by not telling the whole truth about how we caught the villain. But I had to persuade him that I was taking this seriously.

'This is my business,' I said, standing up as straight as I could. I pulled out one of my cards from my pocket and held it up to him. 'Veil Investigations. I have been hired to solve this case by Miss Li of Turner Square.'

He laughed. Of course he laughed. 'And I have been hired by Her Majesty the Queen. *Leave.*'

★ ★ ★

We found ourselves in the retiring room, and desperately in need of a plan.

'Whoever sent that message might well be still in the theatre,' I said as I paced the room. Bones was pacing too.

'Or they could have run for it,' Oliver pointed out. He was perching awkwardly on one of the chaises longues, looking a little out of it. He rubbed his eyes. 'There was no one to stop them leaving out through the front doors. The constables were only guarding the bit by the stage.'

I nodded. The police hadn't expected a threat from above.

Eleni picked at the stitching on her chair arms, which seemed to be a nervous habit. 'And, if it's someone who knows the place, they could have slipped down the ladders and out the back without anyone thinking anything of it.' She shuddered. 'I hate the thought of anyone who works here being the murderer, though.'

I knew what she meant. It had to be frightening and sickening to think someone that her family worked closely with might be involved.

'Well, I say we search the theatre – whatever bits of it the police will allow us to – and see what we can find.'

'We need Niko,' Eleni said, putting her head in her hands. 'Where is he?'

'Oliver, see if you can go and find him,' I said. 'Take Bones.' Bones's ears pricked up, but Oliver looked dejected.

'All right,' he said, getting up to open the door.

I bent down and ruffled Bones's soft fur on the top of his head. 'Bones, find Niko. You can do that, can't you? Find him for us!'

Bones barked in agreement and went trotting out of the door, nose to the ground, with Oliver reluctantly following close behind.

I turned back to Eleni. 'You said there were ladders going up to the top of the stage – can we get to them?'

'I think so,' she said. 'I can show you the way.'

If Pickles had gone up there to investigate too, he had most likely taken the stairs – so, if I climbed a ladder instead, perhaps I could avoid him. It wasn't something I often got the chance to do, given that Mother had always told me that ladies ought not to. But I had been climbing trees in the cemetery for years and years, much to Mother's horror, and I hadn't fallen to my death so far.

With Eleni directing, we went a roundabout way to the back of the theatre, avoiding the corridor where Constable Williams was guarding Lady Athena's dressing room. The backstage area was once again full of theatre workers all shouting to each other, gossiping, scratching their heads. This was quite the shock to everyone. Hopefully so much so that they would pay no attention to two girls that were about to do some investigating.

'Psst,' said Eleni as we moved through the crowd. I leaned down so I could hear her. 'Over there.'

To our right was a mess of scaffolding and ropes, and an enormous ladder. I peered upwards, but could see only darkness.

'There's a walkway at the top,' she said. 'I used to love climbing up there.'

'Did your mother faint at the sight?' I asked, still staring into the black void.

'No.' Eleni laughed. 'She just called me a little rat. It sounded sweeter in Greek.'

I steadied myself, and put a foot on the bottom rung. It was a long way to the top.

'You can do it,' Eleni said, and I felt myself fill with confidence. Of course I could! People went up and down this thing all the time. It would be no trouble.

I started climbing, feeling the wood underneath my fingertips, worn smooth by years of use. I could still hear the nervous chatter from behind me, and hoped that no one was about to shout at me to come back down. I had to move as swiftly as I could.

It went up and up. At one point, my foot slipped, and I grabbed on tighter, feeling my breath catch in my chest.

What if the villain is still up there . . .? a small part of me whispered, but I ignored it. This wasn't the time to have doubts.

The ladder soon emerged on to a wooden walkway, with bars all around it. Cautiously, I peered up on to the platform – there was just enough light to see by, spilling in from the auditorium, and there didn't seem to be anyone there. It looked precarious to say the least. *A lot happens up here above the stage*, I reminded myself. *It must be well built.*

Without wanting to dwell on that thought too much, I pulled myself up and took a few steps along the walkway. From that dizzying height, I could see the stage below: Lady Athena's empty chairs, her askew crystal-ball stand, her mysterious cabinet. It looked as though the thing had a false back on it – more trickery!

But I had to stick to the matter at hand. Whoever had dropped that threatening note had been up here, and I needed to see if there were any hints as to who that might have been. They had to be someone relatively young and fit to make the climb, and to get back down so quickly.

I took tentative steps along, holding on to the bars. There was nothing on the walkway that I could see. I began to feel foolish – what was I expecting? A sign proclaiming: 'I, the dastardly villain, was here'?

I turned to look at the stage again. Assuming the letter fell more or less straight down, the culprit had probably dropped it from the centre to get it close to where Lady Athena was standing.

And that was when I spotted it.

Just below the platform, there was a torn bit of paper sitting on a beam.

It could have been nothing. But, now that I'd seen it, there was no chance of me leaving without finding out.

I got down on to my knees and stretched towards the scrap of paper – and, of course, the blasted thing was just out of reach!

Trying very hard not to think about how far it was to the stage below, I gripped the metal bar and stretched my arm out until it hurt, my fingertips wiggling towards the tiny piece of paper. At last, I was just able to pinch the corner.

'Yes!' I whispered triumphantly. I snatched it back and slumped in the middle of the walkway with relief.

It appeared to be a torn business card. It read:

A.J. CARROTT AND CO
--TAILORS--

24 Cavill Street
Havisham

Purveyors of the finest gentlemen's suits
Satisfaction guaranteed

FOR CRISP AND FRESH SUITS
CHOOSE A CARROTT

For a few moments, I just stared at it. *Well, this is a puzzle,* I thought to myself. *How does this piece fit?*

There was, of course, the possibility that this business card had been up there for years – but it looked relatively new, if a little crumpled and torn from presumably being kept in a pocket. Or it could be that it had been dropped by one of the many theatre workers who climbed up to that walkway each day – but I had seen plenty of those men backstage, and they wore long-sleeved shirts and overalls splattered with paint or oil or sawdust. Would one of them really have a business card for 'the finest gentlemen's suits' about their person?

I gently put the card into my own pocket and went back to the ladder. I had to show this to Eleni.

The climb down was somehow easier and harder at the same time. I was descending backwards, and I kept thinking I would miss a rung and slip off.

The commotion from below got louder again, and I heard Eleni call to me.

'Violet! Did you find anything?'

I reached the bottom of the ladder, hopped off and spun round. I felt my muscles relax in relief. 'Just this,' I said, pulling out the tailor's card and handing it to her.

'Hmm,' she said, her dark brows knitting as she looked

down at it. 'Carrott's is where Baba takes Niko when—Oh!'

She had been interrupted by Bones barrelling through the crowd and nearly crashing into us. I looked for Oliver, and saw him weaving his way between people, muttering apologies. He stopped beside us, a little out of breath, and leaned on the ladder for support.

'Violet,' he said, gasping, 'we really . . . need to talk.'

CHAPTER TWENTY-SIX

'What is it?' I asked Oliver. 'What's wrong?'
He looked dreadfully uncomfortable.
'Can we go outside? Just us?'

'Whatever's the matter that you can't tell me here?' I asked. But then I supposed we were surrounded by theatre workers. Perhaps Oliver had something that needed to remain secret.

'Please?' he begged. 'Quickly?'

I looked down at Eleni, who merely shrugged, looking puzzled. 'I shall wait here, then,' she said.

'Will you be all right?' I asked her, gently putting my hand on her shoulder.

She patted it, and her fingers felt cool against mine. 'I shall be fine. I'll see if someone can find Mama or Baba for me.'

I nodded and, with a sigh, I took hold of Bones's collar and followed Oliver back through the bustling backstage area. We went along the corridors and exited through the stage door – which, to my surprise, was not being guarded by anyone. I wondered if Barrett had been there until everyone was called inside. If not, the culprit could well have escaped that way.

I let go of Bones and he trotted across the cobbled alley, cocking his leg against the wall. *Yuck*. At least we were outside. The sky was dark, and a nearby gas lamp was flickering, sending shadows up the sides of the building. There were pigeons pecking in the gutter and roosting high on the ledges, softly cooing.

I turned to Oliver. 'Well? Out with it, then,' I said. I was aware I was being rather brusque, but I was keen to tell him about the clue I had found.

'Um,' he said, fiddling with his hat. 'Violet, it's Niko.'

'What about him?' I asked with a frown.

He took a deep breath. He was clearly reluctant to divulge this information. 'I went looking for him, an'

Bones took me down to the basement. I thought he was just after a rat or something, an' then he started sniffing at this door with a window that was all . . .' He stopped and made a wiggling movement with his hand.

'Blurry? Frosted?'

'I could see just outlines. Someone Niko's size, an' a bigger man, I think. They were arguing. I think it was a boiler room or something – it was hot an' it smelled like coal and dirt.' He wrinkled his nose. 'I leaned against the wall to listen. Niko was near the door so I could hear him better.'

Oliver was really beating around the bush now. 'Well? What did he say?'

My mind was racing. I shivered, rubbing my arms as the hair on them stood up.

'You're not gonna like it,' Oliver said.

'I shall be the judge of that.'

Oliver fidgeted for a few moments more and then finally explained. 'Niko said, "It wasn't supposed to be this way – this wasn't what we agreed." An' the man said something about taking the reins, or . . . changing the game, maybe. It was hard to tell. An' Niko told the bloke to stop.'

There was a pause while Oliver looked at me expectantly. Bones was staring up at me too, as if I were a ticking time bomb. I didn't say anything. I was trying to process what I was hearing.

Oliver continued. 'Then he got pushed against the door, I think. There was a loud thud, an' I thought Bones was about to bark an' they were gonna catch me. I just grabbed Bones an' ducked into the next room. My head started pounding, an' my chest got all tight, an' I think I sort of blacked out for a moment. I heard footsteps storming away, but when I got up an' looked out the door they were gone.'

'Oh . . . oh no . . .' I managed to stutter. His words had sent a shock through me. 'This is bad. Very bad. Niko could be in trouble.'

'Violet,' Oliver said, his face tight with sincerity, 'I think Niko *is* trouble. If that was the murderer, they've been working together.'

I felt my face flush red. 'He wouldn't,' I said.

Bones curled round my legs protectively, the way that he often did when I was under stress.

'You don't know him,' Oliver insisted.

'We're—'

'Friends, I know!' he snapped. 'I know you think that. But this proves that—'

'It doesn't prove anything!' I said. Bones whined. 'You just heard an argument. We don't even know who Niko was talking to. They could have merely been discussing . . . *horse racing* for all we know. But if this man pushed him . . .'

'You don't hide in the basement to argue about horse racing!' Oliver shot back.

I ignored him. 'We'll find Niko,' I said. 'We'll make sure that he's all right, and he can tell us what really happened.'

'No, Violet, we need to leave,' Oliver said, taking my arm firmly. 'I don't trust any of this lot. I'm just trying to protect you.'

I shook him off. 'How dare you? I don't need *protecting*.'

'There's a killer on the loose an' they've been helping him!' He gestured angrily. 'Probably laughing all the way to the bank too when Lady Athena's shows sell out.' He folded his arms again, wedging his hands under his armpits against the cold. 'I'm telling you, we need to go.'

'That doesn't make any sense,' I said. 'They wouldn't kill their friend. This is a misunderstanding, mark my words. It's some rogue agent and they might have attacked Niko! I'm not running away from this. I'm not afraid. But I'm beginning to think you are.'

'Of course *I'm afraid*, Violet!' he shouted, and it was the loudest I've ever heard him speak.

A few pigeons took flight and Bones jumped and circled

behind me, growling. I was surprised that he would growl at Oliver, but here we were.

'The inspector's right: you think this is a game. You think you can just stop playing whenever you want an' you won't get hurt. I messed with a murderer once an' I woke up *in a coffin*!'

'I'm not likely to forget that, am I?' I huffed.

He rubbed the scar on the back of his head. 'Sometimes I think you have.'

'What's that supposed to mean?'

He shrugged, not wanting to meet my eye. 'All the time, you run on ahead an' leave me behind. In everything. You don't ask how I'm feeling. If I'm all right.'

I felt my anger simmer down a little as shame crept in. I supposed I hadn't considered Oliver very often. I was rather caught up in the mystery and adventure. I breathed out. 'Are you . . . all right?'

There was a pause, heavy with the weight of the question. 'No, I ain't, not really,' he said. 'Haven't felt right since . . . well, you know.'

Being hit over the head with a hammer by a vile villain, I supposed.

'I get dizzy an' out of breath. My head hurts a lot of the time. Sometimes my eyes go blurry.' He waved his hand in front of his eyes. 'It's hard to keep up.'

'I'm . . . I'm sorry,' I said. Bones slunk out from behind me, obviously sensing the change in mood. 'I didn't mean to. You're my friend, Oliver. You know you're dear to me.'

'Do I?' he replied, and though his anger was quieter now I could tell it was still there. 'Because you won't listen to me. But you listen to anything that lot say,' he said, waving his hand at the theatre. 'You've only just met them!'

Suddenly it seemed we were arguing again. 'It wasn't long ago that I'd only just met you,' I pointed out, 'and you were shuffling about the cemetery like Frankenstein's monster. Aren't you glad that I trusted you then?'

'You should trust me *now*,' he said. 'Else I'm worried you'll end up in a coffin too.'

'I do trust you,' I insisted as Bones tried to nuzzle Oliver's leg. 'I just think that you're wrong about them. And I think we need to stay here and get to the bottom of this before it's too late. Even if Mr Hyde is kept safe, the murderer might decide to change target.'

'That's exactly why we need to go home!' He gently pushed Bones away. The dog whined and trotted behind me again. 'Violet, I didn't want to do this, but . . . if you're not going, then I am.'

'Fine!' I snapped as he turned and started walking away down the dark alley, his footsteps on the cobbles echoing up the walls. 'Have it your way! I don't care. I shall solve this all by myself!'

He stopped and turned back to face me. 'That's just it. It's *Veil Investigations*, isn't it?' The unspoken implication hung in the air: *you only care about yourself.* 'Why am I even here? I ain't needed.'

I folded my arms. 'Leave then.'

His face was stony. 'We'll see what your ma and pa think about this, shall we?'

'You wouldn't,' I said, feeling all my muscles tense.

Was he really threatening to tell them? If my parents were to come running down here, that would mean definite and immediate trouble. I would probably be sent straight home to bed.

'I don't know, Violet,' Oliver said quietly. 'Would I?'

And then he was walking away again, and his footsteps faded into the sounds of the city at night.

I clenched my fists, frozen to the spot as I stared after him at the empty gap at the end of the alley. I wanted to march back into the theatre, grab the nearest person to interrogate and crack the case in the next five minutes with my head held high.

Instead, I sank down on to the cobbles and started to cry.

CHAPTER TWENTY-SEVEN

Bones curled round me, his big eyes staring into mine as the tears flowed. I embraced him and leaned my head on his back. He whined sadly.

'I'm a fool,' I said, and I didn't just mean because I was sitting on cobblestones that were undoubtedly dirty and certainly uncomfortable. I wiped the tears from my cheeks. 'What am I going to do now?'

Could I really do this without Oliver? I wasn't sure I was as confident about that as I had sounded. And now I didn't have a choice – I was without him, not to mention the fact that he might be about to bring the wrath of my parents down on me.

I was still angry, could still feel the tension in my body and the burning feeling in my veins. But I also felt a crushing sadness. I hadn't ever quarrelled with a friend before. In fact, I hadn't ever really *had* a friend before. I supposed I had playfellows when I was younger, and there were some girls from my street that I knew. But I had always been aware that they thought I was rather strange, and their mothers often weren't keen on them socialising with me. Father's business put them off, as if death might be catching. Was it any wonder I spent more of my time talking to ghosts?

Oliver was really the first person to have seen me for who I truly was. Now I wondered if I'd just thrown that all away. I thought that I had seen him, too, but perhaps I had not. I hadn't seen how unwell he was feeling, or his frustration at me leaving him out.

I took a shaky breath of cool air, concentrated on the warmth of Bones and the feeling of his soft fur under my fingertips. Slowly, my heart and lungs became calm again. I had to think clearly.

I still thought that Oliver was wrong. I believed Niko was innocent. So how could I resolve this?

By finding Niko.

Of course! I jumped up, sending Bones sprawling. He barked at me.

'Sorry, boy,' I said, brushing off both dirt and painful feelings. 'But I've got it. We need to find Niko. He could be in danger, and if we can find him we can make sure he's safe. Then we can prove him innocent, and Oliver will see that I was right!'

Bones peered at me, head askew.

'Don't look at me like that,' I said. 'Come on.' I stepped back towards the doorway. 'We have a rescue operation to carry out!'

★ ★ ★

My first task was to find Eleni. Thankfully, she was still in the backstage area, talking to her mother. The crowds had thinned out – it looked as though Mr Anastos had started sending the other theatre workers home.

Mrs Anastos was sitting on a bench beside Eleni's wheelchair, rubbing her temples in an exasperated fashion.

'This is too much,' I heard her say as I approached, before muttering something in Greek.

'Mr Hyde will be fine, Mama,' said Eleni. 'He's big enough and ugly enough to look after himself, I'm sure.'

Mrs Anastos frowned at her. 'Don't be rude, Eleni,' she said, but her daughter simply shrugged.

'Um, Mrs Anastos, Eleni?' I twiddled my thumbs. 'I need to tell you something. It's about Niko.'

'What is it?' asked Mrs Anastos, a hint of panic suddenly appearing on her face.

'Oliver heard him having an argument with someone in the basement. Whoever it was pushed Niko against the door, but then Oliver had a funny turn and he didn't see what happened. When he came to, they were both gone.'

'What?' Eleni exclaimed. 'Who was he arguing with?'

'A man, Oliver said,' I told them. 'I don't know what it was about, but it sounded serious.'

Mrs Anastos covered her mouth with a gloved hand. I thought she must be in shock. For a moment, she just stared across the room at the backstage ladders. Then she spoke again. 'He could be hurt,' she whispered.

'I'm sure he's all right, Mama,' said Eleni, putting her hand on her mother's knee. 'You know Niko. He'll be off reading a book and wondering what all the fuss is about. We'll find him. Violet, can you take me to look?'

I nodded and went to grasp the handles of her wheelchair. 'Don't worry, Mrs Anastos, we shall be back soon.'

She stood up, her elegant yellow dress somehow without a wrinkle. 'I will search too,' she said, and bustled away.

I looked down at Eleni. 'Bones has a good nose for people. He can help us.'

Bones seemed keen to look for Niko. He took us back out to the corridors and round to the entrance of the theatre, nose pressed firmly to the red carpet. And then he started pawing at the doors to the auditorium.

'In there?' Eleni asked.

I wondered what Bones was up to. 'Are you sure about that, boy?' I asked him. He simply whimpered and continued to push his paw under the door.

'All right,' I said reluctantly. 'Can we go in?' I asked Eleni.

She shrugged. 'I don't see why not.'

I opened the double doors and secured them on their hooks, and Bones didn't hesitate to go racing down the aisle. I went back and pushed Eleni's chair inside.

I soon spotted what Bones was after.

Niko was, bizarrely, sitting in the middle of the stage. He was surrounded by Lady Athena's set pieces – the spirit cabinet, the table and crystal ball (presumably retrieved from the tuba).

'Niko?' Eleni called to him. 'What are you doing up there?'

He certainly appeared to be a little out of sorts. When he looked up at us, it was apparent he had been crying. He blinked tears from his deep brown eyes, and I noticed his face looked a little bruised under his dark curls.

'Oh,' he said. 'Hello. I was just thinking.' He waved his hand at the empty auditorium. 'You know. Wondering what to do about this whole mess. Baba might have to refund everyone.' He made no attempt to get up.

Bones circled back to me, tail wagging as if to say, *There, I found him.*

Eleni gaped at her brother. 'But Niko,' she said again, 'where have you *been*?'

He stared back for a moment. 'Why?'

I felt deeply uncomfortable, but I knew I had to say it. 'Oliver said he overheard you getting into a fight in the basement.'

'Oh,' Niko said, 'that was . . . that was nothing.' His words were slurring a little, and one of his curls fell back over his eyes.

His sister frowned. '*Nothing?* Honestly, I despair. What trouble have you got yourself into, big brother?'

Niko opened his mouth to speak, but she held up her hand.

'If you say one word that isn't the truth, I'm getting Violet to take me straight to Baba, and you can answer to him.'

Bones suddenly barked and strained towards the stage, but I grabbed his collar and held him back.

'All right!' Niko said. 'All right. Don't, please.' He rubbed his forehead with his fingers, exasperated. 'I've done something . . . rather silly, I'm afraid.' He exhaled sharply. 'I was just trying to help. I . . . it was . . . it was me.'

'*What* was you?' Eleni asked, but I already felt a dreadful knot in the pit of my stomach. One that had begun to form when Oliver told me what he'd heard in the basement.

'I was the one carrying out the prophecies,' he said with considerable reluctance. 'The cat, the letter, the wreath of lilies . . . I wrote the messages and then I did what I had to do.'

'You made the messages appear in Lady Athena's mirror?' I asked. 'And you fooled all those people?' I felt disgusted.

'An old trick with rubbing alcohol and steam.' He shrugged. 'I never wanted to fool people. It was . . . just to help the theatre. Our family.'

The knot grew larger. I thought I might be sick. Niko was confessing. Had I just made a terrible mistake, and lost my only friend, defending this boy?

I thought back to the tailor's card that I had found

above the stage. That was our only clue – and here Niko was in his smart suit. Eleni had told me that her father took Niko to Carrott's tailors, and I hadn't listened. I was such a fool.

But there was something else worrying Eleni. Her face was ashen as she stared up at her brother. 'Not Terence,' she said quietly.

'No!' Suddenly Niko appeared sharper. 'I would never . . . I had nothing to do with that. I wanted to stop. I said I didn't want to bribe people to lose a horse race. I didn't want to hurt anyone, least of all Terence.'

'Well then, who did it?' I snapped. I was losing my patience. *How dare he? How dare this boy fool me with his charm and his friendship?* 'Who's the murderer?'

Bones was growling beside me, his legs quivering. The deafening rumble seemed to grow until it filled the whole auditorium, and I realised it was the rolling thunder from the performance. I clapped my hands over my ears, and Bones whined . . .

And then the lights went out.

CHAPTER TWENTY-EIGHT

leni screamed. The thunder had gone silent, and my eyes began to adjust to the darkness. I realised that there was no outline of a person on the stage. Niko had gone.

'Niko?' I called out. 'Are you there?' But there was no response, my voice just echoing round the empty theatre.

Even Bones seemed confused. He sniffed the air in different directions, his tail pointing straight up.

I heard Eleni muttering something, alongside her heavy breathing. I thought she was trying to calm herself down.

'Eleni?' I whispered, although I was unsure why I was whispering. But the darkness had this oppressive air, like night-time in a cathedral. 'What happened?'

I heard her take a deep breath. 'A distraction,' she said shakily, keeping her voice low like mine. 'I think someone took Niko.'

'Don't worry,' I said quickly. 'We'll find him. Do you think he went offstage?' I peered into the wings, but I could barely see anything. 'Bones, can you find Niko?'

Bones quickly trotted over to the stage and up the steps at the side, running to where Niko had been sitting just a few moments ago. In the darkness, the dog was just a shadow, a hint of movement. I could hear his claws as he padded around on the spot.

'There's a trapdoor in the stage,' Eleni said. 'It goes down to a room in the basement. He could be in there.'

'I think our villain wanted to silence Niko before he could tell us their name,' I whispered back.

Eleni nodded. 'The lights on the gas table must have been cut. That's what we use to control the lighting for the performances. And the thunder . . . well, it could be the thunder run.' She pointed upwards. 'Up in the eaves there's a wooden trough. You can drop heavy balls in to it to make the sound. And we also have a metal thunder sheet backstage.'

'Is the gas table backstage too?' I asked.

She nodded. 'Do you think you can take a look?' she asked, and I could hear the fear in her voice. 'If all the gas has been turned off, you might be able to turn it back on. It's a big red lever.'

'If I can see it, I will,' I said. 'But I don't want to leave you here on your own. What if the person who did this is still around?'

'They're more likely to be up there, aren't they?' she whispered.

I supposed she had a point. But, if this villain had already got Niko, I didn't want them to get hold of Eleni too.

'Bones!' I called, trying to keep my voice low. 'Can you come here? Stay with Eleni?' I heard him clatter back down the wooden steps, and soon he was by my side. 'Stay,' I ordered again. 'Good boy. Right, I shall go.' I was talking to myself in the manner that one does when one is filled with creeping terror.

I tiptoed towards the stage, feeling my way along the seats. I climbed the steps that Bones had just descended, and I knew the wings of the stage were just to my left. I reached out and touched soft fabric – a black curtain. I pushed my way through it, and patted my way along the rough wooden walls. My eyes were adjusting by now, and as I turned a corner I thought I could make out the large gas table – not really a table at all, but a wall of things that looked like taps and levers and wheels.

I paused, searching for movement, but saw none. I reached out with my senses, but the room was eerily quiet. No people, no ghosts. The silence really brought home the fact that I was without Bones – and without Oliver.

I stepped forward, fumbling my way over to the gas table. Closest to me was a huge metal lever, pointing towards the ground – and even in the darkness I could just about make out the flaking red paint. A white sign above it had the word **MAIN** picked out in black.

'Well, it's worth a try,' I mumbled. I wrapped my hands round it and pulled as hard as I could. A blue pilot flame spluttered to life in a tiny lamp on the wall nearby – and then bloomed into a warm orange light. Hopefully that meant the lights were back on in the auditorium too. I had done it, and survived unscathed.

I hurried back out, blinking as my eyes got used to being able to see again. There was already light spilling through the cracks in the black curtains that led to the wings. It must have worked!

I emerged to find Eleni where I'd left her, stroking Bones.

'I did it!' I called out. 'But there's no sign of Niko,' I

added as I descended the steps. 'I think perhaps your trapdoor theory was correct.'

'Can we go to the basement and look for him?' she asked as Bones came over to greet me. Her eyes were wide, her knuckles tight as she gripped the arms of her chair.

'Of course,' I said. 'I wouldn't be much of a detective if we didn't.'

* * *

Eleni, Bones and I took the lift down to the basement. I kept starting to say something to Oliver, and remembering that he wasn't there. It felt like there were a hole in the world where he ought to be.

I shook the idea of him from my mind. At least Oliver was safe at home. Niko was the one in trouble, and I ought to focus on him.

'Remember that we're looking for Niko, boy,' I said to Bones. 'Can you find him?'

Bones wobbled out of the lift and on to the flagstone floor of the basement. He pressed his nose to the ground and trotted away.

The temperature dropped as we followed him, the air dusty and chill. The area we had emerged into was vast, and I couldn't help but gasp as I stepped out under the arched ceiling into the dim flickering light. The smell of the gas lamps underground was even more oppressive, but there were fewer of them. This place was clearly not for the general public.

'This is where we store the props and sets,' Eleni said quietly.

It was like a graveyard of sorts, the memorials of performances gone by, that the modern addition of the lift awkwardly nestled into like a tomb. There were tall set pieces: a doorway that looked as if it belonged in a church, a castle wall, a wooden balcony the likes of which a Juliet might stand on to call to her Romeo. There were racks of painted scenery, and dining chairs, baskets, tables and rugs were piled high. Shelving lined the walls, packed with wine glasses and magic lamps and telephones and just about anything else you could think of.

It appeared a chaotic mess, but one that the people who worked in the Grecian would have understood well. There must have been a method to their madness, if they were ever to find anything they needed in this huge space. It would be a perfect hiding place.

But Bones was heading off to the right, where I could make out a large archway that led to another room.

'Let's follow,' Eleni said, and I turned her chair to pursue him. It creaked as it bumped over the flagstones.

We passed several suits of armour and a rack of swords and shields. A tall wardrobe leaned against the wall, and I almost jumped when I saw a skeleton dangling on a post behind it – real or not, even I couldn't tell without a closer look. Beside it were shelves of animal bones and a garish display of pretend body parts.

Crates of what looked like food and wine teetered over us, threatening to topple. I was surprised Bones wasn't trying to sniff them. Perhaps he was merely concentrating on his task, or perhaps the food wasn't real. It was hard to tell. This was a place where illusions came to life.

Passing under the archway, we found ourselves facing the stairs down to this level that we had avoided by taking the lift. A lady in an apron and cloth cap hurried down them and past us, only pausing quickly to curtsey and say, 'Evening, Miss Anastos,' to Eleni before darting into another room. The walls were covered in red and black pipes, some of them glistening. One gave out a steady *drip, drip, drip* . . .

'The kitchens are down here,' said Eleni. 'And the laundry room, the boiler room, the props department . . .' She trailed off and then suddenly sat upright and pointed. 'Oh, and that's where the trapdoor comes down.'

Bones was sniffing round the area she was referring to,

which had a wooden platform below it. It was surrounded by piles of boxes and crates.

The platform had some sort of winch beside it that must pull it up and down, and a big lever that presumably operated the trapdoor. It looked rather like a coffin lift – something that we used in the cemetery to move coffins into the catacombs below.

Bones seemed puzzled. Had his trail gone cold? He came back over to me and Eleni, his ears flattened.

'Drat,' I said. 'I think we're too late. Bones has lost the scent.'

I perched on the platform, suddenly feeling deflated. Bones pushed his way under my hand, and I rubbed his head gratefully. He had done his best.

Eleni let out a sigh of exasperation. 'I'm sorry,' she said, putting her head in her hands. A few moments later, she lifted it again, and her eyes were glistening. 'I feel useless sometimes. It's frustrating when I can't keep up with everyone else.'

'None of this is your fault,' I reminded her. 'The villain is the one to blame here.'

She looked over at me. 'When Niko said he did it to help our family . . . I think it's because of me.'

'What do you mean?'

'Well, when busybodies ask me what's the matter with

me, I don't fancy telling them a thing. But I shall tell you.' She closed her eyes for a second, as if summoning the strength. 'I had a disease when I was very young. I was completely paralysed at first, but things improved a little. Now I can walk, but it's painful and I get worn out so easily.'

I stayed quiet, listening. Whenever she paused, I could only hear our breathing, the dripping of the pipe and a distant clattering from the kitchen.

'The theatre was doing well – not the best because Baba always spends too much on the repairs. But I needed medicines, and when I was too big to be carried he had this chair made for me. And then he wanted to put in a lift, and that was . . .' Eleni winced.

'Expensive?'

She nodded. 'Whatever I thought of Lady Athena's reputation, it was bringing in the money. And it seems that's what Niko was trying to do, to make Lady Athena even more popular. Someone persuaded him to do this.' She stared up at the trapdoor. 'I hope I haven't just lost my brother,' she whispered.

I felt a rush of anger and my fingertips curled closed. I stood up. 'I won't let that happen. We will find him, Eleni – I promise.'

She looked at me now, and our eyes met. 'What are your promises worth, Violet Veil?'

'My life,' I replied, and I reached down and linked my finger with hers. If I couldn't keep this promise, then what was my life worth?

CHAPTER TWENTY-NINE

We hurried back up to the ground floor as quickly as we could. In the foyer, Mrs Anastos was talking to a policeman.

I winced when I saw them. I wasn't sure that the police ought to be involved with Niko's disappearance, but it was too late now.

'. . . and when did you last see your son?' I heard him ask, his pencil poised. He wasn't a constable I recognised – he had ginger stubble and bags under his eyes. Inspector

Holbrook was standing nearby, talking to the boy in the ticket booth.

'We saw him,' Eleni called out as I pushed her chair nearer, Bones skittering along beside us. 'He was on the stage, Mama,' she said tearfully, 'and someone turned off the gas so all the lights went out, and he disappeared.'

'Is that what happened to the lights?' Mrs Anastos asked. She shook her dark curls in disbelief. Her face was drawn with worry. 'Wait, what do you mean by *disappeared*?'

'We think someone dropped him through the trapdoor,' I explained, 'but when we went to look in the basement there was no sign of him.'

She rubbed her eyes and muttered something in Greek. Then she added, 'What has that boy got himself into?'

The policeman frowned and tapped his pencil against his helmet. 'Can you show me where this trapdoor goes?'

'Yes, yes,' said Mrs Anastos. 'Eleni, come with us. Tell us more about what you saw on the way.'

I moved aside, and Mrs Anastos took the handles of her daughter's wheelchair in her gloved hands. 'Thank you,' she said, although I could tell her mind was elsewhere.

'I'll keep trying,' I told Eleni, who nodded back at me. 'Don't give up on him,' she said to me as her mother took her away, footsteps and creaking wheels echoing in the empty entrance hall as the police constable followed them. I wasn't sure if further inspection of the basement was likely to yield any answers. But, then again, I had no answers whatsoever. It was time for something drastic.

Something drastic like approaching Inspector Holbrook.

I had reservations concerning what I was about to do. If this went wrong, Niko could end up in the same position as my father – faced with a false accusation of murder. But, if I didn't say anything, there might be no hope for him. I had to get this right.

I bent down and stroked Bones, tickling him behind the ears. He looked up at me with his solemn eyes. 'Stay here, boy,' I whispered. I had a feeling that Bones taking a bite out of the inspector's trousers wouldn't help my case.

Steeling myself, I went over to the ticket desk.

'Inspector?'

He turned to look down at me. 'Miss Veil,' he replied in an almost bored tone. 'As you can see, I am rather busy questioning this clerk.'

'Oh no,' said the boy behind the desk, his face flushed with panic. 'Do carry on. I'll just be over here.' He backed away and then spun round to start shuffling through sheaves of tickets. Inspector Holbrook had a certain effect on people, one that I was trying very hard not to experience.

I stood tall, put my shoulders back. I wouldn't let his withering gaze deter me.

'Please, sir, this is important.' A little courtesy went a long way. 'It's about Niko. He confessed something to us, before he disappeared.'

'Oh, did he now?' He raised an eyebrow.

'He told us that he knows who the culprit is, the person behind the murder and the death threat. Whoever this person is, they're responsible for Lady Athena's prophecies coming true. And they pulled in Niko to help because his family need more money, and making Lady Athena a success benefits the theatre.'

Inspector Holbrook scratched his beard. 'You're sure? Are you certain that isn't just an elaborate pretence? That this Niko boy hasn't just hoodwinked you?'

I tried not to flinch at his deft incision into the heart of my anxieties, but instead took a moment to think about it.

'Well, Oliver overheard Niko having an argument with someone in the basement, and he was saying that things had gone too far and he didn't want to be involved any more. So, yes, I think he was telling the truth. Some greater villain is pulling the strings here.'

'And who might that person be?' the inspector asked. His tone of voice suggested he was only humouring me. But I had no choice – it was be humoured or be ignored.

'That's the puzzle,' I said. 'But I believe the Anastos family to be innocent.'

He paused for a moment, and then spoke again. 'Wolves don't get into Grandmother's house by accident, Miss Veil. You have to invite them in.'

'What is that supposed to mean?' I asked, which wasn't good manners at all, but it still elicited a response.

'It means, whatever their intentions, they probably invited the trouble.'

I frowned back at him. 'That's not fair.'

My father had taught me that victims shouldn't be blamed for what happened to them. But then, if Niko were really in on the plot, well . . . that was a different matter.

The inspector pulled out his pocket watch, looked at it and sighed wearily. 'I need to keep working, not playing your nursemaid. I know you are friendly with these people, Miss Veil, but you need to remember that things are not always what they seem.'

'I'm not a baby!' I responded, folding my arms with indignation. 'I thought I had earned your respect!'

He tucked the pocket watch back into his jacket. 'You

have. At least enough that I am giving you one minute of my time. Your information may be helpful. But I need to keep working on this, lest we end up with another body on our hands. You need to go home to bed.'

'I can help,' I insisted. 'Let me join your investigation. We'll find the murderer.'

The inspector laughed in my face. 'You're still a child. A clever and precocious one, perhaps, but it takes experience to catch a criminal. I've learned that over the past thirty years.'

He tapped his head. 'You want a piece of wisdom? When you're young, you take things at face value. You go in wide-eyed and innocent. Don't fall into that trap. Question everything, Miss Veil. Question even the victims. Question *yourself*. Think about that while you stay out of my way.'

★ ★ ★

Night had well and truly fallen across the city, a thick cloak of darkness and smog. I stared out at it as I sat on the front steps of the Grecian Theatre, watching carriages rattle past over on the road and moths fluttering around the streetlamps.

I ought to be helping to look for Niko. I ought to be investigating. I ought to be doing *something*. Instead, I was wallowing in misery, with my greyhound whining on my lap.

'I know,' I said to Bones. 'We've really made a mess of things, haven't we?'

He stopped whining and looked up at me with what I felt was a sceptical expression.

'Fine, *I* have made a mess of things,' I said.

I sighed deeply and buried my face in his fur. Bones was so warm and comforting, and I could feel his little heart pounding away. The smell of dog was only a minor inconvenience.

Oliver was gone, quite possibly to get me into trouble with my parents. Niko was gone, quite possibly at risk of being murdered, and I had no idea where he could be. Even Bones's trusty nose hadn't worked this time. And now the church clock was chiming nine bells, and I was losing all hope.

Don't give up on him, Eleni had said.

I was tired, the cold was pricking at me like icy needles, and I was out of answers.

'I think we need to go home, boy,' I whispered to Bones. I had to trust that the Anastos family and the policemen would keep looking for Niko.

Bones stood up, his slim tail wagging. I think he liked the idea. After all, home was where his food bowl was.

I turned and looked back at the vast theatre with its grand columns and loud posters. Was the villain still inside? Where had he taken Niko? Mr Hyde and Lady Athena were under guard, and I felt sure the entrances and exits would soon be too. The clock was ticking, but perhaps there was nothing more for me to do. I didn't know the theatre well enough to search every crevice of it, and if the culprit was out in the city then it was probably too late already. Not to mention that I thought Inspector Holbrook was likely to throw me out if I didn't leave of my own volition.

Bones nudged me and then began to trot in the direction of home. He had made up his mind.

I scrambled up and followed him, the glittering lights of the theatre watching my back as I retreated.

A few streets away, I passed a pub, the Hook and Anchor. The smell of ale and sawdust hit my nose, and I could hear rowdy shouting from within. I quickened my pace.

As we turned the corner, Bones began to growl. I saw a businessman in a ruffled suit leaning against the wall, his tie undone and a bottle in his hand. His hat was tipped low and the stench of smoke clung to him.

'Hello, little girl,' he said, stepping on to the pavement. 'Out all alone?'

My blood ran cold. 'Stay back or my dog will bite!' I shouted. Bones leaped ahead of me, barking viciously. The man backed away, his hands held up in defence. Bones kept barking, and I ran.

I kept running. I didn't want to stop or look behind me.

Bones caught up, racing just ahead of me. We didn't stop until we were outside the front door of the shop. I put my hands on my knees, panting. I was shaking with fear and cold.

Suddenly the door swung open and I jumped: putting my hands up, ready to defend myself.

'Miss Violet?'

'Ernesto!' I gasped. 'I thought you'd gone home!'

For once, Bones didn't jump up at him. Instead, he trotted into the shop as if he were happy to be home – probably looking for his dinner bowl. I, on the other hand, stood shaking under the gas lamp.

'I was working late in the funeral parlour,' he explained. '*¿Qué pasa?*' he added gently, and I knew that meant he was asking me what was going on. 'What are you doing out here?'

I tried to slow my breathing and piece myself back together, but the panic was still flowing through my veins. 'Please don't tell anyone,' I begged.

'Come inside,' he said, and he led me through the front door and seated me at the desk, before peering out the back – to check if the coast was clear, I supposed. Then he came and knelt down next to me. 'Did something happen? I think your father told you to stay home, no?'

'I was investigating,' I said quietly, pulling out my handkerchief and dabbing the corners of my eyes. 'I know I shouldn't have been. I'm sorry.' I shivered. 'Oliver came home and I had to get back by myself. I was so scared.'

'Oh, Miss Violet,' Ernesto said. 'It is not always good to be afraid. But sometimes fear keeps you safe. Promise me you will not do this again?'

'I promise.' I gulped. And I meant it.

'Then I won't tell them,' he said, tapping the side of his nose. 'But, next time I work late, I will make sure you are not sneaking out.'

CHAPTER THIRTY

That night, I felt grateful for my cosy quilt, for the embers sizzling in the fireplace, and the warming pan that Maddy had tucked into my bed earlier in the evening. I felt grateful for Bones, who was curled up at my feet and daintily snoring. Most of all, I felt grateful to be alive.

My body was exhausted, but my mind was racing. I hated being away from the action. Niko was still missing, a murderer was at large and Mr Hyde's life under threat. And, just to make all of that worse, I'd hurt Oliver and didn't know if he would ever want to speak to me again.

Inspector Holbrook's words were spinning in my head like a merry-go-round. *Question everything, Miss Veil. Question even the victims. Question* yourself.

I asked questions, didn't I? Wasn't that the job of a detective?

Well, I had questioned suspects and the people involved. I had questioned the victims. Had I questioned myself? Perhaps not. I tended to believe I was always right. Most of the time, I was. On this occasion – well, my convictions had not led to a brilliant outcome so far.

Question even the victims.

That phrase was sticking with me. Perhaps Inspector Holbrook didn't just mean asking questions. Perhaps he meant questioning what I believed to be true, questioning whether what I'd been told was real.

Perhaps I had to go back to the start.

Back to Miss Li and her necklace.

That was where this had all begun. She had come to me to ask about the amulet, and how it could have returned from the grave. But I had never thought to ask whether what she had told me had been the whole truth. If there were more that she could tell me, that might unlock this mystery. It could be the key to ending all of this.

I tossed and turned, trying to get comfortable. Bones grumbled and shifted his weight, but my thoughts were wild horses that couldn't be tamed.

How does a necklace reappear after being thrown into a grave and buried under tons of earth, with the grass undisturbed? It doesn't. That's impossible.

Unless . . .

Unless it were removed before the grave was filled in.

If so, then someone who attended the funeral was responsible. The undertaker's men? Someone in Miss Li's family?

I clenched my sheets tightly between my fingers. I had done it.

I had found the question I needed to ask.

★ ★ ★

Dawn broke and I was already up, dressed and racing down the stairs.

'You're so noisy, Violet!' Thomas shouted at me from his room, throwing a pillow at his open door which landed with a *thwump* on the landing, just missing me.

'I have important work to do!' I shouted back. Bones barked happily and raced ahead.

Maddy was tending the fireplaces, the first task of the day, and Mother had not yet emerged. Father and Oliver had been up before the light – there must have been a morning funeral to get ready for. I felt relieved that Oliver would be kept out of my way, but part of me hoped that we would have been able to make amends. At least I now had something else to occupy my mind.

I'd searched my notebook and found the slip of paper with Miss Li's address – she lived at number 4 Turner Square. It was within the Seven Gates borough where we lived, but a fair walk away.

I hastily prepared myself a bowl of porridge in the kitchen, while Bones wolfed down some dog biscuits with a little dripping left over from the previous night's supper.

When Mother came down, yawning and bleary-eyed, I decided I had better tell her what I was up to on this occasion. I didn't want any more incidents.

'There's been a development in my case,' I told her. 'I need to go and speak to Miss Li again. May I?'

'All right, I suppose,' she said, covering her mouth as she stifled another yawn. 'Be back before lunchtime, or I shall send out a search party.'

That was surprisingly easy, I thought. Perhaps I ought to ask Mother's permission when she was barely awake more often. 'When will Oliver and Father be back?'

'Around one o'clock, I think,' she said, shuffling over to the stove and picking up the heavy kettle.

So I had plenty of time, and it was early enough to catch Miss Li before she went anywhere for the day.

As I was putting my coat on and hurrying to leave, I heard a knock at the door of the shop. Bones bounced over, and I followed – nudging him out of the way so that I could open the door.

It was the telegram boy in his uniform, his smart bicycle leaning against the railings. 'Telegram for Miss Violet Veil?'

'That's me,' I said, and took it from him. He tipped his hat and hopped back on the bicycle.

It was from Eleni. I read it with haste:

```
Niko still missing. Mr Hyde not dead
(yet). Come here when you can! – E
```

I folded the paper anxiously and tucked it into my pocket. I was glad to hear that the murderer had not struck again, but it was bad news that Niko hadn't been found. All the more reason why I had to speak to Miss Li, and quickly.

* * *

The walk to Turner Square was bright and sunny, and it almost felt a betrayal. Things were dark in my mind. But perhaps this was a good sign.

The square itself was affluent and pretty, with a tiny park in the centre that boasted pink-blossomed trees. A carpet of blossoms littered the pavements around, and Bones dashed through them with excitement. Even the air smelled better than it did in the rest of the city. The place was mostly empty, save for a few parked carriages and a milkman making his final deliveries.

I hopped up the steps of Miss Li's home and rapped the knocker on her beautiful jade-green door. I stroked Bones's head as I waited. It took a little while for my knock to be answered, but I wasn't surprised given that it was so early in the morning.

Miss Li's surprised face peered round the door. 'Miss Violet?' she asked. 'It's very early . . .'

'Good morning, Miss Li,' I said, pulling out my notebook and clutching it tightly. 'I'm sorry to bother you at this hour, but it's rather important. There have been some developments in the investigation, and I really need to ask you a few questions.'

'Oh,' she said, blinking in the emerging sunlight. 'Oh, you must come in, then.'

She pulled the door open and waved me inside. I saw that she was wearing a beautiful red silk dressing gown with golden embroidery.

I paused on the threshold. 'Um, can my dog come in too?'

Miss Li considered this for a moment. 'Can he wait in the hall?'

I gently pulled Bones in and told him to sit on the tile floor. He seemed quite happy about it, probably because Miss Li had a nice big cast-iron radiator that he could curl up next to.

She led me into the parlour, and I tried not to gasp. The room was grand and filled with stunning furniture – dark wood but painted in the Chinese style with birds and flowers and temples. The wallpaper was golden and intricate, as was the chandelier that hung above. Two ornate blue-and-white vases stood beside the fireplace, and a complex patterned rug was spread across the floor. The chairs were red velvet, not unlike those in the theatre, but in better condition and with far more detailing.

'Please,' Miss Li said, pointing me to one of the chairs. I perched on it, contented by how comfortable and soft it was. She took the other, across from me.

'Where to begin?' I pondered aloud, staring down at my notebook. There was an awful lot to cover in a short time, and I didn't want to confuse her. 'Well, I have established that she is definitely a fraud.'

Miss Li gasped and said something in Chinese. 'I knew it!' she said, switching back to English.

'The tricky part is that I believe someone is acting

out her prophecies, but that she is truly unaware who it is.'

'Really?' Miss Li asked, leaning forward. 'You're sure she is not responsible?'

'As far as I can tell, she and her husband are innocent,' I said. 'She seemed to believe that the prophecies were really coming true on their own. And the pair were locked in their room at the time of one of the incidents, among other things. But I have now heard a partial confession from someone else.'

'Who?' My client was quite literally on the edge of her seat at this point.

'Niko Anastos, the son of the family who own the theatre. He told us that he was helping someone to carry out the prophecies. Unfortunately, he disappeared yesterday. I fear he has been taken away by the real murderer in order to silence him. And now there is a threat on Mr Hyde's life too.'

She put her hand over her mouth, but this time said nothing.

I took a deep, shaky breath. 'I'm beginning to think the only way that we might solve this is to go back to the beginning, to your necklace.' I pulled the golden lock amulet out of my dress, and she almost recoiled at the sight of it. 'I realised that perhaps the only way that your necklace could have returned was if someone took it before the grave was filled in. And, if that is true, then the person behind all of this – the fortunes and the murder and the threats – must have been at your father's funeral.'

She blinked at me for a moment, and I thought that she might not respond. 'Someone . . . at the funeral?' she said eventually. 'But . . . who would . . .'

'Which undertaker did you use?' I asked, my pencil poised to note it down.

'Flourish and Co.,' she replied quickly.

'Oh, hmm,' I said, trying to conceal my reaction on hearing the name. 'Well, they are our rivals. We aren't friendly with them, but I don't think they're untrustworthy. I've never heard a bad word about them. I suppose that's why they do well. But what about the guests? Who was in attendance?'

'There weren't many of us,' she said, her eyes going a little glassy as she tried to remember. 'Some of my father's business associates, and then myself and Zhen. And her husband—'

We were interrupted by the sound of feet skittering across the tiled floor – Bones had spotted something. When I looked towards the parlour door, I was surprised to see Zhen herself peering in at us, while Bones sniffed round her feet.

She was dressed in a dressing gown that matched her sister's, only in blue. Her hair was neatly arranged, but her eyes looked tired and a little red as if she had been crying for some time.

'Violet?' she exclaimed, although her voice was soft and quiet. 'The girl from the theatre?'

'Um, yes,' I said.

'Do you have news of my husband?' she asked with a hint of desperation. 'I heard you mention him.'

Now I was puzzled. 'News? About your . . . husband?'

Miss Li looked at me. 'Oh,' she said, and I think the realisation was slowly looming towards both of us, like a steam train on the horizon. 'My sister's husband didn't come home last night . . .'

CHAPTER THIRTY-ONE

'Has something happened to him?' Zhen asked.

'I don't think so,' I said carefully.

It crossed my mind that, if I began throwing accusations around, Zhen might just panic and leave. I had to think before I spoke, and that was not a speciality of mine.

'When did you last see your husband?' I asked.

Zhen gave her sister a questioning look.

'Tell her,' said Miss Li. 'She is a young detective. Perhaps she might be able to help.'

With a sniff, Zhen nodded and walked into the parlour, taking a seat on one of the ornate chairs. 'We went to Lady Athena's performance together last night, as we always do. But Barnaby disappeared before it started. I went looking for him, but he wasn't there. His seat was empty.'

Aha, so that was why she had been wandering around near the lavatories before the show. I scribbled down what she had told me.

'She came to stay here, with me,' said Miss Li. She gestured around. 'This was our father's house.'

'I thought you said your father didn't leave you with much?' I asked, the memory flickering dimly in my mind. I was remembering Inspector Holbrook's instruction to question everything.

Miss Li flushed a little, and I realised that was rather a rude question – but at this point I needed answers.

'I own the family houses,' said Zhen, sniffing again and pulling out a delicate lace handkerchief. 'But I let my sister stay here. Barnaby and I have a bigger house.'

'Ah,' I said.

'I told you your husband was too interested in your money,' Miss Li said, crossing her legs and leaning back in the chair. Then she added something in Chinese, and Zhen made what sounded like a cutting remark in response.

I had to jump in before they could start a full-blown

argument. 'Did your husband want to give money to Lady Athena? He said you wouldn't ever miss a performance. Is that correct?'

Zhen was still glaring at her sister. 'He did,' she admitted. 'He is a –' she paused, and I sensed some discomfort with this topic – 'a supporter. We both are. He wanted us to be her patrons, and give money to the theatre. He spent a lot of time there.'

I was having to think extremely quickly. The ticking of the clock on the mantelpiece was burrowing into my mind, alerting me to how little time I had. I tapped my pencil on my notebook. 'Did he introduce you to Lady Athena?'

'Yes,' she said. 'Just after our wedding, he took me to the first performance.'

'And that was before your father's funeral?' I asked, looking between the two sisters. They both nodded.

So Barnaby Campbell had married this wealthy woman, only to immediately begin taking her to Lady Athena's performances, and trying to persuade her to donate money. Then Lady Athena's prophecies began to come true, with one of the first being the removal of Miss Li's necklace from her father's grave – at the funeral that Barnaby attended. Which would have only strengthened his wife's convictions and willingness to give away her funds.

And, if that weren't enough, there was also the fact that

Mr Campbell had mysteriously disappeared shortly prior to the threat against Mr Hyde. And then someone had kidnapped Niko, and Mr Campbell was still unaccounted for.

That reminded me – there was one more thing I needed to ask. I took out the torn business card for A. J. Carrott and Co. that I had found above the stage.

'Mrs Campbell, does your husband shop at this tailor's?'

She peered at it. 'Yes. I took him there to buy his suit.'

That was it. It was Barnaby Campbell. It *had* to be.

Means. Motive. Opportunity. I was beginning to think he had all three.

But where was he?

'I have to go,' I said, pocketing my notebook and scrambling up. 'Do you have any idea at all where your husband might be? Is there any place that he frequents?'

She shook her head. 'Only the theatre, and the bank where he works nearby, and they said they have not seen him.'

'Where are you going?' Miss Li asked as I walked over to the corridor. Bones hopped up and trotted over the tiles to stand beside me.

'I'm sorry, but I need to locate Mr Campbell. It's rather important.' I turned to leave, but thought I ought to add something.

'Miss Li,' I said over my shoulder, 'do lend your support to your sister. She may have need of it.'

I left the two of them staring blankly at each other as we dashed out, nearly knocking over a startled servant who jumped out of the way just in time.

Bones and I darted from the square and down the street, his ears flapping with happiness. I didn't feel much of that, it must be said.

Barnaby had to be the murderer, and he had taken Niko. It made my stomach drop and heart pound just to think about it.

He worked at the bank – could that be how he was finding out people's details? And, attending so many of Lady Athena's shows, he could befriend the patrons there too. That could be how he had wormed his way into their lives and discovered such invaluable information as a dead wife or an unexpected inheritance.

But it was hard to fathom how Niko had become involved with such a man. Perhaps Mr Campbell had approached him, and Niko had been driven by his own desperation to help his family.

But why Niko? I snapped my fingers as the answer came to me. Niko knew the ins and outs of the theatre, and that would be an advantage, of course. There was another, though – the fact that Mr Campbell could remain in his seat throughout the performances, unsuspected by anyone. Until this latest performance.

I paused at a crossroads. One way led home, the other to the Grecian Theatre. Did Barnaby really have no other hiding place? But the theatre had been searched, and nothing had been found. Even Bones's nose hadn't sniffed out anything.

He sat on the cobbles and looked up at me.

I had a choice to make – run to the theatre and try to fix this mess on my own? Or . . .

Admit that I was wrong.

Make amends.

I knew as soon as I thought it which choice was the right one.

I couldn't do this alone. I needed Oliver.

CHAPTER THIRTY-TWO

Once I arrived home, I needed to wait for Oliver and Father to finish at the funeral. I made sure all my notes were in order, but I couldn't bring myself to eat. Nevertheless, Maddy eventually forced me to have some sliced bread and ham, and I gave a few scraps to Bones.

After what seemed like an age, they finally returned.

Oliver came into the kitchen and sat down heavily on a chair, exhaling and wiping his brow. 'Afternoon,' he said, and he smiled gratefully when Maddy offered him a spread for his lunch.

Eventually he appeared to notice that I was sitting at the table across from him, and he seemed rather surprised. 'Violet?' he said. 'I thought you'd be at the theatre.' There was an edge to his voice, but at least he was talking to me.

'About that,' I said quietly, when the others were out of earshot. 'We need to talk. Can you meet me outside under the oak tree in a minute?'

He had just taken a mouthful of bread, but he nodded.

I cleared my plate, and went to our bench to wait. I wasn't sure why I felt so nervous. I told myself it was the prospect of catching a murderer that was turning my stomach to fluttering moths and setting my hands aquiver. But, if I were to be honest, it was having to talk to Oliver that was doing it. Would he accept my apology? What if he truly didn't want to be my friend any more?

Bones sensed my discomfort and jumped to sit beside me on the bench, his tail wagging. He took up rather a lot of the space. I hoped Oliver didn't want to sit down.

'There you are,' I said when Oliver finally appeared, brushing some of the crumbs from his shirt.

'Here I am,' he said, and then an awkward aura of silence radiated from us both.

Someone had to break it, and I supposed it might as well be me.

'I'm truly sorry, Oliver. I've been an idiot.'

'Oh?' He raised an eyebrow.

And then it all came pouring out. 'I should have listened to you. I should have made sure you were all right. I should have done a lot of things, instead of blundering about like a fool. And now everything's gone wrong.' I sniffed, and tried to blink back the tears that were coming. 'Niko *was* involved. He was the one carrying out the prophecies for the real culprit, but after the argument you heard, where he tried to back out, the villain decided to take matters into his own hands. And now Niko's gone missing, and, and . . .'

I paused, took a gulping breath and stroked Bones for comfort. 'It's *Barnaby Campbell*, Oliver. I worked it all out. Zhen's husband. He's the murderer. He was in charge of faking the prophecies, and he's got Niko.'

'Wait a minute,' said Oliver, holding his hands out. 'Slow down. Zhen's husband? Is that the bloke we met who was gushing about Lady Athena?'

'The very same,' I said. 'I've just come back from visiting Miss Li. Zhen was there, and she said her husband didn't come home last night. He's been using Niko to do his dirty work while he sits and watches

Lady Athena every night.' I shuddered.

'But why?' Oliver asked, looking baffled.

'I'm not sure yet, but I think he has some sort of obsession with her. It could be that he was using Zhen for her money because he wanted to give it all to Lady Athena. And Niko went along with it all because, well – the more tickets they sell for their "real" medium, the more money they make, and they need it to help pay for Eleni's care.' I put my head in my hands. 'I should have realised,' I mumbled.

Oliver came nearer and placed his hand on my shoulder. 'I accept,' he said.

'You accept what?' I asked, lifting my gaze.

'Your apology. That was all I needed.' He shrugged. 'I just wanted to know if you cared.'

'I *do* care for you, Oliver,' I said, standing up and sending Bones running off again. 'It's just that sometimes I can be rather . . .'

'Pig-headed?'

'Steady on.' I prodded him gently. 'I was going to say obstinate. *Headstrong.*'

'Head in the clouds, more like,' he replied cheekily.

I probably deserved that. 'Well, yes. I was so focused on the investigation that I didn't really listen to you. I didn't notice that you needed help sometimes.'

He nodded and tucked his hands under his arms. 'I ain't quite back to what I used to be. It's gonna take time.'

I supposed that was true. What had happened to Oliver before we first met, well . . . that shouldn't happen to anybody. It was a miracle that he'd survived, but having a head wound and being unconscious for so long was bound to have side effects. In his body and his mind. And I had been pushing him all the time, on top of the hard work he already did for my father's business.

'I'm sorry,' I said again. 'I promise to . . . to pay attention and not to be so hard on you in the future. We should be a partnership. Will you help me again?'

Oliver's arms dropped, and he smiled. 'Sounds good to me,' he said.

I sighed. 'I'm stuck, though. I think Barnaby Campbell has kidnapped Niko, and I haven't the faintest idea where they've gone. I got Bones to search the theatre, but the trail went cold.'

Bones's ears pricked up at the mention of his name, and he gleefully brought me a wet stick in case that was what I wanted. I elected to ignore it.

'And, well . . . I had to walk home on my own last night, and it was frightening. I would really rather not do that again.'

'Oh, Violet,' said Oliver, and there was real understanding in his eyes. He rubbed the back of his head, where his scar carved through his hair. 'That won't happen. We'll go together.'

'But go where?' I exclaimed. 'Zhen said she had no idea where her husband might be. She wasn't aware of any place that he frequented, other than the theatre.'

Oliver stared out at the cemetery for a minute, thinking. 'Well, what if he's still there?'

Now I was staring at him, searching his deep brown eyes. 'What do you mean? Where?'

'That place is enormous an' old. We don't know every bit of it.'

'But Bones found nothing,' I insisted. 'The scent disappeared. We can't walk through walls.'

'Bones ain't all we have,' he said quietly. 'We've got you.'

'Me?'

'Yes, you,' he said, returning my gentle jab from earlier. 'Your . . . powers. You know. There are ghosts in the theatre, ain't there? More than one. They *can* walk through walls.'

It was as if a lightning bolt shot through me, like Frankenstein's monster being brought to life. I instantly knew that he was right. This was what I needed to do.

'Oliver, you're a genius. That's it! If I can communicate with the ghosts again . . . they might well be able to tell us where Niko is.'

It didn't always work that way, of course – I might just as easily get nonsense or nothing but a deathly sigh on the wind. But, if there were a chance, then we had to try it.

'We must go now!'

My friend, and I was relieved that I could call him that again, grinned back at me.

'I'll just get changed,' he said, looking down at his black uniform, 'an' I'll be right there.'

While Oliver hurried upstairs, I found Mother and Maddy and told them we had to go to the theatre for an urgent matter. Mother gave me her usual lecture about being careful and returning before nightfall, and after the events of the night before I wouldn't be likely to forget it. 'And do take the dog with you!' she called after me.

Bones didn't need any more encouragement. He was still gripping his wet stick in his mouth and wagging his tail, his trotting paws having left a trail of dirt through the kitchen. Come to think of it, that was probably why Mother wanted him out of the house.

Some of Father's men and Ernesto were assembled in the shop, having a cup of tea – Mr Dreyfuss with the bushy moustache, young Frankie and Ivan who had recently been hired, and Mr Patel. The last time I had spoken to Mr Patel was when I had put on an accent to sneak into a funeral, and Bones had caused a scene. I felt myself blushing as I greeted him on my way out. 'Um, sorry about pretending to be French,' I added.

'I had my suspicions, Miss Violet, but it was quite entertaining,' he replied, winking at me. I wondered if what we were about to do next would cause a scene too.

I let myself out of the door, Bones hopping from the step beside me, and I was only waiting on the pavement for a few minutes.

'Come on!' I said, about to hurry away, before I remembered myself. I turned slowly back to Oliver. 'If you're all right, that is?'

He grinned at me, and I felt the warmth of knowing that our friendship was healing. 'I'm ready,' he said. 'Just don't run this time.'

CHAPTER THIRTY-THREE

Inside the Grecian Theatre, it always felt like evening. It was another world. No matter how bright the sun shone outside, and even with the windows along the front, the theatre seemed to have a permanent cloak of darkness. Once you were inside, it felt as though it were getting late, and a performance were about to start.

In some ways, there was soon to be a show – but a secret one known only to myself and Oliver. And hopefully Eleni would soon know about it too.

We found Archie manning the ticket booth, although it currently had a **CLOSED** sign hanging over it, so exactly what he was supposed to be doing in there, I couldn't be sure.

'Mr Anastos says no one's allow— Oh! It's you two,' he said. Bones ran over and licked him, before trying to sniff his pockets for treats.

'Us again,' I said. 'Afternoon, Archie. Please, tell me they've found Niko?'

He shook his head. 'No such luck,' he replied miserably. 'Sorry, miss.'

I winced. Part of me had been hoping they would have tracked him down by now. There was a weight in my heart, heavy with the idea that something truly terrible might have happened. But I couldn't think about that. If we still had time, I had to make the most of it.

'What about Mr Hyde?' Oliver asked. 'Is he still here?'

'Nope,' said Archie, gently pushing Bones's probing nose away. 'Inspector Holbrook had him taken home. The police have got their house surrounded, I reckon.'

'And Lady Athena?' I added.

'She went with him, but I saw her dashing back in about an hour ago. I think she was looking for the inspector, and he's been running things here all day.'

'Ordering people about, I assume,' I said, knowing the

inspector. 'Well, that's excellent. Do you think Lady Athena has gone to her dressing room? We need to pay her a visit.'

'I'll come with you!' Archie said. I think both of us were looking at him with a little horror because he shrugged and added: 'Haven't got anything better to do. Mr and Mrs Anastos have been searching everywhere, and they didn't give me a job other than turning folks away.'

I glanced at Oliver, who just raised his eyebrows at me. 'All right,' I said tentatively. This was about to get rather interesting.

★ ★ ★

Knock knock.

The three of us and the dog stood outside Lady Athena's dressing room, me closest with fist still raised in case I needed to knock again. There was no policeman there this time – she and her husband were both supposed to be safe at home.

'Who is it?' came a wavering voice from inside.

'It's Violet Veil,' I said. 'And Oliver and Archie. May we come in?'

Lady Athena opened the door cautiously, peering round it. Her make-up was smudged as if she'd been crying, and her normally luxuriant hair was veering off in multiple directions.

'I ought to be getting home,' she said in a wobbly voice that wasn't far off a whisper. 'That inspector is useless. He still hasn't caught the man threatening my husband.' She sniffed. 'What do you want?'

'We need to talk to your sister,' I said.

She went very still.

'I'm sorry,' I said, ignoring the noises of confusion from Archie, 'but I wouldn't be doing this if it weren't very important. I think she might be able to help us find Niko, and the murderer. And I don't think she'd come out without you here.'

'That's . . .' she started to say with a frown, and I wondered what she was thinking. *Madness? Out of line?* I didn't think there was anything she could say that wouldn't reflect badly on her profession.

I realised, too, that I had acquired two boys whom she might not want to reveal anything in front of. 'I'll only ask about finding them,' I promised quickly. 'And, with the strength of your powers, I'm sure we can get through to her.'

Her face and shoulders relaxed a little. 'All right,' she said, standing back and pulling the door wider. 'Come on in, but be quick about it.'

I heard a whimper, which I soon realised didn't come from Bones but from Archie. I turned to look at him. 'I . . . I can't go in a *dressing room*, miss – it's not allowed! And, and . . . *powers*? Are you talking about g-ghosts?'

'I think it's perhaps better for everyone if you wait outside,' I said and, as the rest of us filed in, I left him anxiously twiddling his thumbs in the corridor.

We settled into the dark dressing room, surrounded by the eclectic collection of skulls. Oliver leaned against the back wall, while Lady Athena stood to the side, still looking pale and drawn. I took a seat at her dressing table and, as Bones lay down beside me, I began to reach out with my senses. I caught the shimmer in the mirror, and almost slid my gaze in sideways – as though I were looking at a postcard with an optical illusion. And now I could see the outline of Mary, see her faint smile and her curious expression.

Please let this work, I thought, gripping the hem of my dress between my fingers to focus my concentration.

'Hello, Mary,' I said aloud. 'I'm sorry to trouble you, but I have an urgent matter.'

The mirror-girl tipped her head sideways as if to tell me to go ahead.

'We're looking for a dangerous man – Barnaby Campbell. He threatened to kill your sister's husband. And we think he's taken the boy who lives here in the theatre. Do you know where he is?'

A soft voice echoed in my ears: *He's here.*

'He's here?' I heard Oliver mutter behind me. I spun round to look at him, and saw that his eyes were closed, while Lady Athena was gaping at him. Had he heard the ghost speak?

I didn't have time to think about that. I turned back to the mirror. 'He's here? In the theatre? Can you tell us where?'

There was a pause, and then Mary simply said: *Follow.*

With that, she turned and walked away, her image getting smaller as she somehow appeared to slip further into the mirror.

I looked round again, to see if Oliver had reacted. He'd opened one eye and was peering at me curiously.

'What did she say?' Lady Athena blurted out, before I could ask what he'd heard.

'She said to follow her,' I said slowly, tiptoeing over the words as I tried to work out what they meant. How did one follow a ghost?

Oliver scratched his head. 'Does she . . . live in mirrors?'

I snapped my fingers. 'You might be on to something.' I jumped up, making Bones bark with excitement. 'Thank you, ma'am,' I said to Lady Athena with a hurried curtsey as I flung open the door.

'Wait—' she started, but I was already out in the corridor, Bones and Oliver hurrying after me.

I passed Archie, who was standing nervously to attention. 'W-what happened?' he asked.

'We need to follow a ghost to find the murderer,' I told him.

This somehow made him turn even paler than he already was. He looked as though he were about to be sick.

'Don't trouble yourself,' I said, patting him on the shoulder. 'But please, tell me where there's a mirror.'

'Um, round here in the corridor, miss,' he said, pointing. 'But why . . .?'

I quickened my pace, turned the corner and found myself in front of a gilt mirror, a little worn with age. I took a deep breath and looked into the glass. It was harder to see in the brighter light, but I could just make out Mary's reflection. I was certain her finger was pointing downwards.

'Downstairs?' I asked, puzzled. That was where the trail had taken us, but we'd had no luck.

Follow, I heard the whisper say again, and Mary's outline disappeared.

I looked round to see Oliver, Bones and Archie staring at me. 'We have to go to the basement,' I said. I patted my knee to call Bones over. 'Bones, can you take us to Niko again? Niko, remember?'

Bones panted and wagged his tail, and then he was trotting away.

As we followed through the corridors and into the backstage area, Archie still trailing behind us, I turned to Oliver. 'Did you hear Mary?' I asked, my curiosity getting the better of me.

'I don't know what I heard,' he said, but he was frowning. I was sure he had sensed more than he was letting on. Was Oliver beginning to share my power? That thought was so large and strange that I had to put it aside.

Finding Niko and catching Barnaby was all that mattered in this moment. I wondered where Eleni was, and whether she were all right. Perhaps she'd taken to her bed.

The four of us rushed down the wooden stairs to the dimly lit basement. I paused at the bottom, wondering where to go next. Bones began sniffing round the wall again, and I thought perhaps he could sense something that I could not.

'Archie,' I asked, 'are there any mirrors down here?'

He shrugged. 'Maybe in the prop storage? I don't come

down here much, miss. Gives me the creeps.' He shivered as he said the words, but perhaps that was just the cold. I saw Oliver pull his jacket round him.

'We're close,' I said. 'I can feel it.'

Whether that was my sixth sense or my intuition, I couldn't say, but some part of me felt certain as we tiptoed through the archway and into the prop-storage vaults.

'Violet, stop a minute,' Oliver hissed. 'What are we gonna do if we find him? The murderer, I mean?'

I paused next to a pile of dining chairs while Bones investigated a rustic wardrobe. Of course, I hadn't thought that far ahead – when did I ever? My mind ran before it could walk.

'Hmm,' I said. 'Perhaps we need some insurance.' I looked at Archie and immediately had an idea. 'Archie, can you hang back and, if you think we need help, run for the inspector?'

'Yes, miss,' he said with an air of both terror and relief that he didn't have to confront the murderer alongside us.

I carried on searching the walls, passing paintings and old set backdrops, and curious miscellany like a candelabra carved with crows' heads and what looked like a witch's cauldron. Suddenly Bones begin to growl.

'Over there!' Oliver whispered.

Bones was poised before a selection of mirrors – three tall standing ones in different woods, and one enormous one leaning against the wall. It was like the magical mirror from a fairy tale. Bones looked up at his many reflections, still growling. I wondered if he had truly found something, or if he were just angry at this imposter.

Oliver and I stared at each other. There was only one way to find out.

I stepped closer and peered into the giant mirror, letting my eyes search for the otherworldly image. It took a moment, but soon I could see her, her pretty curls waving in some unseen wind.

In here, she whispered, and then she faded from view.

I went to the side of the mirror and pulled on it, expecting it to be impossible to shift – but lo and behold it swung out easily, as if it weighed almost nothing. Another theatre trick. Behind it was a solid and rather ancient-looking wooden door. Bones was still growling, and I prayed that if Barnaby were in there that the walls were thick enough to keep out the sound. We needed the element of surprise on our side.

I went back to the others. 'Wait here,' I said to Archie, pointing to a leather Chesterfield sofa close by. He perched on it, jiggling his feet on the floor. 'If we need you, we'll shout . . .'

'Bluebottle,' suggested Oliver.

I raised an eyebrow at him.

'It means police.'

'Fair enough.' I shrugged. 'Are you ready?'

My friend's deep brown eyes met mine. Words went unspoken between us – I knew he'd be afraid. He had encountered a murderer before, and nearly paid the *ultimate price* just as the threat said Mr Hyde would. If I were honest, I was afraid too. I felt the fear prickle at my skin and pound in my heart. But beneath it was exhilaration, the thrill of the chase, and I was showing Oliver that I wouldn't run blindly after that any longer. This would be a team effort. We could end this together.

'Ready,' he said finally.

We headed for the door. It was time to see what awaited us on the other side.

CHAPTER THIRTY-FOUR

We burst through the secret door and into the room behind it.

It was a fairly large space, dark and damp, with just one lamp flickering in the centre of the room, casting shadows up the walls. There were piles of ancient-looking crates, perhaps holding dusty wine bottles or forgotten props. They were stacked up to a metal air vent that looked very similar to the one in Lady Athena's dressing room. Were they connected, perhaps?

Despite the abandoned crates, someone had clearly

been using this place recently because they had dragged in some of the furniture from the storage vaults – a desk and a chair, some buckets, a few books.

And that someone stood in the corner of the room, frozen beside Niko, who was lying on a pile of blankets.

Barnaby. He was holding a letter opener, and it looked deadly sharp.

We had to tread extremely carefully. 'Mr Campbell,' I said, keeping my voice as calm as I could. 'Don't do this.'

He frowned at us. 'What are you doing here?'

He had taken off his hat, and his blond hair and moustache were looking considerably more ruffled than they had before. His elegant suit, the one that I now knew must have held the tailor's card from Carrott and Co., had a rip at one side. He was watching Bones warily as Bones crouched by my side, growling and ready to attack.

'We're just looking for Niko, sir,' I said. 'He's our friend.'

I thought perhaps if I didn't draw attention to Barnaby Campbell's crimes, we might stand a chance of getting out unscathed.

Niko sat up slowly from the pile of blankets, peering at us through bleary eyes. His face lit up a little in recognition, but as he moved I realised with horror that his hands were tied together with rope. Barnaby really was holding him hostage. There was an empty bowl and a glass bottle beside him, so at least he'd not been without food and water.

Barnaby glared at us. We had thrown a spanner in his works, I supposed.

'If you know what's good for you, *children*,' he sneered, gesturing with the letter opener, 'I suggest you run along home. I'm not playing a game.'

I wasn't going to take that bait. We had caught him red-handed, there were two of us and we possessed an angry greyhound, and that meant we had at least a little power in this situation. 'Let Niko come with us,' I insisted, folding my arms.

'I'm afraid not,' said Barnaby, and he took a threatening step closer to us. Bones barked, but the man did not flinch. 'Niko and I have important work to do together, don't we, boy?'

Niko shook his head quickly, his dark curls bobbing. His eyes seemed to plead with us that he did not want to be associated with this individual.

'You should leave him out of this,' I said.

'Strange,' said Barnaby, 'he did seem so keen to be involved. I think perhaps you don't know your friend as well as you imagine you do.'

That stung, but I kept my eyes on Niko.

Help, he mouthed silently.

'I think perhaps you don't know who *we* are,' I said. 'We've confronted a killer before. We aren't afraid of you.' I kept my arms folded, lest they start quivering and betray what I felt deep down.

Barnaby laughed, and it was a laugh full of scorn, not joy. 'A killer? Whatever gave you that idea?' As if the sharp letter opener he was currently brandishing in his hand were merely a toy.

Bones growled lower, baring his teeth, keeping in front of us. At least we had some protection.

'Would you like me to prove it, Mr Campbell? We know what you've been doing, that you and Niko have been making Lady Athena's prophecies come true.'

'And have you told anyone else?' he asked, almost conversationally, holding up the letter opener and examining it so that the light glinted off it.

To my surprise, Oliver suddenly swiped at the air, as if batting away an invisible fly.

'What was that?' I hissed.

'Bluebottle!' he said a little too loudly, and I immediately realised what he was doing. That was the signal for Archie to run. I hoped he had something to say to drown out Archie's footsteps, and he didn't disappoint.

'We ain't seen nothing, sir,' Oliver bluffed, his voice noticeably still rather loud, as Barnaby stared at him with grim curiosity. 'We'll say Niko fell down here an' got a concussion. We'll let you run.'

He knew that we had sent for help. There was nowhere to run . . . as long as we could survive for long enough.

I was expecting that we would have to stall, to stop this unhinged man from attacking us or from hurting Niko. What I wasn't expecting was what happened next.

'Mr Campbell?' came a soft voice from behind us.

We turned to see Lady Athena. She had brushed out her hair and put on her stage gown, and she almost looked like a ghost stepping into the room. She put her hands on Oliver's and my shoulders, and we shared a glance before moving aside to let her through.

Mr Campbell's eyes lit up, and his whole demeanour seemed to change. He ran a hand through his blond hair. 'My lady,' he said. 'Please call me Barnaby.'

She curtseyed low, and I thought she was laying it on rather thick, but it seemed to render him speechless. He let his arm fall behind his back, hiding the sharp letter opener. Bones came out of his defensive stance, but stayed in front of us protectively, looking up at me with some confusion in his celestial eyes.

'Is it true that you did all this for me, Barnaby?' the fortune-teller asked, using her stage voice, silky and mesmerising.

'It was –' he swallowed – 'the least I could do. I . . .' He was stumbling over his words as he focused on her in the lamplight, and he took a deep breath before continuing as if this were a speech he had practised many times in the mirror.

'I was fascinated with you from the moment I first saw you. I am your most devoted patron. Your faithful servant. I wanted you to go down in history. Never to be forgotten. They'll build a statue for you, I promise.'

I was surprised to hear Oliver pipe up with, 'What does your wife think about that?'

'My wife?' Barnaby had a sneer on his face. 'She was the means to an end,' he said dismissively. 'Lady Athena is my goddess.'

I felt a rush of anger. How dare he treat Zhen that way? He had clearly only married her for her money, to get closer to Lady Athena.

'She deserves better,' I snapped, but he barely seemed to register that I had spoken now that his *goddess* was in the room.

Lady Athena glanced at me briefly, and gave me a barely perceptible nod. She knew what she was about to do.

We held our breath as we watched, Niko staring up anxiously from the corner. I stepped closer to Oliver, and took hold of Bones's collar to keep him still.

Lady Athena moved forward. 'Barnaby,' she said, keeping her voice low and soothing, 'I see you now. I see what you have done for me. Come away with me, won't you?'

His eyes moved back and forth as they searched hers. I could feel his desperation to believe her.

'We'll forget all of this ever happened,' she added insistently. 'We'll go to Paris, or New York. I can be a star there. You shall be my manager.'

His brow furrowed. 'But your husband . . .'

'I don't want you to hurt him,' she said, 'but I'll forget him. He'll never find us.'

I stayed silent. In that moment, I felt as if I were balancing on the walkway high above the stage again, teetering on the edge, seconds from falling. This could all go wrong in an instant if Barnaby didn't believe her.

There was a heavy pause.

'Do I have your word?' Lady Athena asked.

He took her hand in his. 'My lady,' was all he said.

She turned and led him over the rough stones towards the door, the expression on his face hypnotised.

No one was more surprised than him when Inspector Holbrook appeared in the doorway.

'Barnaby Campbell?' the inspector said, his two officers flanking him. 'You're under arrest.'

There was a clatter as the letter opener fell to the floor.

CHAPTER THIRTY-FIVE

Barnaby Campbell didn't try to resist arrest. He couldn't take his eyes from Lady Athena. They were filled with disappointment.

'You betrayed me,' he said.

She said nothing, and I didn't blame her. She didn't owe him a thing – after all, she had never asked him to act on her behalf, and certainly not to kill. I prayed that he would confess to all that he'd done.

It turned out that Mr and Mrs Anastos had been following the inspector, and they rushed in to check on

Niko. His mother grabbed his face to look at him and then swept him into a tight hug, saying grateful-sounding words in Greek. Meanwhile, his father stood over them, wiping away a tear of relief. Bones decided to join in the celebration by running over and licking Niko's face, making him laugh.

'I'm all right,' I heard him say. 'I'll be all right.'

We all followed as the police led Barnaby out of the secret room, the villain seeming in quite the daze. I thought that Lady Athena's duplicity had shocked him more than being arrested.

Mr Anastos stopped and stared at the door behind the mirror. 'Twenty years I have owned this theatre,' he said, shaking his head in disbelief, 'and I never knew this was here.'

'Places get lost sometimes,' I said.

The crypt in our cemetery had once been the cellars of a grand house that had stood up on the hill, destroyed by a fire – I only knew that because my grandfather had told me. Times changed, and people forgot the forms things had once taken.

I trotted ahead through the prop storage until I was neck and neck with Lady Athena. She seemed a little dazed too, as if she couldn't quite comprehend what had just happened.

'Thank you,' I said to her. 'Your quick thinking saved Niko.'

She looked back at me. 'Only because I followed you,' she said quietly. 'Your power is . . . magnificent.'

I tried not to blush.

As our procession reached the top of the stairs, we found that Eleni was waiting in the backstage area beside Archie, who was sitting on the floor, hugging his knees.

'Niko!' she cried.

He broke free of his mother's arm and ran over to her. I felt relief deep within me at seeing them reunited. Oliver, Bones and I hurried to join them.

Niko sat down heavily on one of the low wooden benches. Eleni clutched his hand, speechless and tearful.

But things were not over yet. I heard a commotion and then Mr Hyde burst through the door to the backstage area. 'Olivia!' he cried, apparently forgetting to use his wife's stage name. He was wearing his trousers and shirt, but not his signature jacket or top hat, as if he'd got dressed in a rush.

A distressed-looking young policeman appeared behind him. 'I tried to stop him, sir,' he pleaded to Inspector Holbrook. The inspector merely gave him a withering look in response.

Mr Hyde and Lady Athena ran to each other and embraced.

This was the thing that seemed to snap Barnaby out of his trance. He fought against the constables that were holding him, but they didn't let go.

'You *witch*,' he growled. 'I would have given you everything!'

'I don't want anything from you,' said Lady Athena, turning her face away.

'This is him?' Mr Hyde asked. 'The man who threatened to kill me? Who murdered Terence?' He looked Barnaby up and down. 'Pathetic,' he spat finally.

'And you're frauds and liars,' Barnaby shot back, red-faced with anger. 'All of you!'

Mr Anastos immediately looked panicked. 'I won't have any more of this slander,' he said, holding up his hand. I supposed he didn't want his top act exposed in front of the police.

To my surprise, though, Barnaby nodded to Mrs Anastos. 'Why don't you ask your wife?'

Mrs Anastos had gone to fuss over Niko and Eleni and she looked up, her eyes wide and her raven hair falling across her shoulders.

'Yes, you, *Maria*,' he said. 'Did you not hire me?'

My breath caught in my throat. *What?*

Her husband went pale, while Inspector Holbrook just raised an eyebrow. 'Is this true?'

'Tell them,' Barnaby snarled.

'I . . . I am so sorry,' said Mrs Anastos, and she put her velvet-gloved hand over her mouth. Niko touched her arm, but she gently shook him off. Her eyes filled with tears. 'It's my fault. All of this is my fault.'

'Maria, no,' said Mr Anastos, his mouth hanging open.

She ignored him. 'I was the one who hired Mr Campbell,' she said shakily. 'We were struggling,' she added, directing this at her husband. 'We were low on funds. I thought if we didn't have a big success, we would be closed down. We would not have anywhere to go, and we wouldn't be able to pay for the help my daughter needs.'

She sobbed, and Eleni looked up at her, distraught. 'Oh, Mama,' she whispered. Even Bones looked upset, and he curled himself at her feet.

'When Lady Athena came to us,' Maria Anastos continued, 'I noticed that she had some dedicated followers already. I thought perhaps one of them could help us.'

'So you asked Mr Campbell to fake the prophecies,' I said, filling in the gaps.

I couldn't believe it. And Niko had helped, of course, but I wasn't sure I wanted to incriminate him after the ordeal he had just been through. Surely that was punishment enough.

His mother coughed and pulled out a handkerchief, wiping her tears. Then she pointed it at Barnaby. 'You were never supposed to hurt anyone! I never asked you to do this!'

'More of your lies,' said Barnaby, but I didn't trust him. He was on the offensive now, trying to take others down with him.

Inspector Holbrook was watching this whole charade with an expression of bemusement on his face, the other constables' eyes darting back and forth at each new accusation.

'Mr Campbell, do you really expect me to believe that Mrs Anastos asked you to murder her friend and co-worker, and beyond that, that she asked you to kidnap her son and hold him at knife-point? Why, pray, would she do such things?'

'Because . . . because . . .' Barnaby tried to answer, but he was faltering. His eyes looked wild, his hair dishevelled. 'Her theatre, you heard . . .'

Inspector Holbrook shook his head. 'I think what I've heard is that you have an unhealthy obsession with this young woman.' He gestured to Lady Athena. 'I think you took things further and further because you knew it increased her fame and fortune, and hoped that she would feel indebted to you. And you wanted to remove anyone who stood in your way or became a threat to that.'

Barnaby didn't seem to have a defence any longer. He merely glared at Lady Athena and Mr Hyde, staring daggers.

'Take him away, boys,' Inspector Holbrook said, and the constables began trying to move Barnaby, but still he fought against them.

'Liars!' he shouted. 'You're lying, Maria. You made your boy help me, didn't you? And you are a fraud, *Olivia*!' he spat towards Lady Athena.

There was a horrible pause as a variously tearful, shocked, exhausted and horrified group of us stared at one another.

'And *you*, Violet Veil,' Barnaby said, turning to me.

It was as though I'd been hit with a gust of air. I did not know how to react. Beside me, Bones's ears pricked up with curiosity.

'You think I don't know who you are?' He forced a laugh. 'I overheard your little conversation with dead people the other day.'

'What?' I asked, the sensation of dread creeping over me.

'In Lady Athena's dressing room? You should be careful what you talk about. The walls have ears, you know.' He smiled horribly.

But how? I thought. And then it hit me. *The vent.* It

really was connected – no wonder Bones had been sniffing at it. Barnaby must have climbed up the crates in the basement to listen to Lady Athena's conversations.

Barnaby seemed to enjoy my speechlessness. 'I know someone who would be *very* interested to hear about your mystical powers.'

Who was he referring to? If the others knew who he was talking about, they showed no sign of it. But I could have sworn that a shadow passed over Inspector Holbrook's face for a moment.

But there was no way that I could ask without seeming to admit the truth of his accusation. I felt like a rat in a trap. I couldn't give in, couldn't let myself be revealed in front of everyone. I had to think quickly.

'*Mystical powers?*' I said with a hint of confusion. 'I can't say I know what you're talking about.'

Oliver broke into a convincing chuckle. 'She's no more powerful than a mop, sir,' he said.

'Charming!' I shot back, elbowing him in the ribs. Bones barked as if in agreement.

The two policemen restraining Barnaby gave each other a sideways glance and smirked. They clearly thought he had lost all reason.

'I think we've heard quite enough,' said Inspector Holbrook. 'If you want to throw around any more strange accusations, Mr Campbell, I suggest you do it at the station. But please do remember that we caught you red-handed in a kidnapping.'

'Listen to me!' Barnaby shouted as the constables dragged the tall blond man away, his shoes scraping on the floor. 'You'll all listen to me one day! You'll regret this!'

The door to the backstage area slammed shut behind him, only slightly muffling his yelling.

Inspector Holbrook followed and then turned back. 'If I need to talk to any of you lot, I will summon you, understand?'

The assembled group of us nodded gravely. The rest was silence.

CHAPTER THIRTY-SIX

We found ourselves deposited in the Anastos's apartment as we all tried to digest what had just happened. The parents had gone through to their bedroom, where we could hear them arguing. Lady Athena and Mr Hyde had left together.

Niko had taken us to his room where a kitchen maid had brought him some soup, a piece of crusty bread and a glass of water. Oliver and I stood awkwardly in the corner of the room, not quite sure what to do with ourselves, while Eleni sat in her chair beside us. Bones was pestering Niko for his food.

It felt strange to be in an older boy's bedroom, but I supposed these were exceptional circumstances. I was surprised to see that beyond his bed and chest of drawers Niko's room was mostly filled with bookcases. It seemed odd that I hadn't known he was a keen reader. Perhaps I didn't really know much about him, after all.

I still wasn't sure how to feel about Barnaby Campbell knowing my secret. At least nobody had seemed to take him seriously. That was always how it seemed to go – people never believed that I could sense ghosts, and I rather hoped to keep it that way. Who knew what trouble I'd attract if it became public knowledge? Perhaps even some scoundrel that Barnaby associated with, by the sound of his curious taunting comment.

And Oliver, well . . . I looked at him leaning against the wall, hands in his pockets, and wondered what he'd seen as we'd followed Mary's mirror trail. He had brushed closer to death than even I had. Had it left its mark on him?

'Stop staring at me like that,' Niko said to Eleni. 'I'll spill my soup.'

Bones lifted his nose hopefully.

She leaned forward and stared at him with even greater

intensity. 'I don't know what to say to you,' she said. 'I'm thankful you're alive, of course. You know I love you, brother. But really? You and Mother collaborating with a villain this whole time? Why did you keep this from me?'

He lowered his spoon. 'I knew you wouldn't understand.'

She wheeled her chair a little nearer and whacked him on the arm. 'Wouldn't understand what? That you're a fool who could land himself in prison?'

'You can't stand Lady Athena,' he shot back. 'But she was our chance to help the theatre, to keep us off the streets, to help *you*.'

Oliver and I watched them silently as they argued at cross purposes. I didn't feel that we ought to intervene. This was between the two of them. I felt my anger at Niko growing as Eleni's did. Surely he must have known that aiding a man like Mr Campbell with his dangerous obsession was a terrible idea.

'That is not helping,' she said. 'That is gambling with our future.'

'I'm sorry!' said Niko, balling up his fists and sending a little soup spilling to the floor that Bones promptly began licking. 'I really thought I was doing what was best. What else could I do?'

'You could just be there for us,' said Eleni.

'But that's exactly it. I'm there all the time!' He paused for a moment, biting his tongue as if unsure if he really ought to speak.

Eleni's eyes bored into him, daring him to go on.

'I look after you,' he said. 'I help you to get about. I don't have much time for myself. Doing something in secret felt, well . . . liberating. Like I was free of my burdens.'

'I'm not a burden,' said Eleni, and I noticed that she had begun shaking with quiet rage. 'I'm your sister.'

'I didn't mean it that way—' he began, but she cut him off.

'All of us have our problems, Niko!' She waved her arms in exasperation. 'But most of us simply try talking about them. Working things out. Cooperating. We don't all go running about deceiving people because a madman asked us to.'

'I didn't . . . I didn't know he was . . .' Niko tried to explain himself, but it was clear that Eleni wasn't prepared to accept his excuses.

'You may be my older brother, Niko,' she said, 'but you need to grow up.'

There was a pause, where we all remained silent. I stared at the ceiling. Bones buried his nose in the carpet.

'Blast,' said Eleni finally. 'I can't even make a dramatic

exit. A little help, please, Oliver?' She turned her chair to him.

With a shrug to me, Oliver grabbed the handles so he could push her out.

'And slam the door on our way out, would you?' Eleni huffed.

I held it open for her, and watched as they left, Bones trotting alongside. And then I realised that I was now alone in the bedroom, face to face with Niko. My mother would have given me quite the pointed glare.

He was staring at me. 'Violet . . . I'm sorry. You trusted me.'

'Perhaps I shouldn't have,' I said. 'Oliver was right all along. He told me I ought not to believe you.'

Niko sighed and fiddled with his spoon. 'Perhaps you should have just left me down there to rot.'

I frowned at him. 'You need to face your mistakes, Niko, not give up.'

But his mind was clearly still lingering in the cellar as he looked at me. 'I ought to thank you for finding me. How did you do it? I didn't even know that hidden room was there.'

I paused, but Niko knew my secret already. I supposed it was all right to tell him.

'Well, in fact . . . a ghost led us there. It was Oliver's

idea, really. Bones couldn't trace your scent, and he kept getting stuck at the wall in the basement. But I was able to talk to the ghost of Lady Athena's sister, and she showed us the way through the mirrors.'

Niko raised his eyebrows. 'That's . . . incredible, Violet. You are special, you know that?'

This didn't seem like false charm this time – I think he truly meant it.

'I know,' I said with a shrug. No false modesty for me, either.

'I'll make things right with you, somehow,' he said, and our eyes locked for a moment.

But I still felt the anger simmering in me at what he'd done. Lying to everyone, tricking people, helping a stalker and murderer – his good intentions had led him on the path to evil. I folded my arms tightly across my heart like armour.

'It's not me you should be concerned about. It's your sister. You've hurt her deeply.'

He blinked at me, appearing a little shocked that I was so forthright. 'I – I didn't mean to—'

I shook my head and pointed out to the corridor. 'Listen to her. She's her own person, and she's not a broken thing that you need to fix.' The words were just spilling out. 'You make things right with her, you hear me! With your actions, not just pretty words. Or I shall have you haunted!'

And, with that, I turned and walked away – and I slammed the door too.

CHAPTER THIRTY-SEVEN

I had spent the night tossing and turning, worrying about the fate of the Anastos family and the Grecian. I couldn't bear to think what might happen to Mr Campbell – I wanted him stopped from hurting anyone else, but the hangman never felt like justice to me. It was a final cruelty that only added to all the cruelty in the world.

As I had recounted everything that happened to my family round the dinner table, Father went glassy-eyed. I supposed he was thinking how close he had come to that ending.

Mother nearly dropped her cutlery in horror at several points in my tale. Thomas kept putting a potato to his mouth and then lowering it as he came up with yet another question. I eventually told him to be quiet, but secretly I quite liked that he was showing an interest. Perhaps I would have to let him borrow some of my detective novels in future.

'Did you know about all this?' Mother asked Father when I'd finally finished.

Father said nothing. He appeared to be speechless.

'Perhaps we need to have a talk,' Mother said pointedly. Oliver and I tried not to giggle at each other. 'I think our daughter is wayward.'

'She was born wayward,' said Father, taking another bite of his dinner. 'It might be too late to change her.'

When I had finally retired to bed, Maddy came to bring my nightgown, and brush out my hair. She gave me a tight hug. 'You are brave, Miss Violet,' she said. 'We're all proud of you. But can you try to avoid murderers in future?'

'We shall see about that,' was all I said. Bones barked and curled up on my quilt. I wasn't sure whose side he was taking.

* * *

We returned to the theatre the next day, once the dust had settled. How could I move on with so much unsaid? And, to be quite honest, I was hoping to avoid a telling-off from Mother, so keeping well away was probably best.

When we walked through the front entrance, Archie ran over to us. 'You're here!' he exclaimed. 'Mr Anastos has just called a meeting of the whole theatre. I think Miss Anastos was hoping you'd come along.'

'I was indeed,' said Eleni as Niko wheeled her through the doors.

Archie blushed and grinned before running into the next room.

Eleni smiled at us, and I smiled back. It was so good to see her happy again. 'Violet, Oliver,' she said. 'Niko and Mother are going to talk to everyone in the auditorium. Will you join us?'

'Course,' said Oliver.

'I hope you'll like what I have to say,' said Niko with a glance at me.

As we moved towards the auditorium, I turned to Eleni. 'Tell me, what happened with Lady Athena?'

'Unfortunately, the police were not that interested in a theatre act being fake,' she replied, with a clear air of disappointment. 'I was hoping they might throw her in a cell for the night at least.'

'She saved me,' Niko pointed out.

I had to say, I had considered exposing her to the press, but what she had done for Niko had made me see her in a slightly different light. And, of course, she no longer had anyone carrying out her prophecies for her, so her act would have to change. I wondered if she might stop exploiting the dead for the money of the living, too, but perhaps that was too much to ask for.

His sister shrugged. 'Well, we haven't seen her and Mr Hyde since. I think they are probably re-evaluating their lives as we speak.'

'Maybe they really will go to Paris,' Oliver said.

'And never come back?' said Eleni cheekily. 'We can only hope.'

I was not sure what to expect, but as we entered the theatre all the lights were up and everyone who worked there seemed to be assembled in and around the rows.

We took our seats, Bones wandering up and down the aisle before finally settling beside us. Eleni was nearby, looking up expectantly as her mother and brother took to the stage.

Maria Anastos was wearing a beautifully tailored scarlet dress with black trim and matching gloves. She was nervously picking at the stitching on them. Niko wore a grey suit – from Carrott and Co., I presumed.

Maria finally spoke up. 'Everyone, I must apologise. I am sure you have heard some rumours about what has happened. Well, it is . . .' She paused, took a deep breath. 'It is all my fault. It was my idea to hire Barnaby Campbell to make the predictions of Lady Athena come true. I swear to you that I did not ask him to hurt anybody, but I still feel responsible for the loss of our friend. Terence was a good man and a great actor, and nothing I could tell you would bring him back. I'm so sorry.'

She wiped a tear from her eye, and then began to quietly sob. I had heard she was a good actress, but this really felt genuine. The crowd before us murmured among themselves, but it was too soon for me to be able to tell if they were receptive to her words.

'I was also responsible,' said Niko. 'I want to apologise to everyone, too, from the bottom of my heart.' His gaze was lowered but steady, his hands clasped together. He meant those words. 'We were trying to save the theatre, but what we did was wrong. I'll never forgive myself for what happened to Terence.'

I turned to look at Eleni, to see her reaction, but her expression gave nothing away. She kept her chin high.

'And I especially want to apologise to my sister,' said Niko, raising his hand in the spotlight. 'For putting up with me when I have been such a fool.'

Now I thought I saw the quirk of a smile at the corner of her lips.

Back on the stage, I saw that Niko glanced at his mother and noticed that she was still crying. 'I think we both want to say that we promise to change things,' he continued. 'We will make things better.'

Maria nodded silently.

'We'll put on more plays and better acts, in honour of Terence,' he said. 'No more trickery.'

There was a murmur of what seemed like agreement from everyone – the actors, the bar staff, the painters, the stage crew and all the rest. I noticed Mr Anastos standing at the side – I couldn't see if he was smiling, but he was nodding his approval. I wondered if he could forgive his wife and son. It certainly seemed that he was supporting them.

'I have a play you can use!' Eleni shouted, cupping her hands to her mouth.

That broke the tension, and everybody laughed. I suppose Eleni was well known for her passion at the Grecian.

'We will put on one of Eleni's plays,' Niko said with more confidence. 'Are you happy now, sister?'

'Perfectly,' she said, and more chatter and even a few cheers broke out around the theatre.

I leaned over to her. 'You ought to write one about a fraudulent fortune-teller and a brave detective,' I suggested.

'And a reporter called Jack Danger,' Oliver added.

Bones barked.

'And a dog.'

Eleni made a show of thoughtful agreement. 'I shall call it . . . *A Case of Misfortune*,' she said.

★ ★ ★

I had hope for the Anastos family and the Grecian. They were taking steps in the right direction. Now that Mrs Anastos and Niko had apologised, and Lady Athena was gone, how would the theatre change? Perhaps Eleni's plays really would be the key that unlocked their success. I hoped that if Terence were looking down on them that he'd be proud to see them returning to their roots.

After we had said goodbye to our friends, there was one final task of importance. Once again, I had to go back to where this had all begun.

This time Oliver and Bones were both by my side when I met Miss Li.

We sat on a bench beside a little park near her home and I told her everything. I explained why her sister's husband had done what he did, and how it started with him stealing Miss Li's amulet from their father's grave.

She listened with a glazed expression. I had handed the necklace back to her, and she was twisting it through her fingers.

'My sister is devastated,' she said eventually. 'She . . . she believed in him.'

'Sometimes we believe in the wrong people,' I said gently. 'It doesn't mean we've done wrong. Please tell her that, won't you?'

Miss Li nodded. 'I will be there for her.' She stared down at the blossoms on the pavement for a moment, where Bones lay panting in the spring sun. 'I should have kept her away from him.'

Now Oliver spoke up. 'We can't always keep people from harm,' he said, 'even if we want to.'

He didn't meet my gaze, but he didn't have to. I knew that was what he had tried to do for me.

Finally Miss Li got to her feet. 'Thank you for telling me all this,' she said. 'I must get back to my sister. Oh, and of course I will write you a cheque for your services.'

I tried not to seem too excited, given the circumstances, but I perhaps thanked her rather *too* enthusiastically.

Chapter thirty-eight

With everything over, I felt triumphant but somewhat at a loose end. I couldn't deny that I wanted more – more mystery, more thrills, meeting more people outside our house and our street. All the things that my parents hoped I would avoid, in short. But, at the same time, there had been danger and death. I had come closer to both than I'd have liked.

Those things played on my mind. People said one ought to keep one's friends close and one's enemies closer – I thought perhaps I ought to work on keeping my friends closer, and my enemies as far away as possible. But who would my enemies be? That part was hard to tell. As for who my real friends were, that was much easier. I hoped I'd see Niko and Eleni again, and Archie. And there was someone else who was important that I needed to show my appreciation for.

★ ★ ★

It was a bright weekend morning, and I was at the front of the shop, making an addition to my card in the window. I had to wonder whether Father had really not noticed its presence, or whether he'd decided to humour me. He was in the funeral parlour at that moment, and I didn't think it was a good idea to ask.

I poked my tongue out of the corner of my mouth in concentration as I wrote. Bones was lying by my feet, chewing a slipper that he almost certainly wasn't supposed to have. Glancing down at him, I decided to make a further alteration.

Oliver came strolling in, hands in his pockets. 'What's this?' he asked.

I stood back and admired my handiwork. 'I have added some important details,' I said.

VEIL INVESTIGATIONS

Detective Services

(*Mysteries Solved Within*)

ASK FOR MISS VIOLET VEIL
AND MR OLIVER OATS

'Does that say . . . Oliver?' he asked.

I grinned back at him, pleased that he'd been able to read it. 'You are an important part of the team.'

He pointed at the illustration I'd drawn on the side. 'An' Bones!'

'Well, what would we do without him?' I asked. Bones looked up at me, swishing his tail across the floor.

'I'm better behaved,' said Oliver, folding his arms indignantly, despite the clear pleasure on his face.

'That's debatable,' I responded. 'But what do you say? Will you join me in this business venture?'

I put out my hand, and he stared down at it for a few moments. 'Course,' he said, and he shook my hand with great enthusiasm.

'In that case, shall we celebrate our first victory as a detective agency?' I asked. 'I heard Maddy has made some pork pies.'

Bones scrambled to attention, abandoning his chewed slipper.

'I think that's a yes,' said Oliver proudly, scratching Bones behind the ears.

★ ★ ★

We spread out a blanket in a sunny patch of the cemetery a little way up the hill, where daisies and daffodils sprang up among the graves. I had managed to grab some of the pies before Thomas ate them all. There were boiled eggs and fresh bread, too, and Mother had even bought ginger beer as a treat.

Bones rolled in the grass, covered in seeds already. All around, I could sense the familiar feeling of the presence of souls welcoming us. I wondered if Oliver was aware of it too. It made me feel at home.

Birds were chorusing in the branches and there was a fresh breeze on the air. I wrapped my shawl round myself and happily listened to the satisfying fizz as I pushed in the marble to open the bottle.

'Cheers to our success,' I said, holding it up in the air.

'Cheers to that,' said Oliver, and we clinked our bottles together.

I smiled at the refreshing taste of the liquid on my tongue.

Oliver was staring out at the cemetery around us, holding his drink still. 'I wonder if I'll be remembered,' he said quietly.

'Whatever do you mean?' I asked.

He shrugged. 'It's just . . . that's what Lady Athena wanted, isn't it? To be remembered. An' Mr Campbell was trying to give that to her too.'

I sighed. 'You're right, I suppose.' I thought she was wrong to do everything that she had done, but at the same time her motives were understandable.

He ran his hand through the grass. 'It was only 'cause of your pa that I would have got a proper burial at all when I . . . you know. The likes of me don't get that.'

He was right – a penny a week to the burial club could help you, but what if you couldn't spare even that?

'It's wrong,' I said firmly. 'I think everyone should be treated with respect, and get a proper memorial. They shouldn't have to be rich and famous.'

I remembered what Father had told me that day when we had been looking at the sea captain's grave. *There are people as noble as kings with nothing to mark their resting place*. Believing that had meant that Father gave more than he could really afford to help others be remembered.

'It'd be nice if the world was like that,' Oliver said sadly. Bones shuffled under his hand to receive scratches. He always seemed to sense when someone was feeling down.

'It would be nice,' I agreed. 'But who will be the ones to make it that way, if not us?'

I took a sip of ginger beer and looked out at the graves. Our cemetery was the first built in the city, opened earlier in the century, and many of the oldest gravestones were already tilting, or broken, or faded and painted with lichen.

'Look at this poor fellow,' I said, pointing to a carved cross before us – the front of the memorial had slid off, with the name John all that was now left. 'A grand headstone, but who remembers him? Will he still be John in a few years, or will he lose even his name? Perhaps none of us can be remembered for ever.'

Oliver sighed and nodded, smoothing the seeds from Bones's fur.

Something else Father had once said to me was that a graveyard was such a uniquely human thing. That we had the need to say to the world: 'I was here. I mattered.'

'But we *are* here,' I continued. 'We matter *now*. Perhaps no one will remember us – but I believe we can change the course of history.' I felt a rush of pride. 'We are a team. We shall stop more killers and villains and frauds. We'll save lives!'

A smile spread over Oliver's face. 'You think so?'

'I think we shall jolly well try,' I said. 'And that counts for something.'

'Cheers to that too, then,' said Oliver, and we clinked our bottles again as the bubbles fizzed for a perfect moment.

★ ★ ★

We finished our picnic and reluctantly made our way back across the cemetery. Oliver had more jobs to do for Father, and I supposed I would be sitting around and waiting to see if there was any interest in our advertisement.

Bones suddenly veered off the path, and I realised we were passing the grave of Miss Li's father. I had noticed it when it was newly placed as it was an unusual shape – tall and thin with a rounded top, and it bore Chinese characters. The grass had not yet recovered around it.

Now there was something else noteworthy that Bones had spotted and was sniffing round – something glinting at the base of the headstone.

I paused to take a closer look.

'Is that . . .?' I started.

It was the golden lock-shaped necklace, lying where it

was supposed to have been all along. Miss Li was finally free of that reminder of her father's legacy.

'Blimey,' said Oliver. 'Fancy just throwing that away.' He took a step closer.

I put my hand on his shoulder. 'Let's leave it,' I said. 'It's making a point. And, if someone takes it, perhaps they need it.'

Besides, I was getting a vague disgruntled feeling from the area – someone was not best pleased. I chuckled. He had no say in his daughters' lives any longer.

When we reached home, I immediately heard someone calling my name.

'Violet!'

It was Father. He sounded a little cross. I hurried through the house to the shop, Oliver and Bones trailing after me.

To my surprise, there were not only several people waiting in the undertaker's, but a small queue appeared to have formed outside as well.

Father was standing beside his desk, a flustered Ernesto seated behind it.

I looked around. 'Has there been a plague?'

'It would appear, Miss Violet Victoria Veil,' Father growled, 'that these good people are all here to see you.'

The first woman, who wore a fur stole and a jauntily

angled hat, raised her hand. 'I'm a friend of Miss Li,' she said. 'I heard all about your detective agency. I've had a priceless watch stolen . . .'

'Ahem,' said a portly gentleman behind her. 'I read about you in the paper. It said you had stopped both the Black Widow and the Grecian Phantom. I wanted to enquire about your services.'

'Someone stole my bicycle!' cried a boy from back near the door.

Then there was a clamour of voices as everyone tried to talk at once. Bones cowered behind the desk, and Ernesto shifted his chair back.

'Um,' I said, keenly aware of Father's eyes burning into me.

Oliver clapped his hands together. 'Everyone!'

The crowd fell silent.

'I'm Ja—' He stopped himself, cleared his throat. 'I'm Oliver Oats. You can see my name on the card.'

'He's my business partner,' I declared proudly. I was pleased that he had found some confidence and used his real name, rather than his alias.

'If you could form an orderly queue outside,' Oliver said in a businesslike voice, his cheeks flushed, 'we'll see each one of you, all right?'

The crowd nodded and turned, squeezing back out

into the street and jostling each other for a place in the queue.

Oliver pulled out his notebook. 'Sorry about this, Mr Veil,' he said, striding after them.

Father just gaped at his retreating back. Ernesto looked perplexed.

'Are you going to explain this?' Father asked me as I tapped my leg to call Bones to heel.

'Sorry,' I said with glee. 'Customers are waiting. I must be off.'

And, with that, I dashed out of the door after Oliver, Bones trotting happily beside me.

History was already changing. The air was thick with possibility, and this would be a day to remember.

Dear reader,

I'm so pleased that I've been able to take you on another adventure with Violet. This series has lived in my head for so long, and it's really exciting to have it out in the world.

As always I'd like to thank my editor Michelle Misra; alongside Samantha Stewart, Laure Gysemans, Elizabeth Vaziri and all the team at HarperCollins *Children's Books* for their work on this book. They deserve a round of theatrical applause.

Special shiny thanks to the design team and to brilliant artist Hannah Peck for making the series look so good, both inside and out.

Thanks also to my super-agent Jenny Savill and the team at Andrew Nurnberg Agency for their ongoing support.

To my Writing Group of Wonders: Bernie Howley, Charlett Goretzka, Kim Donovan, Ara Shillam and Sue Sedgwick – a team of brilliant writers who have given me invaluable feedback, right from Violet's first chapter.

To everyone who has helped me with my research – including the gang at Arnos Vale Cemetery and Highgate Cemetery, whose tours really helped to shape Seven Gates. This book was largely written in national lockdown, so much of my research and inspiration had to be acquired at home. A huge shout-out in particular to Kate Cherrell from Burials and Beyond – I attended her talk on Victorian spiritualism when I'd just started writing the book, and I ended up an avid subscriber to her blog and Patreon. I've gained more knowledge than you can shake a skeleton at about the acts of Victorian psychics and mediums – as well as undertakers, cemeteries, memorial art and more. As always, though, any errors or bizarre bendings of history are my doing.

To my husband and daughter, family and friends. Thank you for your love and for keeping me in one piece (just about) this year.

And finally – thank you for reading. The show must go on, as they say. I hope you're ready to follow Violet, Oliver and Bones into the darkness for their next mystery . . .

Sophie Cleverly